Also By Barbara Freethy

The Callaway Series
On A Night Like This (#1)
So This Is Love (#2)
Falling For A Stranger (#3)
Between Now and Forever (#4)
Nobody But You (Callaway Wedding Novella)
All A Heart Needs (#5)
That Summer Night (#6)
When Shadows Fall (#7)
Somewhere Only We Know (#8)
If I Didn't Know Better (#9)
Tender Is The Night (#10)
Take Me Home (A Callaway Novella)
Closer To You (#11)
Once You're Mine (#12) *Coming Soon!*

Lightning Strikes Trilogy
Beautiful Storm (#1)
Lightning Lingers (#2)
Summer Rain (#3)

The Wish Series
A Secret Wish
Just A Wish Away
When Wishes Collide

Standalone Novels
Almost Home
All She Ever Wanted
Ask Mariah
Daniel's Gift
Don't Say A Word
Golden Lies
Just The Way You Are
Love Will Find A Way
One True Love
Ryan's Return
Some Kind of Wonderful
Summer Secrets
Sweet Somethings
The Sweetest Thing

The Sanders Brothers Series
Silent Run & Silent Fall

The Deception Series
Taken & Played

PRAISE FOR THE NOVELS OF
#1 NEW YORK TIMES BESTSELLING AUTHOR
BARBARA FREETHY

"In the tradition of LaVyrle Spencer, gifted author Barbara Freethy creates an irresistible tale of family secrets, riveting adventure and heart- touching romance."

-- *NYT Bestselling Author **Susan Wiggs***
on Summer Secrets

"This book has it all: heart, community, and characters who will remain with you long after the book has ended. A wonderful story."

-- *NYT Bestselling Author **Debbie Macomber***
on Suddenly One Summer

"Freethy has a gift for creating complex characters."

-- ***Library Journal***

"Barbara Freethy is a master storyteller with a gift for spinning tales about ordinary people in extraordinary situations and drawing readers into their lives."

-- ***Romance Reviews Today***

"Freethy's skillful plotting and gift for creating sympathetic characters will ensure that few dry eyes will be left at the end of the story."

-- ***Publishers Weekly*** *on The Way Back Home*

"Freethy skillfully keeps the reader on the hook, and her tantalizing and believable tale has it all-- romance, adventure, and mystery."

-- ***Booklist*** *on Summer Secrets*

"Freethy's story-telling ability is top-notch."

-- ***Romantic Times*** *on Don't Say A Word*

SWEET SOMETHINGS

A Coffee Shop Novel

BARBARA FREETHY

HYDE
STREET
—PRESS—

HYDE STREET PRESS
Published by Hyde Street Press
1325 Howard Avenue, #321, Burlingame, California 94010

Printed in the United States of America

Cover design by Damonza.com

ISBN: 978-1-944417-25-3

One

———❦———

Juliette Adams had been at work in her bakery for over an hour when the sun came up over Fairhope, Alabama a little past seven on Thursday morning, the second of February. Her kitchen smelled like cinnamon and sugar, and the heat from the ovens had put a red flush on her cheeks. While she loved serving her customers, there was nothing better than the actual baking: kneading the dough, whipping the cream, layering the pastry—all of it, really.

Her father said she'd been born to bake, and she'd always believed that. Nothing had ever made her happier than early mornings in the kitchen like this—except maybe the mornings when her dad had been the baker and she'd been his trusted assistant. In those quiet and dark hours before dawn, they'd shared their dreams, their triumphs, even a few fallen cakes, but it had all been so special—until it had ended painfully and abruptly.

She drew in a breath as her thoughts moved in a negative direction, and it took all of her will to force them out of her head.

Wiping her flour-covered hands on her apron, she popped the last tray of her Valentine's Day Wish cookies into the oven. Starting every February first her father had made the special batch of cookies in honor of the season of love. According to town lore, dozens of people had found their heart's desire after eating one of the magical cookies.

Now it was up to her to continue the tradition—to give love and fate a little help.

Her cookies were good, but were they the same? Were they magical?

She hoped so. It wasn't just the cookies she wanted to recreate; it was the wonderful life she'd had in Fairhope before her parents died, before she had to move away to New York, before she had to start completely over.

But her big city days were behind her now. She'd been back in the idyllic small coastal town of Fairhope for five months, and she was feeling pretty good about most things.

Her bakery business was growing rapidly, and she'd found a second sales outlet at Donavan's, the popular coffee shop across the street. Between the two locations, she was beginning to show a profit, which would eventually bring her closer to her long-term goal—to buy the house she'd grown up in.

The old Victorian on Primrose Lane called to her every time she walked down the street. The house had changed hands a couple of times since her parents had died, but one day she hoped to make it hers, the way it should have been.

Most of her New York friends—make that all of them—had thought she was out of her mind to leave one of the most exciting cities in the world to go back to small-town life, to consider buying a house before she was thirty or married or living with someone. But they didn't understand that while she'd enjoyed New York and spending time with them, there was still a hole in her heart, and she couldn't seem to fill it no matter how hard she tried.

Maybe she'd have the same problem here; she hoped not, but only time would tell.

As the oven timer went off, she quickly retrieved two trays of cookies and put them on a cooling rack. Then she went into the front of the bakery and refilled the display cases she'd emptied the night before.

Her storefront was small but cozy. She had a twelve-foot glass display case that ran most of the length of the room, showcasing her pastries, cookies, cakes and pies. On the wooded shelf behind the case and against the wall, she featured her homemade breads: rye, seven grain, white, wheat and the occasional sourdough.

In front of the display case was a coffee stand with a large stainless-steel canister for Donavan's dark roast, coffee beans provided by Donavan's Coffee Shop. For the fancier coffee drinks, customers would have to go across the street.

Next to the coffee offerings were two small red café tables for those customers who liked to linger.

As her gaze moved to the window, she caught sight of a man standing outside. His presence startled her—not just his presence, actually, but the dark, compelling gaze that seemed to hold a hint of yearning that she found oddly unsettling.

He straightened when her gaze met his. He gave her a slight nod and then took off.

She walked over to the window and saw him jogging down the street. He wore dark track pants and a hoodie sweatshirt, and he moved with the athletic ease of a long-time runner.

It wasn't uncommon for some of the before-dawn workout crowd to hit up her shop before they went to work, but she'd never seen him before.

Had he just been hungry or had there been something else in his eyes?

Shrugging that odd question out of her head, she turned away from the window and went back to her display case. She'd just finished that task when her assistant manager came in the door.

Susan Montgomery was a fifty-year-old woman whose only daughter had gone off to college in the fall, leaving Susan with time on her hands. She'd been the first person Juliette had interviewed, and she'd known instantly that the perpetually cheerful and dedicated woman would make the perfect assistant manager.

"Morning," she said.

"It sure smells good in here." Susan took off her coat and hung it on a hook by the door leading into the kitchen. "I know I should expect it by now, but every day I'm still a little surprised by the delicious aroma. Oh, and George said to tell you he's gained ten pounds since I started working here and bringing him home extra treats, so I better be more careful about that." She laughed, adding, "We're not going to talk about how many pounds I've gained."

"One of the dangers of working in a bakery," she said.

"Not for you, Juliette. I don't know how you never gain an ounce. Actually, that's not true; I do know. You never stop working long enough to eat."

"I do enough tasting, believe me. I get plenty of calories in. I want you to try my latest Wish cookie."

Susan tied her apron on. "How early did you start today?"

"Four."

"Oh, my goodness. You might as well stay here all night."

"It might come to that. Every day there are more requests for Wish cookies."

"That's because they're so pretty and so good," Susan said, her gaze sweeping over the shortbread, heart-shaped cookies with the purple icing that were not only in the first display but also on a sample plate on the counter.

"I just don't know if they taste the same as my dad's cookies."

Susan picked up a cookie, bit into it, chewed for a moment, then shook her head. "You're right. They're terrible."

"They are?" she asked in surprise.

"No, they're amazing, but you already know that. Maybe they're not the same as your dad's; perhaps they're better."

"But if they're not the same, I can hardly make a claim that they'll make someone's Valentine's Day wish come true."

Susan rolled her eyes. "The only people who believe in

that are twelve-year-old girls, Juliette."

Since she'd been a twelve-year-old girl the last time she'd made a wish on the cookie, Susan was probably right.

"I understand that the wish gimmick sells cookies, but you really shouldn't worry about it so much," Susan continued. "These cookies will sell even if they don't make any wishes come true."

"I'm sure you're right. I'll bake some more this afternoon. I have one more variation on the ingredients that I want to try."

"I know you won't stop until you get it the way you want it," Susan said, with a knowing gleam in her eyes. "You're quite the perfectionist when it comes to baking."

"It's the one thing I'm confident I can get right if I put my mind and my effort into it." She paused. "I'm going to take our delivery over to Donavan's and get an espresso. Shall I bring you back something?"

"No, thanks. I already had two cups at home."

"I'll be back in a bit."

"Take your time."

She grabbed the plastic container of assorted brownies, muffins, cookies, and pastries she'd put together earlier and took them across the street to the coffee shop.

Donavan's wasn't just a place to get your daily dose of caffeine; it was where the townspeople gathered to chat, work on their computers, play chess, and watch the tourists go by. It was also a place where she was starting to sell a lot of baked goods.

As she walked into Donavan's, she saw Donavan, the pretty blonde owner with the big blue eyes behind the counter, whipping up coffees for the early morning crowd of caffeine addicts. Her coworker, Sara, tended the register. Sara had dark hair and dark eyes that were framed by a pair of black glasses.

Donavan and Sara had become two of her closest friends since she'd moved to town and tentatively asked Donavan about selling some of her baked goods at the coffee shop.

Donavan had generously said yes, and it had turned out to be a good business arrangement for both of them.

"Good morning," she said to Sara, as she went around the counter to unload her baked goods.

"So, did you bring more Wish cookies?" Sara asked, eagerness in her eyes. "They were gone yesterday before I got one."

"I've got a dozen here."

"Excellent."

"I am ready to find some love."

She laughed. "It's not just about finding love. It's about wishing for something you want—your heart's desire."

"Great, then I'm going to need more than one cookie. Because I have a lot of wishes."

She opened the container and put the plate of cookies on the counter, then loaded a display case with mini banana bread loaves, chocolate muffins, and raspberry tarts. "I can't quite believe people still remember the Wish cookies from when my dad was the baker here in town. It's been fifteen years," she said.

"Around here, people have long memories. Fifteen years is nothing," Sara told her.

"I suppose." She was happy that her dad had left behind an unexpected legacy, and it warmed her heart that so many people remembered him.

"Juliette, I have something for you," Donavan said, reaching behind the counter to pull out a framed photo. "I was cleaning out the storage room yesterday, and I came across some old photos my mother had hung onto for whatever reason." She turned the photo around so Juliette could see it. "What do you think about this?"

Her heart squeezed painfully at the sight of her father in his baker's hat and white apron. She stood next to him at about age six, dressed in exactly the same outfit. They were standing in front of the display counter in the bakery he'd run so many years ago. It had been located across town, and while she'd thought about getting the exact same space, she'd discovered that bakery had been turned into an Italian café, so she'd rented the property across from Donavan's.

It had actually been a better decision, because Donavan's provided a steady stream of customers and another place to sell her desserts.

"You look adorable," Sara said, peeking at the photo over Donavan's shoulder.

"I loved helping him bake. He was my inspiration to become a pastry chef." She took the photo out of Donavan's hands and pressed it against her heart. "Thank you."

Donavan gave her a sympathetic smile. Having lost her mom, Donavan knew firsthand about parental loss. "I thought you might want to hang it at the bakery."

"Absolutely," she said. "I'm looking for as many photos as I can find that show off my dad or his old bakery."

"If I see any others, I'll let you know."

"I'd appreciate that."

"How's business going?" Donavan asked. "It seems like there is a steady stream of customers going through your front doors."

"It's picking up every month. Christmas was very good. With Valentine's Day looming, sales are staying strong. I just have to be able to keep up with demand. I might have overextended myself by signing up to provide desserts at every pre-Valentine's Day town event. I can't quite believe how much Fairhope gets into the holidays: the romantic movie festival, the love boat parade in the harbor, and the Sweetheart's Dance to name just a few."

"It's a way to turn February into a fun month and bring in some extra tourist dollars that we don't normally see in the winter," Donavan said with a laugh. "And Sara and I'll be right there with you. We signed up for everything, too."

"That's great. I'll be happy to have the company. In between events, I'm also starting to get a lot of orders for private parties, but I'm not complaining; the more business, the better. I love seeing a line at my counter." She paused, as a gust of cool wind drew her gaze to the door. At first she thought it might be the attractive jogger she'd seen earlier, but it was another guy.

"Looking for someone?" Donavan asked curiously as she turned back to her.

"Not really. Well, sort of..."

"That sounds interesting—like maybe you're looking for a guy?" she asked with a gleam in her eye.

"There was a man outside my bakery early this morning," she admitted. "He was jogging, but he stopped to look in the window, and, I don't know...there was something about him—he was kind of unforgettable."

"Like he had two heads or he was super-hot?" Sara put in, curiosity in her brown eyes.

"Definitely not two heads," she said with a laugh.

"So good-looking then," Sara prodded.

"Definitely. He had this super intense gaze." She shivered at the memory.

"That looked right through you?" Donavan asked, a gleam in her eyes.

"Yes, exactly."

"I'm pretty sure that was Roman Prescott," Donavan said. "I heard he's back in town. I haven't seen him since high school, but that man's gaze was searing. There wasn't a girl in the school who didn't think so. If he's looking at you, you won't be able to do anything but look back."

"Did you look back?" she asked, wondering if there had been something between them.

"Oh, sure," Donavan admitted. "But I was two years younger, and far too innocent. Roman was not interested in me in that way. He liked the hot, fast girls."

"In my experience, most high school boys do," she said dryly.

"True, but Roman was different from most of the guys at school. He didn't grow up here, for one thing. He came to town to live with his grandfather when he was a wild, rebellious teenager, and he caused all kinds of problems, but most of them were just pranks. I always thought he had a good heart."

"He sounds—complicated," she murmured.

"The best ones always are," Sara put in. "I haven't met this Roman Prescott, but now I really want to. There's nothing wrong with a good bad boy."

"You have love on the brain, Sara," Donavan told her assistant.

"It's almost Valentine's Day, what can I say?" She gave a helpless shrug. "It's the season for love."

"Well, I don't think Roman was looking for love this morning, more like food," Juliette said. "He was probably hungry from his run, but the bakery wasn't open yet."

"Hey, Juliette and Roman...that sounds a little like Romeo and Juliet," Sara said.

Her nerves tingled at the suggested coupling, but she brushed the comment off with a wave of her hand. "I've heard that joke before, too many times to count. And I'm not looking for a Romeo; I have no time for love. On that note, I'm going back to work."

Work had always been his therapy, Roman thought, as he used a crowbar to rip off a piece of drywall in the living room of the old Victorian his grandfather was restoring.

Learning carpentry and construction had saved him as an angry teenager. He'd found a place to hammer out his frustration and bitterness. He wasn't sure the work would have the same effect on his burned-out, cynical, and weary thirty-one-year-old self, but at least it gave him a few hours of respite each day from the nightmares that haunted his dreams.

After thirteen years in the Marine Corps, it also felt good to be restoring a building, bringing it back to life, making it better. He'd like to believe he'd improved things in other places in the world. Certainly, he hoped he'd made some of those places safer, but the good didn't always balance out the pain and destruction.

"Roman, there you are."

He looked up as his seventy-three-year-old grandfather Vincent Prescott walked into the room. Tall and thin, with dark eyes and dark hair that had never grayed, his grandfather had always been an imposing man. Vincent had done the hard, physical work of construction all his life, and his callused hands and weathered skin reflected those years. He might be moving more slowly these days with his arthritis flaring up, but his sharp gaze missed nothing. His grandfather had been the toughest boss he'd ever had, and that was saying something.

"Where else would I be?" he drawled. "You gave me a job to do, and I'm doing it."

He and his grandfather had had both an antagonistic and an awkwardly caring relationship. While Vince had saved him from the foster care system when he was fifteen, his grandfather hadn't been around the terrible years before that, and Roman had never really understood why. But his grandfather wasn't big on talking. He'd just moved him into his house, taught him how to build, and made sure he had food to eat and a place to sleep while he went to high school.

"Looks like there's some rot behind those boards," Vincent said, tipping his head to the opening behind the sheetrock.

"I suspect we're going to find that throughout the house," he agreed. "You may need to increase the budget on this one or change up some of your plans."

"Can't do that. Just fix what needs to be fixed. Whatever it costs, it costs."

He nodded, wondering again why his grandfather had chosen this particular house to flip.

In fact, he couldn't really understand why Vincent had bought the property at all. He'd been in semi-retirement before he'd purchased the property six months earlier, and he no longer had a crew to do the work. If Roman hadn't been put on medical leave from the Marines, he had no idea who'd be working on the house. But all he said was, "Will do."

"I've got a kid coming in after school tomorrow to help you with the downstairs bathroom demo," Vincent added. "Jeff Dobbs. He's Margaret's grandson," he added, referring to his long-time neighbor. "He needs some cash for college."

"Fine. I could use an extra pair of hands—more than one would be great."

"I'm working on that. I should also be able to get back in here to work later in the week. These flare-ups don't last too long." He flexed his fingers with a painful grimace.

"Whenever you're ready, but you're going to need to hire subs regardless. I am a little surprised you took on such a big project."

"Why?" his grandfather asked, an edge to his tone.

He suspected that suggesting his grandfather was old would not be the best answer. "I thought you were winding things down."

Vincent didn't answer right away, a faraway light coming into his eyes. "I always wanted this property. It has only been up for sale a couple of times in the last fifty or so years, and it was never the right time for me. When it came back on the market last year, I knew I had to get it. I've had ideas for it for a long time. I want to see those ideas come to life before I die."

It was a sentimental reason for a man who wasn't known for his sentiment, and Roman wasn't quite sure what to make of it.

Vincent's gaze swept the room. "The arched doorways and windows, the exposed beams, the details are all here, but they need to be honed, remade, redone. This house could be magnificent. It deserves to be that." Vincent frowned at the end of his statement, as if he regretted showing so much emotion. He cleared his throat, putting his usual cold, stoic expression back on his face. "I'll check in with you later. I'm going to run some errands and then meet Max at Donavan's for chess and coffee."

"Sounds good." His grandfather spent most of his afternoons at the local coffee shop.

As Vincent left, he thought about getting some coffee himself. He hadn't been to Donavan's yet. He hadn't been ready to face the social scene he knew he would find there, but he had always liked the owner, Donavan Turner, and he was curious to see what kind of business she'd built.

Two years younger than him, Donavan had been a sweet kid in high school and fiercely protective of people she considered underdogs. Back then, he'd fit into that category, with half the school judging him before he ever set foot on the campus. He'd been the new kid in the tenth grade in a school where everyone had been together since kindergarten, and he hadn't made it easy for people to like him.

He'd been reckless, pissed off all the time, impatient, bitter, and…lost.

He hadn't had a clue how to release those emotions in a positive way. He'd made a lot of mistakes; he'd hurt people. And he'd been hurt.

Water under the bridge, he told himself. His teenage years had been a long time ago, and the last thing he wanted to do was relive that time in his life. Unfortunately, he didn't think he would have a choice, because a lot of the people he'd gone to school with were still in town, and there was no doubt they would judge him once again.

He'd known coming back to Fairhope would stir up gossip and old problems, but it was the closest thing he had to a home, and after being injured in action, he'd been forced to take a break from the career he loved and the circle of friends who'd become brothers to him. He'd wandered around for two months before finally getting on a plane to Fairhope. He'd needed to feel grounded again, to get his feet back under him, to recover and recharge and be part of a world where he had a connection with at least one person.

His fellow soldiers checked up on him as much as they could, but they were on the other side of the world—where he would have been, if he hadn't gotten injured, if an explosion hadn't damaged his hearing, if bullets hadn't cracked his ribs and torn through his shoulder, leaving him with poor range of motion and nerve damage that went down into his fingers.

He'd gotten a lot better. He could do most things without pain. He was working out every day, and if he could pass the physical he had coming up in a little over a week, hopefully, he'd be cleared for active duty again. It was an optimistic thought, considering the level of skill and fitness required for his job and the damage that he'd suffered, but he wasn't giving up without a fight.

Focusing his attention back on the work at hand, he ripped off another piece of drywall, only to be interrupted again by a shrill, angry female voice.

"What the hell are you doing to my house?" she demanded.

He swung around, not only surprised by the question but also by the beautiful blue eyes spitting fire at him. It was the attractive brunette from the bakery. There was no apron covering her slender but curvy frame now, and she looked even prettier in black jeans, black boots and a body-hugging bright-green sweater. Her long hair was pulled back at the base of her neck, her skin clear and shiny, although he thought he could see a trace of flour along her hairline. He had to fight the urge to lean forward and wipe it away.

"You?" she asked, more surprise in her eyes as their gazes connected.

That question made him stiffen. What did she mean— *you*?

Two

─➤➤◄◄◄─

Juliette could not believe the man she'd seen outside her bakery window early that morning was now ripping down the walls of her childhood home. He'd changed out of his track pants and sweatshirt into well-worn jeans and a navy blue T-shirt that pulled against what appeared to be a broad, muscled chest.

She blinked twice and had to deliberately drag her gaze back to his face. Only then, she was staring into his eyes, his compelling and intense brown eyes. Donavan had been right. He was impossible to look away from.

He couldn't be the owner of this house. She'd heard that an older man had purchased it a month before she'd arrived in town. It had been rumored that he was just going to rent it out, but that didn't appear to be the plan.

She drew in a breath as they stared at each other for far too long. "I asked you what you were doing," she said finally.

"Actually, I think you said, *what the hell are you doing to my house.* But I'm confused, because this house isn't yours."

"It used to be. I grew up here."

"Okay," he said warily. "But you don't own the place now, so you should have no concern about what's happening here."

He was, of course, absolutely right. But when she'd come down the street and seen the open front door and a man ripping down the walls in the entry of her old house, she'd given no conscious thought to the logic of her actions; she'd been driven by pure emotion.

She'd known it would take years to buy the house, but she'd thought she'd have those years. Maybe the place might have been fixed up a little by then—with cosmetic changes, a new coat of paint, a new roof—but what he was doing looked like a whole lot more than that.

The walls in the living room had been gutted, and there was a table saw, stacks of boards, and toolboxes open on the floor in the adjacent dining room. The hall was dusty, with heaps of discarded and torn-up sheetrock piled up near the front door.

When he was finished, she had a feeling her old house would be completely gone. The thought left her shaking, not just with anger but also with sadness.

It was like he was ripping her life apart, one piece of wood at a time.

She put a hand to her mouth, feeling a little sick.

He gave her a sharp look. "Are you all right?"

"Not really," she murmured.

He grabbed an unopened bottle of water off a nearby table and handed it to her. "Drink this."

Her hands were shaking so much she could barely twist off the top. He took it from her with an impatient hand, opened the bottle and then handed it back to her.

The first long swallow of cool water made her feel a lot better. Another drink, and she felt a little less dizzy. "Thank you."

"I thought you were going to pass out for a minute there."

She felt like a fool now that she wasn't reacting to the wave of painful emotions she'd thought she'd buried away a long time ago. "You must think I'm crazy."

He didn't seem interested in refuting that statement.

"Right," she said. "Well, let me explain. I lived in this

house from the time I was born until I was twelve. That's when my parents died. I was here when I got the news. My aunt was watching me. We were both asleep when the phone rang." She drew in a deep breath. "My parents were on a boat cruise in Italy, and the ship went down. They didn't survive."

"Sorry," he muttered, his brows furrowing. "That's awful."

"It was the worst night of my life."

"I'm sure it was."

"I didn't think it was real for the longest time. It happened so far away; it felt like a nightmare. But the nightmare never ended. I would wake up and look for them, but they weren't there. After the funeral, my aunt sold this house and took me to live with her in New York. I always had it in my head that one day I'd return to Fairhope and buy my home back. But when I came to town five months ago, the house had recently been sold. Everyone told me the old man who'd bought it was just going to rent it out, so I didn't think much about it, except that I still hoped to find a way to buy it one day. When I came down the street just now, and I saw you ripping down the walls..." She licked her lips. "It felt like you were tearing apart my past. I saw red. One minute I was on the sidewalk, and the next minute I was in here. I don't even remember how that happened."

"Okay," he said slowly, understanding in his eyes. "I get it. The old man is my grandfather, Vincent Prescott. I think he's planning to sell the place after he remodels it. Maybe you could buy it then."

"Why does he have to tear the walls down? It's such a beautiful old house. It has character."

"And dry rot."

"Can't that just be fixed?"

"It can—after I rip out the walls."

"So you're not going to actually tear down the house?"

"The plans call for an extension into the backyard, so some walls are coming down."

"Oh," she said, feeling faint again.

"It's all good," he assured her. "In fact, it's going to be great. My grandfather wants to maintain the integrity of the architecture while making the house much more livable and better suited for modern families. There will be a bathroom added to the master. The first floor bedroom and kitchen will be expanded and the bathroom will be remodeled. My grandfather knows what he's doing. This place will be better than ever when he's done with it."

"But it won't be the same."

"Time moves on," he said shortly.

She knew he was right, and that he was being nice enough just to talk to her, because the construction was truly none of her business. She should apologize for interrupting his day, but somehow she couldn't quite get an *I'm sorry* to come out of her mouth.

"When you saw me," he continued, giving her a speculative look as he crossed his arms, "you said *you* as if we know each other. But I don't think we've met."

She flushed at the reminder. She really did need to find a way to think before she spoke, but she never seemed to manage that. "I saw you earlier today outside my bakery. You looked—hungry."

"I was hungry. I'd just finished a six-mile run, and your bakery smelled like heaven."

"You should have come in."

"You weren't open yet."

"It was close enough. Remember that for next time—if you're hungry, that is."

"I will. I'm Roman Prescott." He extended his hand.

"Juliette Adams," she replied, as his fingers gripped hers, and a jolt of heat and electricity ran down her spine. She quickly pulled her hand away. "It's nice to meet you. I'm really not a crazy person."

"Okay." He didn't sound entirely convinced.

"So you said your grandfather is going to sell the house after the remodel?"

"I believe so."

"Would he consider selling it as it is right now—if the price was right?"

"I doubt it. He seems very determined to turn this house into some vision he's had in his head for apparently quite a few years. You're not alone in having strong feelings about this place."

"Why? Why does he care about it so much? He never lived here, did he?"

"He didn't live here, and I have no idea why he's so interested, but he is."

"Could you find out?"

"He doesn't tell me much. You can ask him if you want. He's at Donavan's most afternoons. He plays chess there with his old friend Max."

"Okay. Maybe I'll give it a shot. It can't hurt." She paused for a moment. "I heard you just came back to town."

"Who did you hear that from?"

"Donavan. She said you went to high school together."

"We did. I guess bad news travels fast," he said somewhat dryly.

"Why would it be bad news that you're back?"

He shrugged. "Just a guess."

His vagueness intrigued her, but he didn't seem interested in saying anything more. He definitely wasn't a man of many words.

"Sorry I interrupted your work," she said. "Come by the bakery sometime, and I'll give you a pastry—on the house." She hesitated, knowing she should go, but she hadn't been in her old home since her aunt had sold it. "Before I leave, do you think I could look around a little? I haven't been inside since I was twelve. I walk by the place almost every day; I even looked in the windows once, but there was no one living here to ask if I could come in for a minute."

"Sure. Go for it."

"Really?"

"Just watch your step."

"Thanks." She moved toward the stairs, knowing exactly

where she wanted to go first—her old bedroom.

———➤➤◄◄———

There were four rooms on the second floor: the master bedroom, a hall bathroom, and then two bedrooms, with her room tucked away under the eaves of the sloping roof.

She'd always liked the feeling that she had her own little hideaway. She wondered if Roman's grandfather planned on lifting the roof, making the room bigger, with a ceiling you didn't have to duck under on your way to the closet.

Probably.

It would add value to the house. But it would also destroy the cozy feeling of safety, warmth, happiness.

She stepped across the threshold, then paused. There wasn't any furniture in the room now, but in her head she could see the twin bed she'd slept in, the white dresser and matching desk, the shelves filled with books, the big pillows and stuffed animals in what she'd called her reading corner, which was just under the window and the recipient of a bright slash of sun every afternoon when she got home from school.

A wave of sad nostalgia for a life she could vividly remember ran through her, but it was a life she had left fifteen years ago. The last time she'd been in this room she'd been twelve. Now she was twenty-seven. She'd lived more than half of her life somewhere else.

It was probably time to break the tie between her past and her present and move on to the future. But she still didn't feel ready.

She walked over to the window and looked out at the backyard. Weeds had overrun what had once been her mother's garden. Landscaping was no doubt part of the remodel plans, which would bring more changes.

If she hadn't put the cash she'd won from a baking contest into opening her bakery business, she would have been closer to a downpayment, but having to decide between the old house and a new business, she'd chosen the new business, thinking she'd have time to get the house later, and in the meantime she had to live.

Well, it wasn't over yet. She needed to talk to Roman's grandfather and find out what his plans were—for both the remodel and the sale of the house. Maybe she could reason with him. Hopefully, he'd be a little more talkative than his grandson.

She had to admit that Roman Prescott looked even better in the daylight than he had in the early morning shadows. But he had all kinds of walls up. She didn't know where the detachment came from, but he was clearly not interested in becoming friends. She'd obviously misread the interest she'd seen in his eyes earlier.

That was just as well. She had enough on her plate without adding a man into the mix.

She left her old bedroom and walked down the hall, pausing at the door to what had once been her mother's sewing room. There was a double bed in the room now with a sleeping bag tossed over the mattress. A half-filled suitcase was open on a chair. A guitar was propped up against the wall.

Someone was living here—Roman? It had to be him. The male T-shirt tossed on the bed made her nerves tingle. She could almost imagine Roman stripping it off what had to be a sexy, ripped body.

She was getting as bad as Sara... Clearing her throat, she quickly left the room and hastened down the hall, pausing at one more door. The master bedroom had once been her parents' room. Could she go in?

Her heart started to beat faster. Her mom and dad hadn't been in that room in more than a decade. There was nothing to be nervous about, but still...

Roman frowned as he heard Juliette moving around on the second floor. He could silently admit that he'd been a little dazzled by the image of the pretty woman inside the bakery just after dawn, the sweet warmth of her pastries spilling out to the street as he ran by. But while she was even prettier in person, she was also a lunatic, and he'd never been big on drama.

If he'd needed a reason to stay away from her, he certainly had one now. But first he had to get her out of the house.

What the hell was she doing up there anyway? The only furniture was in the bedroom he was using, and that didn't involve much, because he didn't need much. His grandfather had offered him a room at his house, but he preferred being on his own, and he was used to making do with the bare necessities.

He pried off another big piece of drywall and tossed it on a pile on the floor. His grandfather wanted to open up the space between the living room and dining room, making it feel like one big room. It was a good idea, one of many, but again he didn't know how the work was ever going to get done. His grandfather had barely done anything in the six months he'd owned the house. But his job was not to question why, just work. At least these questions kept him from thinking about his very uncertain future.

It was suddenly very quiet overhead. He told himself to leave it alone, but as the minutes ticked by, he knew that wasn't going to happen. He pulled off his work gloves and headed up the stairs.

He found her sitting cross-legged on the floor in the middle of the empty master bedroom, her arms wrapped around her waist. She didn't turn her head when he entered the room and judging by the pallor of her skin and the distant look in her eyes, she was somewhere far, far away. He knew the look of trauma, of a deep, agonizing pain. He'd seen it in his own eyes and the eyes of friends who'd lost people they loved.

"Juliette?" he asked quietly, not wanting to shock her too quickly.

She started as he came around in front of her. He squatted down. "You okay?"

Her beautiful blue eyes were wide and confused. "I don't know why this house bothers me so much…it shouldn't. Logically, I know it's not mine. I even know that owning it won't change anything, not really. But I can't seem to get my emotions in line with my brain."

He had a feeling she operated only on emotion, which was something he never did, or at least he hadn't done in a very long time.

"My mother had always wanted to go to Italy," she told him. "My dad surprised her with the trip. She didn't know until that day when my aunt showed up, and my dad handed her the airline tickets and told her she had one hour to pack her bags. It was so romantic. It was going to be the trip of a lifetime." She drew in a breath and let it out. "They started in Milan and worked their way south through Venice, Florence, Rome and then down to Salerno, where they got on a boat for a luxury cruise. Only, the boat wasn't that luxurious, and the operators had been cutting corners, and mechanical problems led to a fire, and…" Her voice trailed away. "It went down."

His gut churned. "I'm very sorry."

"They were two days away from coming home. There were no good-byes. No chance to say I love you. I don't even remember the last thing I said to either one of them. I know we were on the phone together the night before the cruise. They were telling me about what they'd seen that day. I'm pretty sure they asked how school was going, and I probably rambled on about nothing. I just don't know what it was."

The guilt in her eyes resonated within him. "It doesn't matter if you didn't say I love you or I miss you; they knew. It sounds like you had a happy family life."

"We did. It was great. They were the best parents in the world. But I didn't have them long enough."

"No, you didn't," he agreed.

"I wanted to stay here—in this town, in this house—but my aunt lived in New York, and that's where her job was, and that's where she needed to be. I had to move into a completely different world. Her one-bedroom apartment was tiny. We lived there for almost three years. I slept on a pull-out couch in the living room. Then she got married, and her husband bought us a condo. He was nice to me, but I wasn't very nice to him. It was another change in my life that I didn't want. I kept thinking one day I would have control over my life. I would call the shots. It's taken a long time, but I'm pretty close to being there. I have my own business. I just need—this house."

He could hear the desperation in her voice, but he doubted that the house could ever give her what she really needed. He didn't think she'd appreciate hearing that, so instead, he said, "When did you come back to Fairhope?"

"Five months ago. I won a national baking contest, and the prize was $30,000."

"Impressive."

"I had considered using the money to make a downpayment on this house, but it had recently been sold, and I was told the buyer wasn't interested in selling yet. Plus $30,000 wasn't going to be enough, not if I wanted to open the bakery, too. So I had to choose. I could only afford one dream."

"You're lucky you could afford even that."

She stared back at him. "You're right. I'm sorry. I don't know why I'm dumping all this on you. I don't usually go on and on like this with a perfect stranger."

He'd actually enjoyed it, more than he cared to admit. It had been some time since he'd had a long conversation with anyone. "It's not a problem. But..." He stood up.

"You need me to leave. I know." She got to her feet. "Thanks for letting me look around."

"You can come back if you feel the need," he said, then immediately kicked himself for making that offer. He didn't want her coming back here for any reason. She'd already distracted him and cost him an hour of work. And while he might be working for his grandfather, the old man was as hard-assed as any Marine he'd worked under.

Juliette brushed the dust off the back of her jeans, drawing his gaze to her very shapely rear-end. Which he really did not need to be looking at. He turned and headed toward the door, leading the way down the stairs.

"So where did you come back from, Roman?" she asked as he reached the last step.

He should have known the questions were coming. She was too talkative to just leave without saying anything else.

"I'm on leave from the Marine Corps, so you could say I'm coming back from all over."

"I don't remember you from when I lived here before."

"I think I'm older than you by a few years. I'm thirty-one."

"I'm twenty-seven—so a four-year difference."

"I didn't show up here until I was fifteen, which would have made you eleven. I guess our paths could have crossed, but we wouldn't have been in the same school at the same time."

"And I was gone a year later." She cocked her head to the right, giving him a thoughtful look. "Donavan said you came to live with your grandfather. What happened to your parents?"

His lips tightened. "My father died and my mother wasn't around."

"I'm sorry about your dad."

"I didn't even know him. He died when I was a toddler."

"Still..." She frowned. "You don't like to talk about yourself, do you?"

"No."

"That's unusual. Most of the men I've met lately love to talk about themselves, and none of them have led very interesting lives. While you, on the other hand, don't want to say much, but I suspect you have all kinds of stories you could tell."

He dismissed her hopeful smile by waving her toward the door. "I doubt that, and I have work to do, Ms. Adams."

"Oh, please, it's Juliette. No one is formal in this town, least of all me. I'll let you get back to work. But please come by the bakery sometime and collect your free dessert. You can pick whatever you want."

"I'm not much on sweets."

She laughed in disbelief. "No way that's true. I saw the look in your eyes this morning when you gazed at my display case. It's not a crime to eat a little sugar once in a while." She gave him a dimpled smile that made his heart twist. "It might even sweeten you up a bit."

"I'm never going to be sweet," he said, quite certain of that fact.

"You've already been very sweet to me. But I won't tell anyone. I wouldn't want to ruin your tough-guy, doesn't-talk-much image."

With that parting shot, she finally made it through the front door. He quickly closed it behind her. He couldn't tell her that he hadn't been looking at her display case when he'd stopped outside her bakery; he'd been looking at her. And that hunger churning in his gut hadn't had much to do with cookies and pies.

As for some dessert sweetening him up, it was going to take a lot more than cake to smooth his rough edges.

Not that he intended to try. He liked the calluses and scars over his heart. They were important and constant reminders not to believe in anything or anyone that was too good to be true, and Juliette Adams had all the signs of being in the too-good-to-be-true category.

Three

By four o'clock in the afternoon, his shoulders were aching as well as his back, and Roman decided to call it a day. He didn't want to jeopardize his recovery by overworking his muscles.

Throwing on his black leather jacket, he locked the front door of the house to avoid any more unwanted visitors and headed downtown for some coffee. It was only about a mile and a half to the center of town, and he was happy for the walk.

As he neared Juliette's bakery, he deliberately crossed the street. While he might take her up on her offer of a free pastry one day, that day wouldn't be today. He'd spent far too much time already thinking about her. He needed a break before he saw her again.

Walking into Donavan's, he was immediately struck by the warm, charming atmosphere. With exposed brick walls, wooden tables, and an old piano in one corner, the coffeehouse felt more like someone's living room than a café.

A large chalkboard on one wall detailed the day's specials. A charming array of mugs sat on the counter and inside the display case he saw brownies, cookies, eclairs, and pastries from Sweet Somethings. Obviously, Donavan and

Juliette had a business relationship as well as a friendship.

As he looked around the room, he saw his grandfather sitting at a table in the corner with his friend Max, an African-American man in a wheelchair. Vincent had his back to him and Max's gaze was focused on the chess board, so he left them alone and headed to the counter.

When he stepped up to order, a striking blonde, wearing a bright-red apron, came over to the counter, her blue eyes sparkling a familiar welcome. "Roman Prescott. It's about time you came in here. I heard you've been back almost two weeks, and this is the first time I've seen you."

"Hello, Donavan. Nice place you have here. My grandfather tells me this coffee shop is the best thing that ever happened to this town."

She smiled at the compliment. "It's certainly the best thing that ever happened to me. I'm glad he feels the same way."

As he drew in a breath, his senses were assailed with the scent of coffee. "Damn. It smells good in here."

She laughed. "It's our dark roast. It comes from a small town in Ethiopia." She tipped her head to the map on the wall where several colored tags showed where the different coffee beans were grown.

"You get your beans from Ethiopia?"

"I do. And a couple of times a year we hold fundraisers to send money to some of the poorest of the poor in the areas that grow our coffee. It seems only fair. We're actually having one of those next week. Maybe you can come."

Donavan Turner had always been the kind of person who looked out for other people; she'd looked out for him once. And he'd never forgotten that. Although, she was probably a little too optimistic, always wanting to believe that everyone had a good side, when some people were just bad all the way through.

"I will definitely try to come," he said.

"What can I get you?"

"I'll take the dark roast."

"I'm assuming you want it straight up—no whipped cream or sprinkles?"

"Definitely not."

A dark brunette came up behind Donavan, giving him a curious look.

"Sara," Donavan said. "This is Roman Prescott. We went to high school together."

"It's nice to meet you," Sara said. "I assume you're Vince's grandson?"

"That would be me. And it's nice to meet you, too."

"I'll get your coffee," Donavan said.

"And I'll take your money," Sara added.

"No, this one is on the house," Donavan told Sara.

"You don't have to do that," he replied, handing Sara a five-dollar bill.

"But it's your welcome-back coffee," Donavan said.

"Consider it my donation to the good people of Ethiopia."

"In that case—all right." Donavan handed him a ceramic mug of coffee. "You never did like to owe people. And, yes, I put this in a *to-stay* instead of in a *to-go* cup, because I thought we might chat for a minute."

Seeing the determination in her eyes, he knew there was no way he was going to escape without that chat. And the fact of the matter was he didn't really have somewhere else he needed to be. "Sure."

Her eyebrow arched in surprise. "That was easier than I thought, but I'll take it." She came around the counter, and they sat down at a small table.

"I saw the piano," he said. "Do you still play?"

"Whenever I get the chance. How about you? Still strumming that guitar?"

"Just took it up again recently."

"That's great. How are you doing, Roman? I heard you were injured and had to leave the Marines. The details are murky, though."

That's because no one knew the details, including his

grandfather. "That's pretty much the story. I may still go back. I'm on medical leave."

"Well, I'm glad you weren't too badly hurt. It's been what—eleven, twelve years—since you were here?"

"Thirteen. I left a few weeks after my eighteenth birthday." As he sipped his coffee, he added, "This might be the best cup of coffee I've ever had."

Her smile broadened. "I'm glad to hear that. I have to say I wasn't sure you'd ever come back to this town, Roman. Things weren't great when you left."

"No they weren't, but it was a long time ago."

"I'm sure your grandfather is happy to have you back. He said you're working for him now."

"Temporarily anyway."

"Well, I hope you'll stay as long as you can."

"Thanks, but you may not share the popular opinion when it comes to me staying in town," he drawled, seeing two older women across the room, one of whom was glaring at him.

She followed his gaze. "Don't worry about Martha Grayson. No one listens to her."

"That hasn't been my experience."

"Well, even if people listen to her, they know she's just gossiping. Give the town a chance to show you it has grown up, just like you have. And while Martha can be the ultimate small-minded mean girl, her sister Cecelia isn't so bad, and sometimes she can keep Martha in line."

He smiled at her optimism. "Sure, she can. But thanks. You were always kind to me, even when I didn't deserve it."

"You did deserve it. Most people just didn't see the real you, Roman. And that wasn't their fault; it was yours. You didn't let people in. You had a huge wall up."

"That's true, but I did let a few in, and that didn't work well."

"I never really understood what happened."

"You and me both." He paused as a familiar woman came through the door of the coffee shop, and just like earlier in the day, every muscle in his body tightened and warning bells went off in his head. Juliette's gaze, however, went straight to his grandfather, and as she headed over to the men's table with a purposeful walk, he was actually curious to see what would happen.

To most people, his gruff, short-tempered grandfather would probably be intimidating, but Juliette didn't seem at all worried. Then again, she was on a mission, and she wasn't about to let anyone stop her from making her pitch.

"Who are you looking at?" Donavan asked, then turned her head to see. "Oh, Juliette Adams." She turned back to him with a knowing gleam in her eyes. "Juliette runs the bakery across the street—Sweet Somethings."

"I know. I met her today," he murmured.

"She spent her early childhood here, then came back several months ago. Her bakery has really taken off. We sell a lot of her desserts. She's very nice."

He didn't comment, thinking that the word *nice* didn't fully describe Juliette. Not that she wasn't nice, but she was a lot more complicated than that.

"Donavan," Sara said, waving a hand from the counter, where the line had grown.

Donavan gave him an apologetic smile. "Sorry. I better get back to work."

"No problem."

"Don't be a stranger, Roman."

As Donavan left, his attention shifted back to Juliette, and he was remarkably glad that she was speaking loud enough for him to hear.

"I'm really sorry to interrupt," she said. "I'm Juliette Adams, Mr. Prescott, and I want to know if you might be interested in selling the property on Primrose Lane to me."

Vincent sat up a little straighter at her question. "I'm just starting a remodel on that house."

"Yes, I know that, but I wonder if you'd consider an offer before you do any more work."

"What kind of an offer?" he asked, rubbing his chin

thoughtfully.

"Well, I'm not sure. I'd need to get an appraisal, but do you have a number in mind?"

"Why do you want that house?"

"My parents used to own it. I lived there until I was twelve."

"You said your name was Adams," Vince said. "Frank and Tricia—those were your parents?"

She nodded. "Yes."

"Tragic what happened to them."

"Did you know them?"

"I met your dad a few times. He was a baker."

"And I'm following in his footsteps. I run the Sweet Somethings Bakery across the street. But getting back to the house—"

"Sorry, but I'm not interested in selling right now," his grandfather said firmly. "Once the remodel is done, I'll consider it. You can buy it then if you still want it."

"But I want it the way it is now."

"Why? It's got a lot of problems."

"Because it's part of my history."

"It's just a house. It's part of a lot of people's history. It was there before you, and it will be there after you. You're a young woman. There will be plenty of houses in your life."

A frown crossed Juliette's face. She obviously didn't care for his grandfather's dismissive comment. "Well, if you change your mind, will you let me know?" she asked.

"I won't change my mind."

Juliette looked taken aback by his grandfather's blunt words, but she nodded and then walked away from the table. She headed toward the counter, and she was almost there when she saw him. She hesitated and then changed course, taking the seat across from him.

"You heard all that?" she asked.

"Yes. I'm not surprised."

"I don't understand why your grandfather is being so stubborn."

"He probably thinks the same thing about you."

"I have a personal reason for wanting the house; he doesn't."

"The house will be better after it's remodeled. You might like it even more then."

She sat back in her chair, folding her arms across her chest. "No one seems to understand that I'm not interested in a remodel. I want it to be the same as it was."

"That's your choice, Juliette. But let's be honest. You don't have the money to buy the house now anyway, regardless of what it would be appraised at, do you?"

He could see the truth in her eyes.

"I might be able to make something happen," she said. "I could borrow money from my aunt, maybe get a loan." She blew out a breath. "But that's all pointless if your grandfather won't sell. I really wish you'd talk to him."

"It wouldn't make a difference. He doesn't care what I think; he never has."

She stared back at him with defiance in her eyes. "Well, I'm not giving up."

"I figured," he said, impressed she was still ready to do battle. He liked someone who was willing to fight for what they wanted.

She pushed back her chair and stood up. "I need some coffee."

After she left the table, a cold blast of wind entered the room, and he looked toward the front door. A man about his age walked into the coffee shop wearing black slacks, a cream-colored dress shirt, and a maroon and gray striped tie, his brown hair edged with blond highlights, his hazel eyes very familiar.

Doug Winters had certainly aged well, boasting the same good-looking features that had gotten him dates with half the high school cheerleading squad.

Doug had been the closest thing to a best friend he'd ever had, but that friendship had ended on a summer night a week before he left town to join the Marines.

As their gazes met, he saw surprise and wariness flash through Doug's eyes. Apparently, thirteen years had not been long enough for anyone to forget.

He took the final sip of his coffee and set his mug down on the table, then got to his feet.

Doug moved in front of him. "So, it's true. You lied again. You did come back, even though you said you never would."

"I said a lot of stupid things when I was eighteen." He paused, looking Doug straight in the eye. "So did you."

More discomfort entered Doug's gaze, and his lips drew into a worried line. "How long are you staying?"

"Not sure."

"I don't want any trouble, Roman."

"Why would there be trouble?"

"You know why." Doug drew in a breath.

They stared at each other for a good thirty seconds, and he could see beads of sweat appear on Doug's brow. That surprised him a little. Doug had always been cocky as hell as a teenager, convinced that his father, who'd been chief of police, and his mother, who ran the PTA, would be able to get him out of any problems. And, in fact, they'd done just that. *So why the worry now?*

Doug cleared his throat. "I don't know if you've heard, but I'm running for mayor."

Ah—now he understood the concern. Doug was afraid he would try to damage his reputation. "Good luck," he said.

"I don't want any trouble with you, Roman. Can we let the past be the past?"

He wasn't at all interested in soothing Doug's nerves. "I guess we'll find out."

Juliette tapped her fingers restlessly on the counter while Donavan made her espresso. She probably shouldn't be getting coffee; she felt in more emotional turmoil now than she had in years. But she needed a taste of something strong, something grounding, something to give her the energy to keep thinking and strategizing. Her outreach to Roman's grandfather had been unsuccessful. But she wasn't done trying. As she'd told Roman, she didn't quit easily. She just needed a new approach.

Thinking about Roman filled her with more turmoil...but a different kind—the kind that came with butterflies in her stomach and sweaty palms and a tingly feeling of anticipation, uncertainty.

She was happy he'd left the coffee shop, although she was curious about the tense exchange he'd just had with Doug Winters. She hadn't been close enough to hear their words, but there was no denying the angry, tense body language.

She wondered what it was all about. Doug was one of the most well-liked people in town. He was a lawyer and a city councilman, and now he was running for mayor. Roman might have been a troublemaker in high school, but he'd gone on to become a soldier, a Marine. They both seemed to have a lot going for them, but something from the past was still between them, and she was very curious as to what that was.

"Hello, ladies," Doug said, as he stepped up to the counter. "How is everyone today?"

"Great," Donavan replied. "The usual, Doug?"

"Give me two shots of espresso today, and I'll take a to-go cup."

"Must be a tough day," Donavan commented, a gleam in her eyes. "Or did it get tougher when you saw Roman?"

"Roman has always made my life more difficult," he said, then turned toward Juliette. "I have to tell you that the coconut lemon cake you made for my mother's birthday has won me a lot of points. She said it was the best present I ever gave her."

"I'm so glad. It's one of my favorites."

"The bakery looks like it's doing well."

"Very well," she said.

"That's great. It's nice to have you as part of the business community." He paused. "We should have dinner one night. I'd love to take you out."

"Oh—sure," she said, a little surprised by the invitation.

"Good. I'll give you a call or I'll stop by the bakery." He picked up his coffee, tipped his head to Donavan and then left the coffee shop.

"Sounds like Doug is interested in you," Donavan said, a gleam in her eyes. "Any interest back?"

"Uh, I don't know." She gave a helpless smile. "He's definitely attractive. He seems like a good guy." She paused. "Is there something between Doug and Roman? They certainly had a tense exchange when they saw each other."

"There's a lot of history there. They were friends in high school, but some stuff happened senior year that Roman took the heat for, and I've always wondered if Doug was as innocent as he claimed to be."

"What kind of stuff?"

Before Donavan could explain, a crowd of teenagers came into the coffee shop, overwhelming the counter.

"Sorry, I can't talk now, but later," Donavan promised.

"Of course."

She moved away from the counter to allow more space for the new customers.

Donavan's words had made her curious, which did not make her happy. She'd already thought about Roman way too much; now she had to wonder about Doug, too.

Four

—➤➤◄◄◄—

Juliette beat her alarm by an hour on Friday morning, bringing an end to her sleepless night around four in the morning instead of her usual five a.m. wake-up time. She'd been sleeping so well in Fairhope. She'd actually thought she'd beaten her insomnia until last night, when her mixed-up brain ran around in circles between her childhood home on Primrose Lane, the sexy and somewhat brooding Roman Prescott, his stubborn grandfather, and finally the charming Doug Winters.

Too many men, she decided, as she got out of bed. They were quickly becoming the source of all her problems. She needed to put a stop to that.

Not that Roman wanted to be a problem in her life; he'd probably be happy if he never saw her again. And no doubt his grandfather felt the same way.

Doug—he was another story, a story she wanted to know more about, not just because he wanted to take her to dinner, but also because the first time she'd ever seen him flustered was after he'd spoken to Roman. There was some mystery there, and she couldn't help wondering what it was as she showered and changed into leggings, a long-sleeved tunic top, and her super-comfortable bunny slippers. While she'd slip into her boots once the bakery opened, she'd be on her feet a few hours before that, and she wanted to be comfortable.

When she'd finished dressing, she went downstairs, happy again that her landlord had not only rented her the bakery space but the studio apartment on the second floor. Her commute was perfect.

It was dark outside, and she quickly turned on the lights and started preheating the ovens. Her first job of the day was to get her bread loaves baking, and within minutes she fell into her morning routine. Happy to be doing what she loved, she lost herself in the rhythm of baking, and soon the sun had come up over town.

Once the bread was done, she turned her attention to her Wish cookies. Yesterday's batch had been pretty close to what she remembered. She'd duplicate that and stop trying to tweak the recipe. The cookies were good and as magical as she could make them.

With all ovens firing and timers set, she went into the store and refilled her display cases. Then she made coffee from Donavan's for those customers who didn't hit the coffeehouse across the street.

With that done, she wiped down the café tables by the window. She couldn't help but take a few quick glances outside to see if there were any attractive early morning joggers headed her way, but the block was empty.

Roman had probably decided to take a different route after their two encounters yesterday. Not only had she had a meltdown in her old house right in front of him, but then she'd gotten into an awkward discussion with his grandfather, all over a house that in reality she could not afford to buy.

She didn't know what she was thinking, begging Mr. Prescott to sell it to her when she didn't have any money. She needed to start thinking first before acting. Not that she'd given up on the idea of getting her house back, but she needed to go to Mr. Prescott with a much better informed and planned strategy.

As the clock struck seven thirty, she unlocked her doors

and turned the *Closed* sign around. She'd been opening earlier and earlier since Christmas, as more and more people stopped in on their way to work to pick up a morning sweet or to put in an order for a special cake or dessert for some important occasion in their lives. Since she was still building her business, she'd take customers any time she could get them.

"Good morning," Susan said, as she entered through the front door.

"How are you today?"

"I'm ready for another busy day selling Wish cookies."

"They are popular."

"I can't tell you how many stories I heard yesterday," Susan said. "The cookies bring back a lot of special memories for more people than you would think. I have to admit I was skeptical when you first told me about the tradition, but I have been proved wrong."

She laughed. "I think people want to believe in magic, no matter what form it comes in."

"I think so, too." The doorbell dinged, and the first customers of the day walked in. "I better get to work," Susan said.

While Susan filled orders, she went back into the kitchen and adorned another tray of Wish cookies with lavender frosting and tiny red hearts. Then she took them out to the front of the store and filled the display trays of mix-and-match cookies that were open to the customers to pick and choose their favorite cookies. The rest of the desserts, they kept on their side of the glass.

The line had grown even longer, so she helped Susan out at the cash register, happy to see so many familiar faces coming back for desserts. She was starting to feel a part of the Fairhope family again, and that was an amazing feeling.

As she finished with a customer, she noticed a small boy by the cookie case. He was about eight or nine, with blond hair and blue eyes. She'd seen him in the bakery before and had thought he looked a little ragged. His skin seemed pale and unhealthy, his clothes looking like they hadn't seen a washer in a while.

The kid gave a few furtive looks around him, then grabbed a couple Wish cookies from the help-yourself tray, stuffed them into the pocket of his jacket, and then ran for the door. He ducked under the arm of a woman coming into the bakery, almost knocking her off her feet.

Frowning, she told Susan she'd be back in a minute and went out the door after him.

He was a block ahead of her and moving fast, but she needed to catch him. It wasn't so much that she couldn't afford to lose the two cookies; it was more that she wanted to know who he was, why he was stealing from her, and more importantly, why he looked like he needed someone to go after him.

He cut around the corner, running down an alley behind a row of retail shops. He flung a quick look over his shoulder and then ran faster when he saw her.

As he came out of the alley and darted around a corner, she lost him for a second, then picked him up again when he reached the next intersection. He was heading out of the downtown area and into a residential neighborhood.

Her bunny slippers flopped on her feet, impeding her progress. She really wished she had her boots on, but she'd never had a second to change into her street shoes.

The kid darted through some trees and down a side yard next to a big, two-story house. She quickly followed, but as she went toward the open backyard, a big dog came bounding toward her with a ferocious bark.

Stopping abruptly, she froze, then whirled around and started to run back the way she'd come—only to barrel straight into a hard male chest.

A man's hands came out to catch her—*Roman!*

She stared at him in shock, only to have surprise turn to fear as the big dog came closer, still barking his head off.

"We have to get out of here," she said. "I don't think that dog is friendly."

"Are you kidding? He's super friendly." Roman turned

his head toward the German shepherd. "Barkley, calm down, buddy." He let go of Juliette to pet the dog, whose barks of warning had turned into woofs of joy.

"You know this dog?" she asked in amazement.

"Yeah, he chases me almost every morning for about two blocks. He likes to run with people."

Her racing heart began to slow down. "Good to know. I thought he was going to take a bite out of me."

"Why were you running into his backyard?"

"I was following someone."

"That little kid?"

"You saw him?"

"Yeah, I saw you chasing him."

"So you followed me?"

"Well, you were following him," he returned. "I was curious as to why."

"He stole some cookies out of the bakery."

Roman raised an eyebrow. "And you always chase down eight-year-old thieves?"

She felt a little foolish now. She really wasn't giving Roman the best impression of her. "Not normally. But this isn't the first time he was in the bakery, and he has a look about him that worries me. I wondered what his story was. But I lost him when Barkley here decided to come after me." She paused. "Have you seen the little boy before?"

"Nope—not that I've noticed anyway."

She glanced toward the neatly landscaped property and the stately house. "I don't think he lives here."

"You don't think rich kids can steal cookies?" he asked, a sharp note in his voice.

"I didn't say that."

"It's what you were thinking. You'd have felt much better if he'd taken you the other direction, to the apartment buildings on Randolph Street, or the run-down area off Gardner."

"I wasn't thinking anything. He stole two cookies. I followed him. That's as far as my thought process got." She realized her defense wasn't painting her in that good of a light.

"You're right. I forgot how impulsive you are."

"Considering you've known me for less than a day, I don't see how you can make that statement."

He smiled—*the man actually smiled*—and it sent a crazy shiver down her spine. It was the first time he hadn't looked annoyed or closed off, and it was shockingly sexy.

"I could have made that statement five minutes after you burst into my grandfather's house," he said. "First you want to stop a remodel on a house you don't own, then you want to buy a house you can't afford. Now you're chasing a cookie thief in a pair of bunny slippers."

"I wear them when I bake," she said defensively. "They're comfortable for standing up for hours on end. I was going to change, but I didn't have a chance." She paused. "Just so you know, I wasn't going to yell at the kid; I was going to ask him if he was hungry, if he needed help. There was something in his eyes. It looked like—desperation." She shook her head. "You wouldn't understand."

"Now that I would understand," he said quietly.

She stared back at him, sensing there was more behind his words than he would ever tell her. "Would you?"

He nodded, but didn't elaborate.

"Well, maybe he'll come back another day," she said, taking one last glance around, but she knew the child was long gone.

"Probably not for a few days if he saw you chasing him."

"He did see me." She thought for a moment. "I wonder if I should go by the closest elementary school and see if I can find him."

"Whoa, seriously?" he asked in surprise. "You're going to scout out the school now?"

"What if he's in trouble?"

"What if he just wanted to see if he could steal a cookie right out from under your nose?"

"I don't think it was that."

"It could have been."

He had a point. "Well, I'll think about it. I should get back to the bakery. Mornings are my busiest time. Susan probably wonders where the hell I went."

He fell into step alongside her, which surprised her even more. "Maybe I'll take you up on your free dessert offer. I'm hungry," he said.

"I thought you didn't eat sweets."

"Since I came back to Fairhope, I'm doing a lot of things I normally don't do."

"Like what else?" she asked, as they walked back toward town.

He shrugged. "Chase women who are chasing little boys."

She made a face at him. "No one asked you to do that."

A smile played around his lips again. "The bunny slippers intrigued me. I couldn't resist."

"They slowed me down. I would have caught that kid if I'd been in regular shoes."

"I'm sure."

She cast him a sideways glance, knowing he wouldn't like her next question, but she couldn't stop herself. "What's the story with you and Doug Winters? Your conversation at Donavan's didn't look friendly."

As she'd expected, his expression shut down, his profile turning hard. "We were friends before. We're not now."

"That's it? You can't be a little more expansive? What happened between you? Why did you stop being friends?"

"It's not your business, Juliette."

He was right about that, but she was too curious to back off. "Maybe it would be good for you to talk about what happened. You could get rid of bad feelings, release the past."

"I doubt that would occur." He shot her a look. "You seem to talk about everything that's on your mind, and you're still trapped in the past."

Now it was her turn to frown. "That's not true."

"It's completely true. That's why you want to buy your

old house, isn't it? You can't let go of the past."

"Well, my past was happy. Yours apparently wasn't."

"You've got me there, but it's my business. You need to stop meddling in everyone else's life. That little kid probably doesn't need your help, and God knows I don't need your assistance." He stopped walking and gave her an irritated look. "I've changed my mind about the pastry. I think I'll stick to an all-protein breakfast."

"Hey, hang on," she protested, impulsively grabbing his arm. "Don't be like that. I was just trying to help. You can keep your secrets. And I have the perfect breakfast bread for you, so please come with me to the bakery."

He sighed. "You're a lot of work, Juliette."

"You're not the first person to tell me that." She gave him a pleading smile. "Others have said I'm worth it."

"I'd like to meet some of those people," he muttered.

"If you come with me, I promise not to ask you any more questions about your mysterious past with Doug Winters."

"Fine. I'll come to the bakery."

She let go of his arm as they continued walking toward downtown. "So, what are you doing on the house today?"

"Nothing you want to hear about," he said dryly.

"I'm surprised you're living there during the construction. I saw your stuff in the upstairs bedroom."

"My grandfather and I don't make good roommates, and since I don't know how long I'll be in town, the house suits my needs. I've got a bed to sleep on, a TV in the kitchen, running water and electricity; what more do I need?"

"I would want a lot more, but you don't seem to require much."

"I've lived in a lot worse places."

"Like…" she began, knowing she was probably treading back into dangerous waters, but while she'd agreed not to ask about the distant past, maybe the more recent past would prove less bothersome.

"Like dry, sandy, monochrome deserts that go on for miles, that are unbearably hot, and feel a little like hell on earth."

"I think that's the longest sentence you've ever said to me. Since you're not giving me an exact location, I'm guessing that's somewhere in the Middle East."

"Somewhere," he agreed.

"I heard you were in the Marines."

"I still am—for the moment."

"What does that mean?"

He hesitated, then said, "I was injured and put on medical leave a few months ago."

"So you're going back."

"That's debatable. I have to pass the physical and that might not happen."

She was surprised by his words. He looked like he was in the peak of physical health. "You seem pretty fit to me. You run every day."

"I have some hearing issues that haven't resolved completely, as well as a shoulder injury with some lingering weakness. If I'm not one hundred percent, I won't be able to do my job and any weakness could jeopardize the other members of my unit."

"But there must be other jobs you could do."

"Not that I necessarily want to do," he countered. "What if someone told you that you could still be a baker, but you could only make vanilla cookies and nothing else?"

"I'd tell them the business would fail quickly. But I get your point. When will you find out?"

"I have a follow-up physical a week from Monday, then a decision will be made."

She could hear the tension in his voice and knew he had a lot riding on that decision. "What will your grandfather do if you go back to the Marines?"

"He'll have to find other workers."

She wondered if Roman's departure might slow down the remodel. While that thought was interesting, the idea of him leaving before she really got a chance to know him was not nearly as appealing.

"I have to admit that the construction has been a nice change," Roman continued, surprising her by volunteering information that wasn't in direct response to a question. "It feels good to be in a house, to be tearing out something that will actually be made better."

She heard a deep sadness in his voice and suspected Roman had been through things she couldn't even imagine. *What must it be like to put your life on the line every single day?* It made her bakery business seem quite inconsequential. "Maybe you could do construction if you have to change jobs," she suggested.

"Perhaps. I can't consider it right now. My life has always been the Marines. I'm a soldier. That's what I do well." He stopped abruptly, as if suddenly realizing how much he was telling her.

"You know what you need besides my extra-special banana walnut bread?" she asked.

"I have a feeling you're going to tell me."

"A couple of my Valentine's Day Wish cookies. Legend has it that if you eat them, your wishes will come true."

The tension in his face eased with her words. "Legend has it?"

"Yes. The tradition started with my father. He ran a bakery here in town when he was alive, and he made these special Wish cookies every February. He'd sell them from the first to the fourteenth, and a lot of people have told me their wishes came true after eating the cookies."

"The wishes are for love?"

"Actually, for anything that brings you love or joy. You could wish for a full recovery from your injuries."

"So all I have to do is eat a cookie to change my life? If that's true, and you're the cookie maker, why aren't you already a millionaire?"

"Maybe that's not my wish," she countered.

"That's everyone's wish."

"Actually, I've never been that motivated by money. I respect that I need money to do what I want, but it's not what drives me." She paused. "I don't think it's what drives you."

"You don't know me."

"Well, I don't think anyone becomes a soldier to get rich."

"You've got me there."

"These are very special cookies," she said. "You might be surprised at their power—if you can keep an open mind."

"I can do that."

"Really?" she asked doubtfully as they neared the bakery.

"Yes," he said with a nod. "And I am a little curious to see just how good these cookies are." He paused and opened the door of the bakery to allow two older women to walk out.

The first one—the gray-haired, stern-faced, Martha Grayson—gave Roman a sharp, killing look. Her sister—the red-haired, much sweeter, Cecelia—stumbled into Martha's back as she stopped abruptly.

"*You!*" Martha said, glaring at Roman.

"Ma'am," Roman muttered, his lips drawn in a tight line.

"Good morning, ladies," Juliette said cheerfully, trying to lighten the tense moment.

"I can't believe you had the nerve to come back here," Martha said to Roman. "Haven't you done enough damage in this town? You think we've all forgotten what kind of boy you were?"

"I'll see you later, Juliette," Roman said, letting the door go.

Cecelia caught it with her hand, which probably wouldn't have made Roman happy, since no doubt he'd wanted to smash it in Martha's face, but he hadn't bothered to look back.

Juliette frowned at the Grayson sisters as they came onto the sidewalk, letting the door close behind them.

"You should not be talking to that man," Martha said.

"Why? What happened? What did he do?" she asked.

"So many things," Martha said. "I don't know where to start. As soon as he came to town as a teenager, there was nothing but problems. He got into fights. Good kids were following him down bad paths. He even started a fire that burned down Phil Marson's house. The poor family had to move. He caused nothing but pain and misery, and I can't believe he had the nerve to come back here—or that his grandfather would let him. I don't know what Vincent was thinking."

She was taken aback by the spew of nastiness coming from Martha's mouth as well as the barrage of incidents that apparently had Roman's name on them.

"We don't really know if Roman did all those things," Cecelia put in, giving her sister a pained look.

"Of course we do," Martha said. "Vincent should have sent him back where he came from as soon as he realized there was a problem, but he didn't want to see what was right under his nose."

"You've said enough, Martha," Cecelia said, giving Juliette an apologetic smile. "We'll be going now."

"You'll stay away from him if you know what's good for you," Martha added, sending one last parting shot before her sister urged her down the street.

She considered Martha's words. The man she'd met didn't seem quick to anger or explosively violent, but it was certainly possible he'd changed since he was a teenager. Martha wasn't the only one who had a problem with Roman; Doug Winters did as well.

But she'd make up her own mind about Roman. She wasn't going to let Martha dictate her actions. She also wasn't going to let the butterflies in her stomach distract her from seeing him for who he really was.

Five

~~>≫≪<~~

Roman had always liked his own company, always felt comfortable by himself, but for some reason the solitude was getting on his nerves and by five Friday afternoon, he was itching to get out of the house again.

He didn't know why; it wasn't like yesterday's trip to the coffee shop had gone that well. And this morning's run-in with the Grayson sisters at Juliette's bakery had only reminded him that he could spend a lifetime trying to defend himself—if he was at all interested in doing that, which he was not.

He suspected that Juliette had gotten an earful from Martha and her sister after he left. She'd already been curious about Doug and the tension she'd witnessed at the coffee shop. Well, she probably knew quite a bit more about him now—or at least the teenager he'd once been. He wondered if she'd believe everything she heard.

Probably. Everyone else had.

With a frustrated sigh, he set down his tools, grabbed his jacket and headed outside. Avoiding the downtown shopping area, he walked toward the water. It was a route similar to the one he ran most mornings, but now he wasn't interested so much in exercise as in taking a long breath of cool, crisp air and getting away from his thoughts.

As he walked past a mix of modest and stately houses, most of which were set on large lots with canopies of trees overhead, he remembered the first time he'd come to Fairhope. He'd thought he'd landed in the middle of a Norman Rockwell painting. It was small town America with a charming downtown area and shop owners who knew each other, people who said hello when you passed by. It was a place where community mattered, where friends and families came together to celebrate holidays and birthdays and even sadder moments.

It had been a huge change from his life in Southern California, with a mother who barely talked to him, much less any kind of family or community to support him.

Deep down, he'd really liked Fairhope, but he'd refused to admit it. He'd been sent there against his will, forced to leave what few friends he had, to live with a grandfather he'd never met. He'd barricaded his feelings behind anger and sarcasm.

But inside he'd been vulnerable, worried that if he got too comfortable, if he liked something too much, it would disappear, because it always had before.

So he'd pretended to resent his grandfather's rules: breakfast at six, school at eight, job after school, dinner at six, homework, then bed. It had been more structure than he'd ever experienced in his life. But it had felt good to actually know what he was supposed to do and when he was supposed to do it.

He just hadn't been willing to let anyone else see that. He'd been judged before he even got off the plane as Vincent's troublemaking teenage grandson, and it had been easier to be that than to try to be anyone else. So he'd acted like he hated the hokey small-town traditions, the busybody neighbors, the town's desire to celebrate everything, the emphasis on culture, on art and design and music and writing. He'd made fun of the artists who painted by the pier, the musicians singing in the square for pocket money, the idea that life could be pretty and perfect, even though in Fairhope it certainly seemed like it could be.

With a sigh, he paused as he dug his shoes into the brown sandy shores of Mobile Bay. Off to his right was the long pier that jutted into the bay. He'd stood in this very spot many times as a teenager, wondering what his future held. Would he go back to California? Would his mother ever get better and come and get him? Would he stay here forever?

The answers had never come, but looking at the water, the horizon, had helped keep things in perspective.

He needed some of that perspective now. Just like when he'd come to town before, he wasn't sure how long he'd stay. He'd left Fairhope to make a life for himself in the Marine Corps. He liked the man he'd become, the job he'd done, the people he'd done it with. To think he might have to actually give it all up was difficult to swallow, but he was too much of a realist not to consider that possibility. He wasn't giving up, though—not yet—not until they told him he was done. But in his gut he knew things were going to change. He would have to decide how he wanted to change with them.

His cell phone buzzed, and he pulled it out of his pocket, happy to see Cole Kenner's name run across the screen. Cole had served with him for the past seven years. They'd been through a lot together, and they'd always had an instinct about when the other was in trouble.

"Cole, what's up?"

"Checking in. How's sweet home Alabama?"

"Not home, not sweet, but I'm here." As he made the statement, he realized he was wrong. There was sweetness in this town, and her name was Juliette.

"When do you see the doc again?"

"A week from Monday."

"I'm hoping for good news."

"You and me, both. What about you? How are things going?"

"Same as always. I'm stateside for a few days. Loving a little beach action."

Which meant Cole was probably in San Diego at Camp Pendleton. "I'm at the beach right now, too—different view, though."

"Are you and your grandfather getting along?"

"We are. I'm actually helping him with some construction."

"Your shoulder is up for that?"

"I think it's good to work the muscles." He didn't mention that the shoulder was not as big of a concern as his hearing.

"We need you back, Roman."

"I'd like to be back. Anything new with anyone?"

"Jimmy got himself engaged."

"What?" he asked with a laugh. "Again?" Jimmy had been engaged three times in the five years Roman had known him.

"You know Jimmy. He falls in love every other day."

"And out of love, just as fast."

"True, but he thinks this one will stick."

"I hope it does."

"I gotta run. Let me know what happens after you see the doc."

"I will. Stay safe, Cole."

"Always."

As he slipped his phone back into his pocket, his gaze returned to the water, but he wasn't seeing the scene in front of him; he was seeing Cole and his buddies playing cards to pass the time, running drills, passing out soccer balls to kids, rebuilding a school, getting ready for their next mission. So many memories—both good and bad. He should be with them, but he wasn't.

Letting out a sigh, he told himself to stay in the moment and stop dwelling on what he couldn't control or predict. He turned away from the view. He needed a distraction…maybe some food.

Spying a café down the road, he quickened his steps, and a few minutes later he was sitting at the counter of the Sea Bird Café.

A cheerful woman named Ruth took his order for a bowl of turkey chili and a salad, which he ate while watching a basketball game on the television behind the counter.

"Are you new in town?" Ruth asked, as she cleared his empty plates.

"Not exactly. I lived here a long time ago; now I'm back."

"Welcome home. Are you going to the movie fest tonight?"

"I don't know what that is."

She looked at him as if he'd just crawled out from under a rock. "You must not have been back in town long if you haven't heard about the film festival. It starts tonight in the town square. They put up a big screen, and they'll be showing romantic movies the next two nights. Tomorrow, they'll also be having a costume contest for best romantic couple in history. My boyfriend and I are going as Rose and Jack from *Titanic*."

"That sounds..." he could hardly say *really bad*, so he settled for, "like fun."

She laughed. "The look on your face matches the one my boyfriend gave me when I showed him our costumes the other day."

"Doesn't Jack die, and Rose ends up with someone else?"

"Yes, but they still had the love story of a lifetime, and he died for her. What greater love can you have than that?"

He could not argue her point.

"My boyfriend is being a good sport," she continued. "Of course, he agreed, because if he wants to keep getting lucky, he has to put in a little work ahead of time," she said with a mischievous smile.

He grinned back at her. "I suspect he'll do whatever is necessary."

"I suspect he will, too. Are you married?"

"Nope," he said, seeing the interested gleam enter her eyes.

"That will make a lot of single women in this town very

happy."

He finished off his beer and then put enough cash on the table to give Ruth a generous tip.

"That is too much," she protested.

"Not at all. You made my dinner very enjoyable."

"That's good. Sometimes I get in trouble for talking too much. You have a nice night. Maybe I'll see you at the movies."

"Maybe you will."

Despite his words, he really had no intention of going to the movie fest, but as he got closer to downtown, the sparkling lights in the trees around the square drew his attention. He could just check it out for a few minutes; he didn't have to stay.

The park was packed with people. In the center of the square, a dozen or so rows of chairs had been set up in front of a big screen, and *Casablanca* was already playing. Beyond the chairs, couples and families were also at picnic tables, sitting in beach chairs or sprawled out on blankets on the grass. Around the outskirts of the square were several tables set up to sell coffee, desserts, and other snacks.

He saw Donavan first, selling her Ethiopian coffee, then his heart sped up as his gaze moved to the next table—to Juliette.

She had on a red sweater and dark jeans, her long, brown, wavy hair flowing around her shoulders, her smile bright in the evening light. She had a middle-aged woman helping her sell desserts, which looked to be a good thing, since they had a line of eager customers. He wondered if they were all buying her Wish cookies.

He smiled at the memory of that ridiculous story. Who would ever believe a cookie could grant your deepest desire? But he supposed it was no different than believing in Santa Claus, the tooth fairy or the Easter bunny.

Not that he'd ever believed in any of those mythical characters. There certainly had never been any dollars tucked under his pillow at night after a tooth fell out, and Santa had never seemed able to find his house, but then they hadn't had a chimney. His mom had told him once that was the reason. It hadn't made him feel any better.

He thought about saying hello to Juliette, maybe buying one of her desserts, but he'd wait until the line died down. Glancing away from her table, his gaze caught on a child standing under the trees some distance away. He looked like the child Juliette had chased after earlier in the day.

He seemed too young to be all alone, and there was a wistful expression on his face, as if he wanted to be part of the crowd, but he just didn't know how he could be. It felt like he didn't belong there. There was certainly no family on a blanket or at a table, waving for him to come over.

He'd been that kid once—and probably at that age.

He didn't know what the child's story was, but he knew down deep in his gut that it was a story he'd heard before— lived before.

The question was: what to do about it?

He could try to talk to him, but the kid would probably run.

"Roman?"

Juliette's voice turned his head. He was surprised and bemused to see her standing in front of him. She had a small paper plate in her hand with two purple heart-shaped cookies on it.

"I saw you and thought if I couldn't get you to come inside the bakery, maybe I should bring the bakery to you. These are the infamous Wish cookies," she told him.

"They're pretty," he said, thinking she was even prettier than the cookies with her sparkly blue eyes, rosy-colored cheeks and soft pink mouth that he was itching to taste.

"They're also good. Care to try one?" she asked.

He was tempted—and not just by the cookies. He swallowed hard. "In a second." He tipped his head toward the trees. "Does that kid look familiar?"

"Oh, my goodness. That's the little boy from this morning. I have to talk to him."

He put a hand on her shoulder as she started forward. "Are you ready to run again?"

She frowned. "No. Why?"

"He saw you this morning, right?"

"Yes."

"Let me take him the cookies."

"You? A strange man, in the dark woods, at night, offering him cookies..."

"Good point."

"Let's do it together."

The boy was looking in the other direction, so they were able to get within a few feet before the boy saw them. He tensed and looked immediately ready to bolt.

"I thought you might want some cookies," Juliette said quickly, holding out the plate in her hands.

The kid's eyes widened, but he made no move to take the plate of cookies.

"I'm Juliette. I own the bakery. This is my friend, Roman. Everything is okay. I'm not mad about the cookies you took this morning."

"I have to go," the kid muttered.

"Hang on," he said, grabbing the kid's arm as he tried to leave. "We just want to talk to you for a second."

"I'm not supposed to talk to strangers," the boy said.

"That's smart," Juliette said, squatting down in front of him, so she was at his eye level. "I was worried when I saw you this morning. That's why I ran after you. I thought you might be hungry, or you might need help. What's your name?"

The boy hesitated, then said, "Cameron."

"It's nice to meet you, Cameron," Juliette said. "Are your parents here?"

The little boy shook his head.

"Is anyone with you?" Juliette asked with concern.

"My grandma," he said, with a vague wave of his hand. "I have to go. Sorry I took your cookies."

"Can I meet your grandma?" Juliette asked.

"She doesn't want to be bothered during the movie," Cameron replied.

"You're a little young to be out here in the trees alone," Roman put in.

"I'm not afraid," he said, a defiant note in his voice as he looked up at him. "Let me go."

"I'll let you go after you take us to see your grandmother," he told him firmly.

Cameron measured his words, then let out a sigh. "Fine."

Roman kept a grip on Cameron's arm as the child led them into the park and over to an older woman sitting in a beach chair next to another woman. Then he let go.

"Grandma," Cameron said. "I brought you some Wish cookies."

"Oh, my, are these the cookies I've been hearing so much about?" the grandmother asked.

"Yes," Juliette said, stepping forward. "I'm Juliette Adams. I run the Sweet Somethings Bakery."

"Adams? You're Frank and Tricia's daughter? I remember you when you were a little girl. I'm Donna Mays, and I see you've met my grandson, Cameron." She gave Cameron a shake of her head. "I told you to stay in the playground, not go over to the dessert tables."

"Sorry," Cameron muttered, not admitting he'd actually been in the woods.

Donna bit into one of the cookies. "So delicious," she murmured. "And I hope it makes my wish come true."

"Can I have the other one?" Cameron asked.

"Of course, you can. Georgia, we'll need to get you a cookie, too," Donna added, speaking to the woman sitting next to her.

"I've had far too many cookies already," Georgia said with a laugh. "I love your bakery, dear. I'm Georgia Rogers."

"It's nice to see you again," Juliette said.

"Your bakery is filled with so much sweetness and delight; you're very talented," Georgia added.

"Thanks," Juliette replied.

"Are you enjoying the movies?" Donna asked.

"I haven't had a chance to watch yet," Juliette said. "But I hope to catch some of the films."

"She doesn't need a romantic movie," Georgia told Donna. "She's young enough to have her own romance going on." Georgia's gaze encompassed them both. "The two of you are such an attractive couple."

"Oh, we're not a couple," Juliette said hastily. "We're not together."

"You look together now," Donna said, with a pointed smile.

"Just friends," Juliette said, giving him a look suggesting that he join in, but he didn't feel like saying anything.

No one had asked him who he was, and he was fine with that. Donna looked vaguely familiar to him, but he couldn't quite place her. Maybe she was one of his grandfather's friends.

"I should get back to my table," Juliette added. "Have fun."

"Oh, we will," Donna said. "We just love romantic movies, especially tragic love stories. Those are the best. So much drama."

"You and your drama," Georgia said with a laugh.

As the ladies teased each other, Roman and Juliette walked back to her dessert table. "What do you think?" she asked.

"Cameron has a grandmother."

"Who wasn't paying very close attention to him."

"He wasn't that far away."

"Yes, he was," she argued. "And he was alone when he took the cookies from my bakery. I should have asked her about Cameron's parents." She paused. "Maybe I should go back and tell her what happened this morning."

"You can if you want, but he's with a responsible adult, Juliette. She might not be watching him the way you would, but she seems nice."

She glanced back at Cameron, who was sitting on the

ground next to his grandmother's chair. "She does seem nice. I just have an uneasy feeling. There's something we don't know."

"I'm sure there's a lot we don't know, but we can't butt into their lives. It's their family business. And the fact that she told him to stay in the playground and he didn't isn't a crime."

"But you think there's something off, don't you?"

He took another look at Cameron, who was now flat on his back, gazing up at the stars. He remembered doing that, too, hoping to find some sort of divine intervention. "I think the kid has some problems, but I obviously don't know what they are."

She looked at him in surprise. "Really? I thought you were going to disagree with me."

"Cameron seems sad, but that could be due to anything. And I don't think he's in any immediate danger."

"No, not tonight anyway. I'm going to find out more about him, though."

He was amazed by her persistent bullheadedness. "Don't you have enough to worry about? You're building a business. You're trying to buy a house you can't afford. Now you want to figure out why one little boy is sad?"

"I can find time to do everything I need to do." She paused. "I know what it feels like to be sad, Roman. I guess there's something about that child that resonates with me. You wouldn't understand."

"Actually, I would," he said quietly. "I know what being sad as a kid feels like, too."

She stared back at him and as their gazes clung together, he felt a strong and intense pull of attraction, not just physical, but emotional. He didn't know why he'd just told her something so personal. He barely knew her, and he never spilled his guts—not to anyone. There was only one person who knew even a few things about his childhood, and that person was his grandfather. He'd never talked about his past with anyone else. He didn't know why he'd come so close to the subject now, and judging by the gleam in Juliette's eyes, he was going to regret his brief lapse in judgment.

"You said your dad died, and I know you came to live with your grandfather when you were fifteen. What happened to your mom?" she asked.

"She had a lot of problems—addictions, mental issues. I was taken away from her a couple of times. The last time, my grandfather stepped in and brought me here."

Her gaze filled with compassion. "I'm really sorry."

"It is what it is. I learned early on that the only person I could count on was myself."

She stared back at him with her big blue eyes, and he could see a dozen more questions brimming in her gaze. He needed to cut those off right now.

"I don't really want to talk about my past." He waved his hand to the crowd of customers at her dessert table. "You should get back to work. Your assistant looks like she's going under."

She started. "I do need to help her. Can we talk about Cameron again, maybe tomorrow?"

"What's to talk about?"

"How we can help him."

"We don't know if he needs help."

"Yes, we do. And I don't want Cameron to think that the only person he can count on is himself," she said, throwing his words back at him. "I don't think you do, either."

He wanted to deny her words, but he couldn't. *And why fight her on a desire to help a little kid?* Maybe sticking her nose in Cameron's family business was exactly what the child needed.

That didn't mean he had to help her.

But he was starting to realize that she was really hard to say no to. There was something about her pretty blue eyes and those tantalizing lips, and the fact that every time she walked away, he wanted to call her back. But he shouldn't call her back, and he shouldn't make himself available to her. She was the kind of woman who would want too much from a man. She'd want to get inside his head, his heart, his feelings... He did not need that. He'd locked away a lot of stuff a long time ago, and he wasn't breaking that safe open for her or giving her a key. He wasn't that reckless—at least, he didn't think so.

Six

---→→➤➤◄◄◄←---

Saturday morning, Roman rolled out of bed a little after five, put on his running clothes and hit the streets before the sun came up. He put in six miles of hard running before he turned down the street where Juliette's bakery was located. He slowed his pace down, but forced himself to stay on the other side of the street.

He could see the lights on in her bakery, and as he stopped to stretch, she came into the front of her store and started filling up her display cases.

His heart flipped over in his chest.

He'd thought about her most of the night.

He couldn't have her. He was leaving. Even if he wasn't, she'd soon figure out that they were as opposite as night and day, as light and dark, as sweet and sour. He felt comfortable here in the shadows, where his secrets and his pain stayed hidden. She was bright lights and sweet smiles, serving up warm, delicious goodness. She even had half the town believing in a magical cookie.

While he had half the town believing he was a troublemaker, a liar, a cheater.

Yeah, he needed to keep running—as far away from her as he could get. She couldn't bring him up, but he could bring her down, and that was the last thing he wanted to do.

He started back down the street, arriving at the house a few moments later. After a shower and a quick breakfast, he got to work. He didn't take a break until his grandfather arrived around eleven.

"Looks good, Roman," his grandfather said as he perused the work he'd done so far.

"Thanks."

"Jeff been helping you out?"

"He came for a few hours yesterday, but he said he had a basketball tournament this weekend so he won't be able to work again until Monday after school."

His grandfather's lips tightened. "He didn't tell me that. He said he was free today."

He shrugged. "It's fine. I've got a good handle on the demo, and he's not that great of a worker. Where are you on hiring more crew, or subbing out some of this job?"

"I'm talking to people," his grandfather said vaguely.

"You've been saying that since I came back."

"Well, it's still true."

"You know that I can't commit to being here long enough to help you finish this."

"I'm aware," Vincent said shortly.

"You could scale back your plans," he suggested. "You could improve the house and add value without pushing out the back or moving as many walls around. Or you could stop right now and sell it to Juliette Adams. She'll take it as is."

Vincent's brows furrowed together as he frowned. "She can buy it when it's done, but I doubt she'll be able to afford it. She's young. There will be other houses for her."

"Not ones she grew up in." He didn't know why he was fighting Juliette's cause, because in truth he thought she'd be weighing herself down with this house, and it would never make her happy the way she thought.

"Like I told her, houses have many stories. Hers is only one. She'll be all right. You just worry about what needs to be done now. I'll take care of the rest of it."

"Fine."

"Max and I are going out on Hank's boat this afternoon. You need anything from me before I leave?"

"Nope. I'm set for now."

"I'll check in with you tomorrow then."

"Sure."

His grandfather had no sooner left when the doorbell rang.

He couldn't stop the sudden jolt of anticipation that ran through him. He wasn't expecting any workers today, so he was guessing there was only one person who could be on the other side of that door. He just wasn't sure he was ready to see her.

The bell rang again, reminding him that Juliette was stubborn and persistent.

"I know you're in there, Roman," she called out.

He took off his gloves and opened the door, his pulse racing a little faster as his gaze ran down her body. She wore jeans better than anyone he'd ever met, with curves in all the right places. Her brown hair was pulled back in a ponytail, her blue eyes bright, her cheeks as pink as her soft, clingy sweater.

"What took you so long?" she asked.

"I had my hands full," he said, shoving those hands in his pockets before he could do something far more dangerous with them.

She held up the plastic container in her hands. "I *still* have my hands full, unless you're willing to help me out."

"What's in that?"

"Wish cookies. Cameron and his grandmother ate yours last night, so I brought you some more."

"I'm really not a big fan of cookies."

"Eat these and I dare you to say that again."

He took the container out of her hands. "I suppose you want to come in."

"Yes," she said without hesitation. "I want to talk to you about Cameron."

"I figured." He stepped back as she moved past him.

She paused in the middle of the hallway. "You got rid of the closet."

"It opens up the living room."

"I can see that," she said tightly.

"It's just a closet, Juliette. Nothing stays the same."

"Believe me, I know that as well as anyone," she said, a sharper edge to her voice. When she turned to look at him, there was pain in her eyes along with a question. "Have you ever gone home...to wherever you lived before you came here as a teenager?"

"No."

"Have you ever thought about it?"

"I didn't leave a happy house like you did. I don't have memories of a place where life was wonderful."

"Really? Nothing in your life with your mom was good?" she asked tentatively. "No memories that were sweet?"

"Sweet, huh?" he asked with a frown. "I don't think so." But even as he said the words, flashes of his mom smiling, laughing, running along the beach as she tried to launch a kite into the air went through his head.

"There's something," Juliette said with a triumphant smile. "I can see it in your eyes. What was it?"

"It was nothing."

"It was a memory that wasn't bad."

"We were flying kites on the beach."

"What beach?"

"Santa Monica. We lived in Los Angeles. Not on the beach; we couldn't afford that. But occasionally we'd take the bus down there on a hot day. We didn't have air conditioning, and it was hot a lot. Sometimes we'd go to the market, just so we could stand in front of the freezer section for a while."

"What did she do for a living? How did she make money?"

"She did a lot of stuff—retail, restaurant cashier, dog walker, holiday elf."

"Holiday elf?" Juliette echoed.

He found himself smiling again. "Yeah, she got a job at the mall, one of Santa's elves. I was about ten. I'd go there with her and wander around while she put little kids on Santa's lap."

"But you didn't believe in Santa by then?"

"I never believed in him."

"Never? Not even when you were really young?"

He shrugged. "I tried, but he didn't show up at my house. And when my mom worked at the mall, I saw Santa throwing back shots in the parking lot."

"That's not something you should have seen."

"Trust me, that's the least of the *somethings* I shouldn't have seen."

"It sounds like a hard childhood, Roman." Sympathy filled her gaze.

He thought about her words. "I didn't really know how hard it was until I got older."

"What do you mean?"

"I don't know why we're talking about this."

"Because I asked, and we're friends."

"Are we?"

"I'd like to think so."

"We just met."

"Is there a mandatory time requirement on friendship?" she asked. "Why didn't you know how hard you had it until you were older?"

"Because it was my life. It was my normal. And when my mom would go into rehab or just disappear, and some social worker put me in foster care, I was with other kids who were bad off, too. But when I came to Fairhope, I saw an entirely different world. I thought I was on a movie set for a while."

She smiled. "It can feel that way at times. You kind of liked it, though, didn't you?"

"I didn't want to. I didn't want to be here. I wanted to go home."

"Even though it wasn't great?"

"Even though," he admitted. "It was what I knew."

"That makes sense. I just wish it hadn't been so bad."

"Well, we don't get to choose what family we're born into."

"Which brings us back to Cameron."

He was actually relieved they were moving off his past, because once again he'd said far too much. "What do you want to do now?"

"I got Donna and Cameron's address. I think we should pay them a visit. We can take them some desserts. She seemed to like the Wish cookies last night. Maybe if we get into the house, we can see how things look."

"It's really not your business."

"If there's a child who's in danger, it's everyone's business." She paused. "I know I could call Family Services, but that could cause a lot of problems, and if I'm wrong, Donna will be horribly insulted and embarrassed. I'd rather check things out myself."

Having been the recipient of several social worker visits, he couldn't help but agree. "Fine, but you don't need me for this plan."

"I do, actually. I was thinking that I might need someone to distract Donna while I ask to use the restroom."

"On the guise of looking around."

"Yes. It will take twenty minutes, tops."

"And you want to do this right now?"

"Preferably. I have two helpers in the bakery until three, so it's a good time for me."

"You know, I am working here."

"Can't you take a little time off? We can go now, and then I'll buy you lunch after. Do you like burgers? There's a new restaurant that serves the most amazing, fantabulous burgers. You will die when you eat one."

"*Fantabulous*? Is that even a word?"

"If it's not, it should be; it's the only word that adequately describes these hamburgers."

"I do like burgers," he said slowly, thinking he liked her

even more. He also felt a kinship with Cameron, which was the real reason he was contemplating saying yes to her plan. "Don't you have any other friends you could take with you?"

"I haven't made a lot of other friends here."

"How is that possible? You're one of the most outgoing people I've ever met."

"I've been busy. I love Donavan and Sara, but they work as much as I do."

"What about friends from when you lived here before?"

"I lost track of all of them. I was twelve when I left. That was fifteen years ago. I've run into a couple of kids I went to school with, but no one who's turned into a good friend. Just say yes, Roman. You'll spend more time arguing than it takes to just go over there."

"You are very persuasive and stubborn. All right, I'll go with you." He raised the container in his hand. "Are these the cookies we're taking? They're not actually for me, are they?"

She gave him a mischievous smile. "Well, they could be. We could go to the bakery and get more, or..."

"Or we can take these to her."

"And get you more later," she finished.

"I wonder if I'm actually ever going to get to eat one of these cookies," he murmured.

She laughed. "I promise you will. But this way you'll have time to think of a good wish, make the cookie count."

He already had a wish ready to go, but it was probably one he shouldn't make. He handed her back the container of cookies. "Let me wash my hands and change my shirt."

"Take your time," she said. "I'll just wander around down here."

As Roman went up the stairs, she let out a breath of relief. She'd been hoping he'd say yes to going with her to Donna's house, but she hadn't been sure of it. And as much as she wanted to help Cameron, she felt a lot more confident making the visit with Roman. Hopefully, it would just seem friendly and nothing more than that.

While he was changing, she walked around the downstairs, feeling a mix of emotions with every step she took. Flashes of the past still moved through her head, but the construction, the ripped-out walls, and the clutter of tools did keep some of the memories at bay. The house was starting to feel different than the one she remembered.

She entered the kitchen and saw the first sign of life in the downstairs area: a couple of boxes of cereal on the counter as well as a bag of apples and a bunch of bananas. She set down the container of cookies and opened the cupboards, finding plastic plates and cups and a few coffee mugs. Roman really was living the minimalistic life.

But then, he wasn't planning on being here for long. She frowned at that thought, then moved through the back door, onto the weathered deck that had definitely seen better days. No one had tended to this yard in a long time; it was filled with weeds and overgrown brush. She'd heard that the house had been rented for years, before being sold to Roman's grandfather, so the tenants probably just hadn't cared that much.

It was sad. The corner of the garden where her mom had grown tomatoes, zucchini, and herbs was now just dirt and weeds. She put her arms around her waist, feeling colder than the outside temperature. This yard felt like a reminder of the pain of her past, not the joy. But it would be better once the yard was landscaped, when flowers bloomed and grass grew. She could still recapture its glory—if she had the chance. At the moment, that was doubtful.

She thought about what Vincent Prescott had told her— that the house could and would tell many stories, not just hers. She'd never really thought of it that way before. Who would move in next? Would it be a family? Would there be kids who would want to help their mother grow vegetables, the way she'd done?

"Juliette?"

Roman's voice brought her back to the present. She turned around and pushed a smile on her face. She'd learned how to hide her sadness a long time ago.

"Ready?" she asked.

"Are you?" he countered, giving her a speculative look. "You looked lost in thought."

"I was back in the past."

"We both seem to be taking trips there today."

"This yard was my mother's pride and joy. Now it's a mess."

"It won't be for long."

"What is your grandfather going to do with it?"

"Replace the deck with some built-in benches, build in a barbecue area and redo the landscaping, but that's at the end of a very long list."

"Well, this yard could definitely use all of that. I'm always surprised when people who live in a beautiful house like this don't take care of the yard. If they don't want land to tend, they should live in a condo. It's just not right."

"If we're going, Juliette, we should go."

"You're right." Following Roman into the house, she grabbed her cookies and put thoughts of the house behind her as they went out to the front.

"We can take my car," she said, waving her hand toward her small white Mini Cooper.

He raised an eyebrow. "I don't think I'll fit in that."

"It's roomier than you might think."

"We can take my truck."

His weathered, charcoal-gray truck was definitely a lot bigger, but it also looked like it had seen better days, with dents on the passenger door and peeling paint on the hood. "How long have you had this?" she asked.

"I bought it right before I came here."

"From where—the junkyard?"

"A contractor," he said dryly. "It may not look pretty, but it's got everything I need."

"Do you ever want more than you need?" she asked, as

she got into the passenger side.

He shot her a questioning look. "What do you mean?"

"You seem to exist at survival level, but I don't think it's necessarily because you can't afford nicer things. So I wonder why you don't want to live in a nice place or buy a new truck?" She gave him a questioning look.

"I'm happy with what I have," he said with a careless shrug. "I don't get attached to things. I don't usually keep them that long."

She wondered if *things* included people. Knowing a little more about his past, she thought probably so. Roman had had to protect himself from a very young age, not just from danger but from heartbreak, and he'd probably learned as a child that attaching himself to people who would disappoint him and things he would lose was only going to cause him pain.

She wondered where his mother was now, but that was a question for another day.

Seven

---⟶≫≪⟵---

"It's pretty," Juliette said, as Roman parked in front of Donna's two-story house.

The white house with dark-blue shutters had a big front porch with a seating area of wicker furniture and hanging pots of plants. The yard was well-tended, a colorful array of flowers lining the path to the front steps. She didn't know what she'd been expecting, but she was starting to have doubts about her gut instinct that Cameron's living situation was not good.

"I hope this isn't a mistake," she said as she got out of the car and met Roman on the sidewalk. "Maybe you were right, and Cameron is just an unhappy, bored kid and his grandmother is a wonderful person."

"Do you think only happy things go on in pretty houses?" he asked.

She frowned. "You said that before, when we were running after Cameron. I'm not a snob, Roman, and I don't think I'm naïve."

"Not naïve, but you tend to live on the bright side of the street. Wish cookies and miracles and sweet somethings fill your days."

"Now they do. But I have been through my own personal

hell," she reminded him. "If I choose to make my life sweeter and happier now, then who's to say that's wrong?"

"Definitely not me."

"Good. And I wouldn't be here if I wasn't willing to find out what's really going on with Cameron—pretty house or not." She strode forward and rang the bell.

They waited for a few moments, and she was beginning to wonder if no one was home.

"I feel like I've been here before," Roman muttered as his gaze swept the yard. "Someone lived here. One of the guys I hung out with, I think."

"Really? But you didn't know Donna."

"She looked a little familiar, but I don't remember any kids with the last name of Mays."

Cameron opened the door, interrupting their conversation. His eyes filled with alarm when he saw them.

"Hi, Cameron," she said, trying to ease his worry. "Is your grandmother here? I thought you both might like more of my Wish cookies."

"Uh..." He looked over his shoulder. "She's sleeping. She doesn't like to be woken up. You can leave the cookies with me."

She tried to peer past Cameron, but he didn't seem interested in letting her into the house.

"Cameron," a woman's voice rang out. "Is someone at the door?"

"Sounds like your grandmother is awake now," Roman said, pushing past Cameron.

Juliette followed him inside, feeling a little guilty for just walking in, but they weren't going to learn anything from the porch.

Donna came down the stairs, wearing a robe over a nightgown. "Oh, dear," she said when she saw them. "Goodness, I didn't know we had company."

"We're sorry to bother you," Juliette said. "I wanted to bring you some more of my Wish cookies."

"Well, that was sweet," Donna said, patting down her

hair, then pulling her robe more tightly around her. "Excuse my appearance. I didn't sleep well last night so I stayed in bed this morning."

"It's fine. We're disturbing you, and that wasn't our intent." Actually, it was exactly their intent, but she couldn't say that. She glanced over at Cameron, who had taken the lid off the container and was biting into one of her cookies as if he were really hungry. That reminded her of why they were here. "Would you mind if I use your bathroom before we go?"

"It's down the hall," Donna said with a wave of her hand.

"I'll just be a second," she told Roman, who didn't look thrilled that she'd left him with Donna, but he simply gave her a nod.

"You look familiar," Roman said, as she left the room.

"Do I? Maybe you saw me in one of my plays. I used to be an actress at the Center Theater. It was a wonderful time. I played all the good parts—Stella from a *Streetcar Named Desire* and Scarlett from *Gone With The Wind*."

Their voices faded as Juliette made her way down the hall. She moved past the bathroom to peek into the kitchen. There was a pile of dishes in the sink and an odd smell in the room, but nothing overtly horrible. The bathroom was in the same condition—not exactly dirty but not exactly clean, either. There was an office next to the bathroom and as she looked in there, she saw a lot of clutter.

Moving inside, she perused the desk which was stacked high with mail: flyers, catalogs, fundraising requests, and what appeared to be bills with second and third notice stamped on the front of the envelopes. She frowned at those.

Why wasn't Donna paying her bills?

Was she just lazy or did she not have the money?

That question was still going around in her head when she returned to the entry. Roman gave her a relieved look while Donna was laughing about some story she'd just told. Cameron was sitting on the stairs, working his way through the container of cookies, and Donna didn't seem to be paying any attention.

"Save some for your grandmother," she told Cameron with a smile.

Guilt filled his eyes as he set a half-eaten cookie back in the container.

"Oh, that's all right. He's a growing boy," Donna said, waving her hand. "You go ahead and finish that, Cameron."

"Is the cookie really magic?" Cameron asked her.

"Some people think so," she replied.

"Why?" he asked.

"Good question," Roman muttered.

She ignored him and focused on Cameron. "The cookies are made with a special kind of sugar that comes from the sap of a coconut tree. I can only get it at this time of year, and because it's so special, it gives the person eating the cookie a little bit of magic."

Cameron's eyes widened. "So whatever I wish for will come true?"

"Not all wishes come true, but some do."

"I want mine to come true." There was suddenly a serious and purposeful look in his eyes, and Juliette wondered what he was wishing so hard for.

She looked at Donna. "I hope you don't mind my asking, but I was wondering where Cameron's parents are. Do they live here, too?"

"My son, Travis, brought Cameron to live here two months ago, but he had to tie up some loose ends in New Orleans before he could make the move himself. He's actually coming home today; he should be here soon. Cameron's mother isn't around," she added, a tart note in her voice.

So Cameron's dad was coming back to help his mom take care of Cameron. That sounded good. She felt immensely relieved, because she didn't think Donna was capable of being the sole caregiver. "I'm glad you'll have help with Cameron."

"Oh, he's such a sweet boy; he doesn't need much," Donna said. "Thank you again for the cookies; it was very thoughtful. I'll have to stop in at your bakery sometime."

"I hope you will."

A door slammed somewhere in the back of the house, followed by heavy footsteps. A man came down the hall a moment later. He was short and stocky, with a muscular build. His clothes looked worn and like they hadn't seen a washer in a while. His face was covered with a scruffy beard. His eyes were weary and red, and a new uneasiness ran down her spine.

"Daddy," Cameron squealed. He got up and ran to his dad, throwing his arms around his father's waist. "I didn't think you were ever coming back."

"I told you I was," the man murmured.

"Travis, I was just talking about you," Donna said. "This is Juliette and Roman."

Travis's gaze swung first to her, then to Roman. His face paled. "You?" he asked, giving Roman a hard stare. "What the hell are you doing here? I didn't think I'd ever see you again."

"Likewise," Roman said, a clipped tone in his voice.

"What's going on?" Donna asked in confusion and concern. "You two know each other?"

"Of course we know each other," Travis said to his mother. "This is Roman. The kid from the park, the one who started the fire... Don't you remember?"

"Oh." Donna looked taken aback. "I—I didn't realize. I didn't recall the name. I should have. I didn't."

"Get the hell out of my house," Travis said.

"No problem. Time to go," Roman told her, as he moved toward the front door.

"Uh, all right," she said. "Enjoy the cookies."

She followed Roman outside and they didn't speak until they got into the truck.

"So what was that about?"

He put his key into the ignition and started the engine. "The past."

She frowned. "Martha told me that you were accused of setting fire to someone's house or something along those lines. Is that what Travis was referring to?"

"Yes. Travis, Doug and I were in a park one night after high school graduation. A house next to that park caught fire sometime after midnight. We were the prime suspects. I didn't start the fire. I had left the park before them. But they both pointed their fingers at me. They lied to protect themselves." He paused, shaking his head. "I knew I recognized Donna and that house; I just didn't put it together. Travis's last name is Hastings. I guess Donna used her maiden name because she was an actress."

Finally, he was being forthcoming. She had a lot of questions about the fire; she just didn't know where to start. "Putting your past with Travis aside for the moment, didn't you think he looked...beat-up, exhausted?"

"He didn't look good," Roman said tersely, as he pulled away from the front of the house and drove down the street.

"Cameron obviously loves him, but I still wonder what's going on with that family. When I was looking around the house, I saw stacks of unpaid bills with final notice on them. Maybe the pretty house is just an illusion for what's really going on."

"Donna told us that Travis's wife isn't around, so something happened there. But beyond that, who knows?"

She shifted in her seat. "When she first said her son was coming back, I was relieved. I thought now Donna has the help she needs, because she clearly isn't up to taking care of Cameron on her own. But Travis didn't look like he had a handle on things, either."

"You need to let this go, Juliette. Cameron has a father and a grandmother and probably other family or friends in this town for support. You need to stop trying to fix his life."

"I'm just trying to help."

"I'm getting the feeling your desire to fix Cameron's life is more about the fact that you couldn't fix your own problems when you were a kid."

"That's not true."

He shrugged. "I think it could be."

She thought about it for a moment and decided he was wrong. "I feel for Cameron because he reminds me of when I was a sad, scared kid, and I think he reminds you of your past, too. That's why you came with me."

"Yes, but I can accept when it's time to let go and move on."

"I can accept that, too. I'm not crazy."

His hard profile eased at her comment and he gave her a small, dry smile as he stopped at a light. "All evidence to the contrary."

"Okay, getting back to you."

He groaned. "Let's not."

"I just want to say one thing."

"I seriously doubt you'll stop there."

"Let's find out," she said. "I noticed something interesting about your former friends. When Doug saw you at Donavan's, and when Travis saw you just now, they weren't just wary or angry, they were afraid. Why? Do they think you'll somehow get back at them now for pointing their fingers at you? Do you have something on them? Could you get them into trouble?"

"Just because you don't take a breath in between questions doesn't make it one long question," he pointed out.

"And you're stalling."

"Aren't you going to give me directions to the hamburger place?"

"Stay on this road for the next two miles and then I'll tell you where to go. In the meantime…"

"I don't know why they would be scared of me," he said. "I have nothing on them, no proof of anything. They probably just don't want me around. I'm a reminder of that fire and some of the other stuff we did together that wasn't so great."

"You said the fire started in a park?"

"In the bushes next to a house. Travis and Doug had been smoking."

"Not you?"

"I was drinking beer, but I didn't have a taste for

cigarettes." He paused. "The next morning, I was picked up by the police for questioning. I told them the truth, but no one believed me."

"Were Doug and Travis also picked up by the police?"

"Doug's father was chief of police. So he never actually went down to the station. Travis was taken down there, but his father was vice president of the bank and personally controlled a lot of loans for a lot of people."

She didn't like the sound of that. "So you get tagged for the crime because you didn't have a powerful father?"

"Yes. And because Doug and Travis both swore that I did it. The fact that I'd gotten into some trouble before didn't help my cause."

"What about your grandfather? What did he do?"

"He came down to the station and told the chief I was going home unless they were prepared to charge me. It was the only time in my life anyone ever stood up for me."

"He believed you were innocent."

"Maybe. He never asked me. He's not much of a talker."

"The two of you must sit in silence a lot," she said dryly.

"We can definitely do that."

"So whatever happened? No one was held responsible for the fire?"

"Nope. The truth is they didn't have any evidence about anything, at least as far as I know. A week later, I joined the Marine Corps and left town, swearing I'd never be back." He flung her a look. "Yet here I am—at least for the moment."

"You can't let them run you off again."

"They didn't run me off the first time. I'd been planning to join the Marines after graduation. And it was a good decision. Coming back here now—maybe not so good."

"Why did you come back?"

"My grandfather said he could use some help, and I'd been kicking around different places for a few months, so I thought I'd give him some time while I waited for everything to heal. I thought the town might have forgotten some of what happened back then, but I was wrong about that."

"Most people probably have," she said. "And let's not forget all the people who've come to Fairhope in the last thirteen or so years who have never heard of you. You may not be as famous as you think."

"I think the word is infamous, and you do like to pick the optimistic viewpoint."

"It's better than going negative." She sat up, realizing the road was splitting ahead. "Take the right turn to Evans Road. We're almost there."

"Good, because I'm ready for—what did you call it—a *fantabulous* hamburger?"

"I hope I didn't oversell."

He smiled. "I hope you didn't, either. I'm starving."

The name Burger Palace was obviously meant to be ironic, Roman thought, as he parked in the lot in front of the deliberately weathered shack that sat on a bluff overlooking the bay. But when he followed Juliette inside, his stomach rumbled with the delicious aroma of onions, hickory, and barbecue.

They got into a fairly long line to peruse the menu of burger magnificence. "What's good?" he asked her.

"Last time I got the Princess Burger," she replied. "But I don't think you want that one. I doubt it's manly enough for you."

He grinned, reading the colorfully written description of a petite burger topped with lettuce, tomato, and sweet pickles. "Definitely not enough meat."

"You should go for the Royal Flush burger. Three patties, two layers of cheese, topped off with veggies and secret sauce."

"And that's a little too much meat. Maybe I'll get the Prince." He stepped up to the counter to order.

As he finished, Juliette said, "I'm paying, so just move aside. I'll take the Princess Burger," she added. "No sauce, please."

"Got it. One Prince and one naked Princess," the kid manning the register yelled back to the line of cooks.

Roman laughed. "Naked princess. Now that I like."

She smiled back at him. "Don't get any ideas."

It was a good warning. Unfortunately, it was coming too late. He'd been getting ideas about her since the first moment they'd met—actually before that. His body had been stirring with attraction since he'd spotted her through the bakery windows.

Pushing that thought away, he decided to grab a table while Juliette paid for their order.

He found one outside on the deck. It was a sunny, brisk day and he figured they might as well take advantage of the weather with a seat near the railing overlooking the water.

Juliette joined him a moment later with two glasses of water. "This is nice," she said, settling in the chair across from him. "It's been awhile since I've been out to lunch. What about you?"

"I eat out a fair amount."

"That's right. I saw the empty cupboards in the house."

He sipped his water. "You've been snooping a lot today."

She made a face at him. "I could try to deny that, but I won't. What kind of stories was Donna telling you while I was looking around?"

"She told me all about her days as an actress. Apparently, she was breaking a lot of hearts back then. She did mention that her husband died of a heart attack three years ago."

"I wonder if that's when she stopped paying attention to her bills. In her generation, the woman often left that kind of job to the man. I remember my parents arguing about the bills, but it was reversed. My mother cared about the bills; my dad was all about the baking."

"What about you? Whose footsteps do you walk in?"

"Both of them. I love the baking, like my dad. He was my inspiration to become a pastry chef, but I have to care about the business or I don't have enough money to buy ingredients to bake. It's different, because it's just me. I don't have a husband or an investor; I have to make things work."

"Do you have any family besides your aunt?"

"Some distant cousins I never see."

He rested his arms on the table, curious to know more about her. "Did you like New York at all?"

"Not in the beginning. You thought you didn't fit in when you came here, well, I was definitely a fish out of water in New York. I had a Southern accent. I dressed funny. I was sad, so sad, in the beginning that I couldn't talk to anyone. I couldn't even go into my aunt's kitchen. It felt wrong to bake without my father. So I did pretty much nothing but sleep and watch mindless TV. I don't think I made a friend for at least a year."

"That's hard to believe. You're such a friendly person."

"I was lost for a while. I know you can relate. We both had to make big changes in our teen years. Even though the reasons were different, the result was the same."

"That's true."

"But New York eventually grew on me. My aunt tried hard to make a home for me. She used to take me bike riding and horseback riding in Central Park so I could see trees and sit on the grass and feel like I wasn't living in a concrete jungle; it helped. Eventually, I made friends and I started to appreciate the museums and the theater and the excitement of the city."

"But you still wanted to come back here."

"I always knew I would. When you left, you swore you'd never come back, but when I left, I made the opposite promise—that I would one day return and live in the place that's really home to me." She paused. "My friends thought I was insane to move here, but I just knew I had to do it, especially after I won the baking competition and I had the money. The amount wouldn't have let me do anything in New York City, but here I could pay rent on bakery space and an apartment—my landlord offered me the studio upstairs for practically nothing. And I still have enough money to buy my ingredients and make my desserts."

"What was the prize again?"

"$30,000. I never imagined I could actually win, but I went through six regional contests before becoming one of three finalists to bake the perfect seven-layer cake on a television food show. And I won. It was shocking and amazing."

"It looks like you put the money to good use and your bakery is successful."

"Customers are coming back, and repeat business is always a good sign. Donavan has been awesome about sending people my way as well, along with selling my baked goods in the coffee shop."

"Donavan has always been a very caring person."

"Yes, she is. Did you know she sends money back to the villages in Ethiopia where her coffee is grown?"

"She mentioned that," he said with a smile. "It actually didn't surprise me."

"There's a fundraiser next week. I'm going to try to go in between my manic baking sessions to get ready for all my Valentine's Day orders, but I'm not complaining. Busy is good."

Juliette was one of the few women he'd met who actually didn't complain much, even though she'd certainly had hard and unfair things in her life to deal with.

She sipped her water, then said, "I know you're going to shut down again when I ask this, but I'm curious…"

"You're always curious."

She smiled. "That's true. My mom used to say it was a sign of an intelligent mind."

"That's a good way to spin it. What are you curious about now?"

"Your mother."

He stiffened. "I already told you that sordid story. There's nothing more to say."

"I'm sure there's a lot more, but I was just wondering— where she is now? Do you see her, talk to her? Has she been in your life at all since you were fifteen?"

"She lives in Los Angeles. She got sober about three years ago. She emails me occasionally, but we haven't actually seen each other since I was taken away from her and brought here."

"Is that her choice or yours?"

He thought about that. "It's probably mutual."

"Really?" she asked doubtfully.

"We're not good for each other. She needs to focus on keeping her sobriety and her mental health, and when she thinks about me, she feels guilty. That's not a productive emotion for her."

"But it's not just about her. How do you feel?"

"I don't really want to see her, either. I tried so hard to protect her when I was a kid. But I couldn't. I failed. And I don't want to get back into that impossible place again. I'm glad she's better. I hope it stays that way. I wish her well, but for now that's as far as it goes. Maybe someday that will change, but it's too soon."

"I understand. I'm happy she got better. I was afraid the story was going to end on a darker note."

"You don't like darkness, do you?"

"No, because I've been there, and it's a scary place to live in. So I choose not to."

As he met her gaze, he realized he'd made a different choice. He'd embraced the darkness so it would feel normal. In the shadows, his life had always looked so much better than it really was. He still had trouble with the light. It revealed too much.

Thankfully, their far too personal conversation ended as the waiter set down their plates.

The sight of his thick, juicy burger made his mouth water. "This looks good."

"Wait until you taste it." She bit into her burger and sighed with delight. "It's better than I remembered."

He smiled at her enthusiasm. "Happy to hear that," he said, as he took a bite.

"Well, what do you think?" she asked, wiping her mouth with a napkin.

"Fantabulous."

She laughed. "It's the perfect word, isn't it?"

Everything about the moment was perfect: the scenery, the food, the beautiful woman across from him. There weren't that many times in his life when he wished he could freeze time, but this was one of them.

They ate in happy silence for the next few minutes.

When Juliette was done, she let out a sigh of satisfaction and sat back in her chair. "That was amazing. I only wish I had another one."

"You can get one."

"No, I'm full. And since I don't run miles every morning like you do, I need to have some restraint."

"You could go with me."

"Oh, no, I couldn't," she said, shaking her head. "I am not a runner. I will do yoga, a spin class, maybe the elliptical, but running…not my thing. It's too boring."

"I don't think it's boring at all, especially not when you're outside. You get to breathe in clean air and enjoy nature at the same time you're exercising."

"Yeah, but there's weather to deal with. It's too hot or too cold or too rainy. And I have never felt that rush of endorphins that runners talk about. When I try to run, all I can think about is how tired I am, and I've only gone like half a block."

"You ran farther than that when you were chasing Cameron."

"But that was because I had a goal."

"So that's what you need to run…something to run for."

"I played soccer when I was younger. I like running after a ball and kicking it in a goal. But to run just to run…" She shrugged. "Not really my thing."

"Well, it doesn't have to be. It works for me, whereas trying to turn myself into a pretzel in a yoga class sounds painful and not at all interesting."

"The positions are to get your mind ready for meditation."

"Yeah, okay."

"I take it you don't meditate."

"Actually, I have done some meditation."

She raised an eyebrow. "Seriously?"

"In the Marine Corps. There are certain jobs and skills that require absolutely no movement. You have to be able to control your breath, your brain, be completely still. While it wasn't the same kind of meditation you're probably talking about, it was similar."

"I can see you being very good at controlling your breath."

"Should I take that as a compliment?"

She smiled. "You should. I meant it that way. I'm scattered. My mind jumps from one thing to the next. I always seem to have a million ideas at the same time. Focus is something I have to work at."

"Maybe all those ideas are what make you creative. Don't try to stifle them too much."

"As if I could."

He liked how easy it was to talk to her, how open she was about her strengths and her weaknesses. He also liked how the sun captured her face and how the breeze lifted her hair and warmed her cheeks. Looking at her could become a lifelong obsession if he wasn't careful.

"What?" she asked. "Do I have lettuce in my teeth?"

"Not that I can see."

"Then you're staring, because..."

"It's hard not to when you're around," he admitted.

A nervous gleam entered her eyes. "Really? You're the one with the compelling gaze that makes it hard to look away—not me. Donavan said all the girls in high school used to talk about your intense eyes."

"And I thought it was my muscles, damn," he joked.

"I'm sure your body got some looks, too." She cleared her throat. "I guess we should go. I should get back to the bakery, and I'm sure you have work to do as well."

"Yes, I do. Thanks for lunch," he said, as they got up.

"Thanks for going with me to Cameron's."

"I really do think you should leave that situation alone now that Cameron's dad is back."

"I will…unless there's a reason not to."

"Well, I'm out. I don't need to get more involved with Travis."

"I understand."

He opened the door of the truck for her and then walked around and got behind the wheel. Fifteen minutes later, he was parking in the driveway of her old house. He saw the yearning look she gave the home, but she didn't ask to come in.

"Will I see you at the movie fest again tonight?" she asked. "They're having the costume contest featuring famous couples or lovers from books and movies."

"What are you going as?"

"No one. I'm just manning my table."

"And you're not wearing a costume for that? Doesn't sound like you're getting into the spirit of the event; I'm surprised."

"Can I tell you a little secret?"

He wanted her to tell him all of her secrets, but that was dangerous, because knowing someone's secrets could be a huge burden. "Go ahead."

"I don't like dressing up that much. I do it on Halloween and that's it."

He smiled at her guilty expression. "That might be the sanest thing you've said to me."

She laughed. "So you're not a costume guy, either?"

"I don't think you even have to ask that."

"But you wear a uniform for work."

"That's different. That's part of the job. It's not a costume. The materials that we wear can actually save our lives."

"I was just teasing," she said. "I wear an apron to bake, and that might not save my life, but it does save my good clothes."

"Exactly. But to answer your original question, I don't think I'll be going. Romantic movies aren't my thing."

"Well, I might not like costumes, but I do love romantic movies. In my book, there is nothing wrong with *happily ever after*."

"I think there's a lot wrong with that phrase. It sets too high of a bar."

"I like a high bar, Roman. You can't get it if you can't dream it. That's what my dad used to say."

"You know what my grandfather always says?"

With a frown, she said, "I don't think I want to know."

"Dreams are for suckers. Don't waste time wanting something—go out and get it. Work hard. That's all that matters."

"I don't just think; I also act," she reminded him.

"That's true," he said with a smile. "I almost forgot. You definitely act more than you think. So you don't need my advice. You're a force to be reckoned with."

"Thanks. I guess I'll see you around. Don't forget to come by the bakery sometime and get your cookies."

"I won't."

Their gazes clung for a long moment. He wanted to kiss her good-bye or at least give her a hug, but any move felt fraught with complications.

Damn!

He'd never been so indecisive about his actions, but as he watched her walk away, he knew he was hesitating because Juliette was important.

He wanted her, but he also wanted her to keep living in her sweet, happily-ever-after world, and the two ideas didn't seem to go together. So he dug his hands in his pockets and watched her leave, wondering how long he could stay away from her. Because her car had no sooner rounded the corner when he started to miss her.

Eight

The festival began at six p.m. Saturday night. Juliette arrived at the coffee and dessert tables to find Sara wearing a hoop skirt dress that made it appear as if she'd just stepped off the set of *Gone With The Wind*.

"Let me guess—Scarlett," she said, as she set down a large plastic container of baked goods.

"Of course," Sara said, doing a little twirl. "It was my favorite movie. And I loved Scarlett because she was beautiful, bold, and passionate. But I have to admit I don't know how women ever wore these hoops. I keep bumping into things."

She smiled. "I have no idea, either, but you look good. So do you have a Rhett Butler showing up tonight to be your partner?"

"As a matter of fact I do. He's a guy I met at the coffee shop a few weeks ago," Sara said with a happy smile. "His name is Tim Mueller. He's the manager at the hardware store, and he's super cute. We've only been out a few times, so it's still really new, but I have a big crush on him."

"That's fun. I would love to meet him."

"He should be here soon. Where is your costume?"

"Dressing up as half of a couple didn't seem that

exciting," she confessed, not willing to admit to Sara what she'd told Roman earlier that costumes weren't her thing. "But I'll be behind this table most of the night so hopefully no one will care."

"How are sales of the Wish cookies going?"

"Flying out the door so fast I can barely keep up. Do you want one? It's on the house."

"I would love one."

She opened up the bin and pulled out a baggie with two cookies wrapped in red ribbon. "Enjoy."

"You're so sweet. Do you want a coffee?"

"Maybe later. I better get set up," she added as more people poured into the park and a group of teenagers hovered a few feet away, looking longingly at her desserts.

"I can help you," Sara said. "I'm all ready to go."

"Great. What's the first movie tonight?" she asked as they set out her desserts.

Sara laughed. "Funny you should ask. It's *Romeo and Juliet*."

"Awesome," she said dryly.

"So if anyone asks about your costume, just say you came as yourself."

"Good idea."

"Speaking of *Romeo and Juliet*," Sara said, giving her a sly smile. "How are things going with you and Roman?"

"I wouldn't say there's a me and Roman."

"Really? My friend, Tami, said she saw you at the Burger Palace with Roman today."

"We did have lunch there," she admitted. "That was just a couple of hours ago. The gossip mill churns fast."

"It goes even faster around eligible and appealing men. I've heard all kinds of rumors about Roman since he got back. What do you think of him? Is he the dangerous bad boy everyone says he is?"

There was an edge to Roman, no doubt about that, but he was a lot more complex than Sara's description. "He's interesting. Complicated. And I suspect very few people know who he really is. He doesn't let people in."

"It sounds like he's letting you in. It also sounds like you have a crush."

"Oh, no, don't be silly," she said, avoiding Sara's questioning gaze. "We're just friends."

"Really? You're friends with the guy who's helping his grandfather tear down your old house?"

"It's not Roman's fault. I can't blame him for helping his grandfather." She shook her head at the gleam in Sara's eyes. "Stop matchmaking."

"Why? It's fun."

"I like Roman, but we're not having some great tragic love story like *Romeo and Juliet*. We're not taking poison and dying for each other while our families feud."

Sara laughed. "That's good. Because I don't want you to die. Your desserts are too good."

"Thanks, and I have my priorities straight. I'm building a business right now. That's my focus. Speaking of customers…"

Sara nodded and got behind her table as the head of the movie festival stepped up to the microphone next to the big screen to announce the opening of the festival and the schedule of events.

Romeo and Juliet would begin the night, followed by the costume contest, and then the movie *The Notebook*. The organizer encouraged them to get their coffee and desserts before the movie began and almost immediately the line at her table doubled.

For the next hour and a half, she was swamped with customers. When it finally began to slow, she asked Sara if she'd mind watching her table for a few moments, while she went back to the bakery to get more cookies.

As she walked through the trees, her gaze caught on the big screen, and she stopped to watch for a minute, her interest caught by the passion on the screen. While she didn't want the tragedy—she'd had enough of that—she did want the big love story, the greatest love of all time kind of moment.

Her parents had had it. They'd been madly in love with each other; they'd told her so dozens of times. She definitely wanted what they'd had.

"Well, isn't this appropriate?" a man said. "Juliette watching Juliet."

She turned to see Doug Winters approaching. He wasn't wearing a costume, but he looked more relaxed than he usually did, out of his usual suit and tie, wearing jeans and a jacket. "Hi, Doug. How are you?"

"I'm good. Tell me, did your mother watch the movie while she was pregnant and then name you after it?"

"Yes. She loved the movie, but it has never been a favorite of mine. Two kids killing themselves for love? I might be a romantic, but that's stupid."

He grinned. "A girl after my own heart."

"Love stories should be happy," she added.

"I agree. I'm glad I ran into you. I'd like to take you to dinner. What about tomorrow? Are you free?"

She hesitated. While Doug was attractive and charming, she didn't feel anything else for him, certainly not the butterflies that zipped around inside her when Roman was nearby.

Plus, there was all the bad blood between Doug and Roman, and she didn't know how she felt about Doug's actions in any of it. Although, to be fair, she hadn't heard his side of the story. Maybe she should.

"If tomorrow is no good..." he began.

"No, tomorrow is fine," she said, making a quick decision. "I'd like that."

"Good. Where shall I pick you up?"

"I live over the bakery."

"That's convenient."

"It is."

An awkward pause followed her statement, which didn't bode well for dinner the next night.

"So, six," he said.

"That's perfect. I was just going to run back to my store

to get more desserts, so—"

"So I'll see you tomorrow." He put his hand on her arm and gave it a squeeze, then walked in the other direction.

As Doug left, she saw Roman standing nearby watching her. She was shocked to see him. He'd made a point of saying he wouldn't be coming to the festival. He gave her a brief nod, but before she could move in his direction, he turned and walked away.

Frowning, she wondered why he'd given her the brush-off.

Was it because of Doug? Had he seen them talking together? Was he jealous?

A shiver ran down her spine as she debated what to do.

She should let him go...shouldn't she?

Juliette was interested in Doug.

That pissed Roman off more than he would have imagined. But seeing Doug with his hand on Juliette's arm, giving her that smooth smile that so many people fell for, made his blood boil.

He'd been a fool to come to the movie fest, to go looking for her, but after lunch he'd thought about her all the damn day, and he just hadn't been able to stop himself from seeing her again.

"Roman, wait."

He heard her voice behind him and picked up his pace.

"Roman, stop," she called again.

The last thing he wanted to do was stop and talk to her, especially since he was behaving like a damned idiot. But he could hardly keep going with her chasing him down and calling his name every other minute. The people nearby were already looking in his direction.

So he stopped and waited for her to catch up. "What?" he asked shortly.

"Why are you running away from me?"

"Do you have to talk so loud?" he countered, moving away from the moviegoers and deeper into the trees. "People are trying to watch the movie."

"And you didn't answer my question. What's going on? Why the cold shoulder?"

"You were busy; I didn't want to bother you."

"I wasn't busy; I was talking to Doug, but you saw that."

"Are you going out with him?" The question left his mouth before he could stop it.

She hesitated. "He did invite me to dinner tomorrow night."

"And you said yes?" He shook his head. "Okay, fine, do what you want."

"I will do what I want," she snapped back. "But why are you so mad?"

"I told you about the fire—about the way he hung me out to dry."

"You did tell me your side of the story. I'm curious to hear his."

"So you can decide if I'm lying? I thought you believed me." He'd been crazy to think she'd taken him at his word.

"I don't think you're lying, Roman, but it sounds like there are things you don't know."

"You mean things you don't know. You always have to stick your nose where it doesn't belong. This isn't your business, Juliette."

She frowned. "If you could stop seeing red for a minute, you might be able to hear me when I say that my real interest in having dinner with Doug is to ask him about the fire and the rumors floating around about you. Do you really want to live in this town with a cloud hanging over your head?"

"I'm not going to be here that long, and while I am here, I'll deal with it. This isn't your fight, Juliette."

"You're my friend. I fight for my friends."

As he looked into her fiercely beautiful blue eyes, he felt the ice around his heart start to crack. Juliette wasn't like anyone he'd ever met before. *Was she telling the truth? Was the date with Doug about him? Or did he just want to believe that?*

"Friends, huh?" he muttered, not exactly happy with the description of their relationship.

"I think so. Don't you?"

"I don't know." Actually, he did know. The last thing he wanted to be was her friend.

Driven by a mix of emotions and a desire that had been smoldering since he met her, he impulsively leaned forward and kissed her parted, surprised mouth. She tasted like sugar, vanilla, and coffee—three of his favorite things. He wanted more.

He cupped her head with his hands, taking another kiss while he had the chance.

Her surprise turned to acceptance, to passion. Her arms came around his neck, as she kissed him back with the same kind of enthusiasm she brought to every other part of her life.

Now he was the one who was surprised…and maybe a little rattled. He'd crossed a line he probably shouldn't have crossed. He should pull away, but it wasn't easy to end the best kiss of his life, even though he knew it would only lead to liking her more than he already did—which was probably too much.

But all he could think about was how long he could go on kissing her before he had to come up for air.

Finally, she pulled away and they stared at each other with the heat of their breath creating swirling clouds in the cold night air.

She put a hand to her mouth. "That was—unexpected."

"Was it? I've been thinking about it for a while," he murmured.

"You have?" Wonder filled her blue eyes. "I didn't know."

"Didn't you?" he challenged.

"I—I don't know what to say."

"Well, that's a first," he said dryly.

She made a face at him. "Really? You kiss me like that,

and then you're sarcastic?"

He grinned, liking how real it always was between them. "Sorry, but you usually have plenty to say."

"You surprised me."

"It was just a kiss—a kiss between friends, right?"

She stared back at him. "Right. Friends. I have to go to the bakery. I ran out of cookies. I was on my way there when…"

"Do you want me to go with you?"

She immediately shook her head. "No. I'll see you later."

As she walked away, he let out a breath, nowhere near as unshaken by the kiss as he'd implied. He'd definitely never had a *friend* like her. Only problem was he wanted to be far more than her friend.

⟶⟫⟪⟵

Doug was charming and handsome, and having dinner with him Sunday night at probably the most expensive restaurant in Fairhope made Juliette feel a little like she was back in New York again. The food at Gladstone's was excellent. Her date was more than a little attractive in slacks and a charcoal-gray shirt, his light-brown hair styled, and his face cleanly shaven.

She looked better than she had in a while, too, putting on heels and a dress for the first time in forever. She'd even worn makeup and curled her hair a bit. It was all so sophisticated…but also a little dull.

Doug was happy to talk about himself: his law firm, city council business, and his upcoming run for mayor, which she found somewhat interesting. She always liked getting to know what made people tick, and it was clear that Fairhope's future was a big part of Doug's future. She supposed it was a big part of hers, too, so she should probably be excited to get the inside scoop from one of the more powerful people in town. But their conversation felt more business than personal, and they couldn't seem to find any other subjects to talk about.

She wanted to bring up what had happened years ago between Doug and Roman, but so far Doug had stayed almost deliberately away from his past, from his childhood. Because he didn't want to talk about being a kid in Fairhope, he also didn't seem to be that interested in her life before she'd come back. If she was going to find out Doug's side of the fire story, she was probably going to have to force an unwanted trip down memory lane. And as the waiter set down coffee and a dessert menu, she knew she was running out of time to do that.

"They make an excellent chocolate lava cake here," Doug said. "Want to try it?"

"I'm sure it's great, but to be honest, I never eat dessert out, unless I'm doing research into someone else's cake. I do so much tasting during the day; I have to save my calories."

"You don't look like you need to watch your calories," he said, an appreciative gleam in his eyes.

"Thanks, but I do. You should have some, though."

"No, I'm full," he said, setting down his menu.

"You know, I kind of remember you from when I was a kid here," she said, making a vague statement that wasn't true at all, but she had to find a way to open up the past.

"Oh, yeah?"

"Your father was the chief of police, wasn't he?"

Doug nodded. "Yes, he was—for almost twenty years. He retired about five years ago. Now he and my mother spend their time traveling or in the desert heat of Palm Springs. He's a big golfer."

"That sounds warm—relaxing."

"It's nice. They have a condo there."

"So they don't spend much time here in Fairhope?"

"No, not really. They didn't even come back for Christmas this year. My dad could never travel when he was chief. He worked most holidays, so my mother felt she'd earned their retirement. And he'd earned it, too. He took good care of this town. Now it's my turn."

"It's good that you care so much. That's one thing I've noticed being a business owner here—how much everyone cares about keeping the city great."

"It's all about supporting each other." He paused. "I hope I'll have your support for mayor."

"Of course," she said, even though she had no idea who was even running against him. She needed to get a bit more involved in town business, too.

"Great. I'm happy to hear that." He gave her a beaming smile.

She smiled back, knowing she was probably about to burst his happy balloon, but she was starting to feel like it was now or never. "There's something I want to ask you about."

"Shoot. My life is an open book."

She seriously doubted that, but she was about to find out. "It's about Roman Prescott."

His open-book face immediately closed as he sat back in his chair. "What about him?"

"I saw your tense exchange in the coffee shop on Friday. I asked Donavan about it. She said you and Roman were friends and then you weren't—that there was some mystery about a fire that started in a park and spread to a house."

"There was no mystery. Roman was smoking in the park the way he always did. Drinking, too. He got careless and set the brush on fire and ran away, letting the Marsons' house go up in flames. Then he tried to blame me."

She could hear the bitterness in his voice and the note of betrayal, the same note she'd heard in Roman's voice. "I spoke to Roman about it. He said he wasn't smoking that night, and he'd left the park hours before the fire started."

"Why would you talk to Roman about that old fire?" Doug asked sharply.

"We've become friends."

"How did that happen?"

"Well, he's remodeling the house I used to live in. I stopped by one day, and we started talking."

"Being friends with Roman is not a smart idea. He's trouble. He always has been. We were friends once, and Roman led me down a lot of paths I should not have gone. A lot more happened than just that fire."

"Like what?"

"Roman got into fights on a daily basis. Did he tell you how a test he hadn't studied for suddenly went missing from Mrs. Stewart's desk? Or did he mention how money raised for the high school football team disappeared? Or how the high school mascot ended up on a raft in the middle of the lake?"

"The bulldog?" she asked in surprise. "He put Billy the bulldog in the lake?"

"Yes, right before the big game."

She couldn't help the smile that teased her lips, but she could see Doug didn't appreciate her reaction.

"Okay, maybe that wasn't a big deal," Doug said. "But he caused a lot of people a lot of trouble."

"If you knew he was stealing tests and money, why were you friends with him?" she challenged.

"I didn't know at the time. And Roman was...fun," he said, the word coming with great reluctance. "He shook things up. He was new to the school, and he was from California. He had ideas that I had never had. I was stupid to follow him anywhere. When he turned on me after the fire, I saw what he was really about. I could have lost my admittance to college because of him. And don't think it was just me he tried to take down. Our friend, Travis, also got thrown under the bus by Roman. He had a baseball scholarship that was put into jeopardy by Roman's actions. Roman was the only one who had nothing to lose, but still he pointed the finger at us."

Doug was a completely different person in this moment. He was fired up. He was angry and bitter and there was real emotion behind his eyes. It was almost like seeing a different person. She actually liked this guy better than the one who wore the smooth, charming mask.

"I don't know why we're talking about all this," Doug

added, starting to pull himself together. "It was a long time ago."

"What I don't understand is if Roman did it, why wasn't he arrested?"

"There wasn't enough evidence to hold him. My dad had to let him go."

"That's right. Your father was the chief of police."

He frowned. "He did not try to railroad Roman to protect me—if that's what you're thinking. Is that what Roman told you?"

"He actually didn't say that much about it, but I saw his face when Martha Grayson verbally attacked him in front of my bakery. She said some very hateful things."

"Martha doesn't like anyone, and I doubt her opinion mattered to Roman."

"I think it bothered him more than he might admit."

Doug gave her a sharp look. "Am I missing something? Are you two seeing each other?"

"No, we're just friends. We only met the other day." She felt heat run through her at the memory of their kiss in the park the night before, but she didn't plan on telling Doug about that.

"Well, good, because like I said, he is trouble you do not need to have. I'm just hoping he doesn't stay long. I heard he's recuperating from some injury and then going back to the Marines."

"That's what he said," she agreed. "I don't know who's going to finish the house remodel when he leaves."

"I saw the plans for the house when Vincent brought them before the planning commission. I'm interested in buying the place after it's done."

"Really? Why?" she asked in surprise.

"It's going to be a beautiful house."

She frowned. "It was beautiful before."

"And old. It needed massive updating."

The last thing she needed were more practical opinions about her old house. "Well, we liked it—my parents and me."

"It's a great family house," he continued. "I could see having a family there."

"I can, too," she said, not caring at all for the idea of Doug in her house. He'd turn it into some centerpiece for town events and political dinners. "I'd like to buy the place myself. I just have to figure out how to pull some money together to do that."

"Well, let's not get in a bidding war," he said with a smile. "Maybe we can work something out together."

"Maybe," she said vaguely. She put her napkin on the table, relieved to see the waiter bring over their check. She was ready to be done with their date.

Doug paid the bill, then escorted her to the car. They made some small talk on the way back to her apartment, mostly about how cold it was, which just showed how little they had to discuss when at the end of the night all they were talking about was the weather.

He parked down the street from her apartment and insisted on walking her to the door. On the way, he said, "Do you have a date for the Sweetheart's Dance next Saturday?"

"I'm actually going to be working the dance. The organizer talked to me about providing a dessert table."

"So bring your desserts and then be my date. I'm a good dancer. I promise not to step on your feet," he added with a smooth smile.

"I—I don't know," she said, not wanting to hurt his feelings but also not sure another date was in the cards. "It's hard to mix business and pleasure."

"Just think about it," he said. "You can give me your answer later."

"I don't want to stop you from asking someone else."

"You're the only one I want to go with."

"That's very flattering and I'm sure quite untrue. Donavan and Sara told me you're one of the most eligible bachelors in town."

He stopped in front of her door, the tension leaving his eyes at her comment. "You asked them about me?"

She realized quickly that she'd given him the wrong idea, but she could hardly take it back. "Your name came up one day."

"I'm single for a reason, Juliette. I've been waiting for the right woman, and I have a feeling you and I could be good together. You're a businesswoman. You're ambitious and hardworking, and I respect that."

"Thank you. But we barely know each other."

"It doesn't have to take long to know someone is right for you."

She actually agreed with him. Unfortunately, things didn't feel right with him, and she didn't think they ever would.

"Anyway," he said. "I know I'm rushing you. I'm just a man who likes to go after what he wants."

He leaned over and kissed her. It wasn't more than a brief peck, but it still felt cold. She wondered if it felt that way to him.

Apparently not. He lifted his head, gave her a smile and said, "I'll see you soon."

After he headed down the street, she unlocked her door and stepped inside. She paused on the landing. She didn't feel like going upstairs to her apartment. She felt unsettled, not because the kiss had had any impact, but because it hadn't—because she'd wished that it was Roman's mouth on hers.

She never should have gone out with Doug. Her real motivation had been to learn more about the fire, and she'd done that, but she'd also given Doug the wrong idea. She didn't want to hurt his feelings, but she needed to end things before they went any further.

She'd like to do it now, but it seemed a little too cruel to run after Doug just to tell him she never wanted to date him again.

But she had to do something with her restless energy, which meant she had to bake. It was the only way to burn off some steam.

She opened her door and stepped back out on the

sidewalk, shocked to see Roman walking away from her door. "Roman," she called.

He turned around, giving her a wary look.

"What are you doing here?" she asked. "Were you coming to see me?"

"I was taking a walk. I was going to say hello, but I saw you kissing Doug good night," he said, a terse note in his voice. "I didn't want to interrupt."

"Oh, I didn't see you."

"It didn't look like you did. How was the date?"

"It was all right."

"Well, I'll see you around."

"Wait," she said, not ready to let him go. "Do you want to come up for a minute? My apartment is upstairs."

He hesitated. "It's getting late."

"Not that late." Her restless feeling had vanished, replaced by excitement and anticipation.

"I could come up, I guess," he muttered. "But weren't you just going somewhere?"

"I was thinking about doing some prep work for tomorrow's baking, but I can leave it until morning. That's only a few hours from now anyway." She opened the door. "Come in."

"What time do you start work?" he asked, following her up the stairs.

"Five, sometimes four, depending on how much I have to do."

"Seriously?"

"How do you think all the cakes and cookies get made and put into the display case?"

"I guess I didn't think about the actual baking part."

"The most important part." She unlocked her door and moved into the studio apartment, taking a quick look to make sure she didn't have any underwear lying around, but thankfully she'd done laundry earlier in the day, and everything was neatly folded in the basket by the bathroom. "As you can see, it's not very big."

"But it is very you," he said, his gaze sweeping the room, noting the double bed, the desk by the window, the dresser with the small, ancient TV on the top, the armchair and ottoman where she spent any spare time she had reading. There was a small bathroom off the kitchenette, which boasted an oven with stovetop, a refrigerator, a microwave, and a couple of cabinets. But while the furnishings were worn and simple in design, she'd added colorful throw blankets to the bed and the chair, a couple of plants by the window, and some family pictures on the desk to make it feel more homey.

Roman wandered over to those framed photographs. "This is your family," he said, picking up the last picture she had of her family together.

"Yes, it was taken the Christmas before they died. We always cut down our Christmas tree, which was what we did that day. Then we decorated it while drinking hot cocoa with marshmallows and listening to Christmas music. My dad loved the oldies. He'd sing along at the top of his voice with Dean Martin doing '*Baby, It's Cold Outside*.'" She stopped, feeling the moisture gather in her eyes. She blinked it away, but not fast enough for Roman not to see.

"Sorry, I didn't mean to make you sad," he said.

"You didn't. I like talking about them. I don't get the chance very often, especially now that I don't see my aunt, who is the only one in my life who knew my parents."

"What about your grandparents? What happened to them?"

"My father's parents died before I was born. My mom's parents were divorced, and she never saw her father after she got married, so I've never met him. Her mom was around when I was a child. She was very cool. She was an artist. She painted beautiful landscapes. She died about six months before my mom did. I think it hit my aunt really hard to lose not only her mother but also her sister in such a short period of time."

"But she had you—that must have helped."

"I wasn't so great the first year. In fact, I was a pain in the ass. But thankfully she let me get through it on my own."

"What does she do?"

"She works in finance for a commercial real estate firm in New York."

"She never had kids?"

"Nope. I used to ask her if that was because I was such a headache she couldn't think about having another kid, but she said no, she'd just never really wanted to fill a house with children. She and her husband travel a lot. They're very happy."

"Not everyone is meant to have kids." He set down the family photo and picked up the one next to it—the one Donavan had recently given her. "I like this," he said with a smile. "You were born to be a baker."

"Yes, and I finally grew into that hat. Donavan actually found that among her mother's possessions. I don't know how it got there, but she gave it to me the other day. I should put it in the bakery; I just haven't had a chance."

"Your father would be proud that you followed in his footsteps."

"I think he would be. We talked about it a lot when I was a kid. It was our thing. We'd bake together most weekends. He didn't cook anything else. My mom was in charge of all the other meals. But he was the king of dessert."

"What was his favorite dessert?"

"Chocolate soufflé was his favorite and his biggest challenge. Meringues are extremely sensitive to humidity, temperature, and movement—you have to delicately and carefully whip and fold the meringues and then be super patient and resist opening the oven door until the timer goes off. When it all goes well, it's heaven. When it doesn't, it's a flop."

"Do you sell those downstairs?"

"No, but I occasionally make it for a private party. Actually, I should think about doing that for Valentine's Day. I'm catering the dessert for four private dinners."

"It sounds like you're going to have a working

Valentine's Day," he commented.

"It's a busy time for sweets, but I'm happy about that. And then there's Easter not too long after."

"What's the slow season?"

"Probably the summer. It gets too hot and people think more about Popsicles than cake. But it never falls off entirely."

He set the photo down and took a seat on the ottoman in front of the armchair.

She perched on the end of the bed. "So why did you really come to see me, Roman?"

"I told you I was taking a walk."

"You get a lot of exercise."

"I do, and this block is on my route." He paused. "So did you get the information you wanted from Doug?"

"Finally, you ask the question I know you came here to ask."

"I actually don't care what he said, but you were curious."

She didn't buy that for a second, but she'd let him keep his pride. "I asked him about the fire. He told me that you did it and blamed it on him and Travis."

"Of course, he did," Roman muttered. "I told you he would."

"He also said you were trouble, and I should stay away from you."

"He's singing the same old song."

"Did you really put Billy the bulldog in the middle of the lake?"

He tipped his head. "It seemed like a good idea at the time. I thought he'd jump off the raft and swim back, but it turned out that he didn't like the water. He barked all night until someone from the fire department got in a rowboat and went out to rescue him." He paused. "What else did Doug tell you?"

"Not much. He made a lot of vague references to things that he wanted to pin on you."

"So, there you have it. You've heard both sides. Who do you believe?"

Now she knew what he'd really come here to ask, and there was a tension about him that told her that her answer was important. "I believe you."

His expression lightened as he took in a quick breath. "Why?"

"Because you haven't lied to me yet. Have you?"

"No. But going by that criteria, has Doug lied to you?"

"Not exactly lied, but I got the feeling that he took me to dinner more because he was interested in getting my support for his run for mayor than because he found me wildly attractive."

"I don't believe that was the reason he took you to dinner. Doug is ambitious, but he's not blind, and I'm sure he's very interested in you. He did kiss you good night, after all." Roman got to his feet. "I should go and let you get to bed. I know your morning is coming early."

She stood up, not ready to see Roman go, but asking him to stay was probably not a good idea.

When they got to the door, he paused and looked back at her, and her stomach fluttered with anticipation under his dark gaze.

He reached out a hand and slid his thumb along her jaw, and her heart beat faster. "You are so beautiful, Juliette, more so because you have no idea just how pretty you are. And if you hadn't already had one good-night kiss from a man I really don't like, I'd be tempted..." His voice trailed away.

She wanted to say that good-night kiss had already been completely forgotten, but Roman's hand fell away from her face, and he headed out the door and down the stairs, leaving her with a racing pulse and the feeling that she'd missed out on something amazing.

For a split second, she was tempted to go after him, but she had enough sense to fight against it. Things were already getting too hot too fast. She needed to turn down the heat before she burned everything up.

Nine

---><><——

Roman thought about Juliette all day long. He kept putting her out of his head and then she'd pop back in again. He couldn't remember the last time a woman had been on his mind so much. But this woman was the wrong woman.

Juliette was amazing, but she would want so much more from a man than he could give her, and he wouldn't be good for her. She was sweetness and light, and he was not. He'd just drag her into the darkness with him, and that was the last thing he wanted. She'd had a rough childhood—losing her parents, being ripped out of her home. But she'd rebounded, and she was making a life for herself—a good life. He didn't want to get in the way of that.

Nor did he honestly believe he could ever be part of the kind of life she wanted. It was one thing to hang out in Fairhope for a while, help his grandfather, but it wasn't a long-term move, just an interim stop on the way to somewhere else. He just didn't know where that somewhere else was, but he doubted it would be this town—a place filled with people who didn't think much of him and probably never would.

As his thoughts ran dark, he got up and flipped on some lights. It was after five and the sun was sinking low in the sky. He was about to head into the kitchen when he heard the front door open and a male voice call out.

He left the downstairs bedroom and walked into the hall as Doug stepped into the entry. "What do you want?"

"I need to talk to you." Doug shut the door behind him.

"I can't imagine why."

"Yes, you can," Doug said, giving him a pointed look. "We need to get a few things straight, Roman. Juliette brought up the fire to me last night. Why are you talking about that with her? Why are you drumming up the past? I would think it's the last thing you'd want to discuss."

"Juliette asked me about the fire after hearing about it from Martha Grayson."

"Why don't you just admit you did it? Take responsibility and move on."

"Because I didn't do it, and I don't confess to things I didn't do."

"You're lying, Roman."

"I'm not. If someone needs to confess, look in the mirror."

"I didn't start the fire."

"Looks like we're still going around in circles." He paused. "Look, I get why you couldn't confess back then, Doug. Your dad was the police chief. Your mom was head of the PTA. You were their golden boy, their pride and joy. Knowing you weren't perfect, that you could be as stupid and reckless as anyone, would have ruined them. I almost couldn't blame you for putting the blame on me. I'm sure you felt you had a lot more to lose than I did, and I suspect Travis felt the same. But that doesn't excuse either of you from putting a knife in my back."

Doug stared at him like he was out of his mind. "What are you talking about? I didn't put the blame on you. I told my dad I didn't know what happened."

"Sure you did," he said.

"That's the truth. If anyone put the blame on you, it was Travis."

"It was both of you. You were a team. You'd been best friends since childhood. I was the easiest one to blame. Admit it."

"That's not the way it went down, Roman. My dad told me that you said Travis and I did it, and you weren't even in the park that night."

He stared at Doug, wondering if it was possible the chief had lied to each of them about what the other said. "Whatever. I don't actually care anymore."

"Well, I'm starting to care again, because I can't have that old mystery haunting my campaign for mayor."

He shrugged. "I don't know what you're going to do about it. You can't keep people from talking. You certainly can't stop Martha from spreading rumors."

"How long are you here for?"

"I haven't decided."

"But you're not planning to stay, right? You always said this town was too small for you."

"I'll leave when I'm ready to leave."

"Look, Roman, we've both grown up. We're men now, not stupid boys. I'm sure you've changed, and so have I. I don't want us to be trapped by the past."

"Then let's end this conversation."

"I wouldn't have started it if Juliette hadn't grilled me last night."

He wasn't surprised Juliette had put Doug on the defensive. She did have a persistence about her that could be unsettling. "I'm sure she'll drop it. There's nothing left to discuss. There's no evidence, no truth to be found; it is what it is."

"What's going on between you and her?" Doug asked.

"Why do you care?"

"She's trying to build a business in this town, a business that's going to require goodwill, people who want to buy their baked goods from her. That might change if she hooks up with you."

"You must be one hell of a lawyer, Doug, always

thinking of the angles."

"You didn't answer my question."

"Whatever is between us is between us."

"So I'm going to have to get around you to get to her?"

"That's a question you'd have to ask her."

"I used to beat you when it came to the girls," Doug reminded him, a familiar, cocky note in his voice.

"We'll see if your luck holds up."

"I guess we will." Doug turned and left, shutting the door forcibly behind him.

He stood there for a long minute, thinking about their conversation. He'd always thought Doug had turned on him—Travis, too—but now he wondered. Had Doug's father made him believe that in some effort to protect his son? It made sense. He could clearly remember the chief sitting him down, looking him in the eye, and telling him that Doug and Travis had both given sworn statements that he'd lit the branches of the tree on fire for fun, and then had run when the fire got too big. They hadn't even said it was an accident; they'd sworn he'd done it on purpose.

Doug was telling a different story now. But he was also desperate to be elected mayor. How could he believe anything Doug had to say? And the reaction Travis had had to him when they'd run into each other had been filled with anger and bitterness. The chief had probably told him a different story, too.

Maybe the person Doug should be talking to was his father.

On the other hand, he doubted the chief would tell his son anything that contradicted his past story. The Winters had always been a family that protected their own. And his friendship with Doug had been seen as a cancer. They'd wanted to cut him out of Doug's life long before the fire. He was probably lucky the chief hadn't found a way to send him to jail, but fortunately there really hadn't been any evidence that pointed to him.

Shaking his head, he told himself to stop thinking about

it. He couldn't change the past, so there was no point in going back there. He needed to stay in the present.

The door opened again, and this time his grandfather walked in.

"Was that Doug Winters I saw driving away from here?" Vincent asked.

"It was."

"Why?"

"He wanted to know if I was going to cause him trouble in his run for mayor."

"Because of the past," Vincent said with an irritated nod. "I can't believe his nerve. You're not thinking of leaving early because of him?"

"No. He won't have anything to do with any decisions I make."

"Good. I need your help on this job as long as you can give it."

"About that. You keep promising me some helpers, but no one shows up."

"There are some other contractors running big jobs right now. Everyone is busy."

"This project isn't going to get done with just me working on it. And I could be gone in a few weeks depending on what happens with my next physical. What are you going to do then?"

"I'll find some help." His grandfather walked down the hall, and he followed him into the bedroom he'd been working on.

Vincent looked at the stripped-down walls. They were going to eventually push the back bedroom wall out three feet into the backyard.

"It's coming along," Vincent said, never one to heap too much praise on a worker. "You're going faster than I thought. You haven't forgotten your skills."

"They came back to me faster than I thought they would."

"It's good work, Roman. You'd make a fine contractor. If

you can't continue as a soldier, you should think about construction."

"It's definitely on the list," he said.

"All right. Do you want to get some dinner? I'm headed downtown."

"No, I think I'll keep going awhile longer."

"I'll check in with you tomorrow then."

"Great." After his grandfather left, he got back to work on the last part of the room, the closet. He ripped up the carpet that covered the floor and tossed it aside, then pulled up several loose boards. As he did so, he saw something unexpected: an old metal box about eight by ten inches in size. He squatted down and pulled the box out of what had obviously been a hiding place.

His heart beat a little faster. *Did the box belong to Juliette? Or to someone in her family?* She'd told him her bedroom had been upstairs, but who knew what they'd used this room for?

There was a latch on the box, and after a moment's hesitation, he pulled it open.

Inside was a stack of folded notes. He picked up the first one and read a few words of what was clearly a love letter. *Was it between Juliette's parents?* There were no names on the note, just a reference to a great love.

These letters could belong to more recent tenants or to people who had lived here before Juliette's family. But he had to show them to her. If there was any chance they were letters between her parents, then she'd want to see them.

On the other hand, the letters had been hidden away. Maybe the letters weren't between a husband and a wife, but something more illicit. What if one of her parents had been having an affair? She'd be devastated.

He debated his options. He didn't want to hurt her, but he also didn't want to make the decision for her. Juliette could decide for herself if she wanted to read the letters.

Taking out his phone, he punched in her number.

"Hello? Roman?" she said.

"I found something in the house you need to see."

"What is it?" she asked warily.

"Can you come over?"

"You can't tell me over the phone."

"No."

"Then I'll be there in ten minutes."

———— ➤➤◄◄ ————

Juliette couldn't imagine what Roman had found in her old house. It had to have something to do with her parents. She was both excited and nervous about what that could be after all these years.

When she arrived, the upstairs was dark, but there were lights on throughout the first floor. Her heart was pounding as she went up to the door. It was open, so she walked through it, calling out for Roman.

He met her in the hallway. "It's in here."

"What is *it*?"

He didn't answer, just led her into the first-floor bedroom. The room was completely torn apart. Roman picked a metal box off the floor.

"I found this hidden under the carpet and the floorboards in the closet."

"What's inside?"

"Looks like love letters."

"What? Really?" she asked in surprise. "From my parents?"

"I'm not sure. There aren't any names mentioned."

"Can I see?"

"That's why I called you. Why don't we take them into the kitchen?"

"Okay," she said, following him across the hall. She took off her coat as she sat down at the kitchen table.

Roman placed the box in front of her, and she opened the lid. As Roman had said, there was a stack of letters wrapped with a ribbon. The first one had been taken out of the pack, probably the one Roman had read.

She picked it up and unfolded the notepaper, then read the note aloud.

To My Love,

I can't believe we finally met today. I've thought about how that would happen for so long. I had made up scenes in my head where we accidentally ran into each other, but I never expected it would be in the cold medicine aisle at the drugstore. I'm sorry you're sick but I'm not sorry that we bumped into each other, that you said my name the way I'd dreamed of hearing you say it.

Maybe your voice was deeper because of your cold, but I prefer to think it's because I took your breath away. Isn't that silly?

I'm a silly girl. Everyone says so. I'll never send you this letter, but maybe one day, if things work out, I'll show it to you, and I'll tell you that I knew the first second we met that we were destined to be together.

With all my love

She looked up at Roman. "It sounds like the writing of a very young woman."

"Do you think it was your mother?"

She shook her head. "She met my dad on a vacation she took to Miami Beach."

"Was it possible he had a cold at the time?" Roman said lightly.

She thought about that for a moment. "I suppose it's possible, but I never heard that story."

"There are about ten more letters. Maybe it will become more clear who's writing and who they're writing about as you read through them."

She stared down at the beautiful cursive handwriting and wondered who had taken pen to paper at the first feeling of love and amazement. And why had they hidden the letter in a box under some floorboards in the closet?

"What did you use that bedroom for?" Roman asked, drawing her attention back to him.

"What?" She had to think for a minute. "The bedroom was my dad's den. There's no way he wrote the letter. He was not romantic at all. My mom used to complain all the time about the gifts he'd get her. They were always practical, like a vacuum cleaner or a new microwave oven."

"Those can be good gifts."

She smiled. "My mom wanted jewelry or lingerie or something personal."

"So we can rule out your father, which makes sense. It sounds like a woman. And you just said your mom liked romance."

"But this doesn't sound like her." She paused. "I'd have to read more."

"Do you want something to drink before you get into that?" he asked, getting to his feet to open the refrigerator door. "I've got beer and orange juice."

"I'll take the beer," she said, feeling like she needed a drink.

He opened a bottle and handed it to her. She took a long swig, then set it down and reached for the next letter in the pile.

To My Love, she read aloud. "It would have been nice if she'd used a name."

"Keep reading," he said, sitting back down at the table.

She turned her attention back to the letter.

It's been three magical weeks since we met at the drugstore. You gave me a scare those first few days when you didn't call. I was afraid I'd ruined things by being too friendly. My sister says a man likes to chase, and I should learn to be more elusive. It's just not in my nature to pretend, at least not with you. I feel like you're too important to play games with.

Anyway, I was so happy when you asked me to go to the game with you. I don't even like football, but it didn't matter. Sitting there with you was enough for me.

You're funnier than I imagined. I bet most people don't think you can be funny, but your wit is sharp and quick. I liked talking to you. I wanted to keep talking to you. But then we went back to my house, and I didn't want to talk anymore.

"Now we're getting to the good stuff," Roman interrupted.

She made a face at him. "I don't think it's getting that good that fast."

"Let's find out."

She looked back at the note.

It was the perfect first kiss. I thought it would be awkward, but it wasn't. It felt so right to have your mouth on mine. I wanted it to go on forever. But of course we had to stop. My parents were right inside.

I'm going to miss you so much. I can't wait until we see each other again. I feel like I'm standing on the edge of a cliff, but I'm not scared, because you're there to catch me.

See you soon, my love.

Juliette set down the letter and looked at Roman. "Definitely not my mother. This woman was living with her parents when she wrote these letters. And it's like she's writing to him but also to herself. She didn't mail these, did she? Are there any envelopes?"

"I just saw the notes," he said. "But we don't know if she was living here and hiding the notes away like pages in a diary or if she sent the notes to her love and he was the one who lived here and hid the notes in the box. Maybe he didn't want his friends or his father or his brothers to see them."

"That's a good point."

"But if they don't belong to your mom and dad, then we should probably just toss them."

"What? No," she said, annoyed at the suggestion. "We should find out who they belong to, and return them."

"Why would we do that?"

"Because…" The handwriting caught her eye again. "Because they are about love and they feel important."

"They would only be important to the people involved."

"Or their kids. I want to keep reading and find out what happens next."

He gave her a knowing smile. "I'm not surprised—not with your curiosity."

"Can I take them back to my place?"

"I think you should read them here," he said.

"Oh, so you're curious, too."

"I might be a little interested," he admitted. "Have you eaten dinner yet?"

"No, I was working late at the bakery."

"So was I. Why don't I order us a pizza? We can read the letters while we're waiting."

"Okay," she said. "Piazza's has the best pizza in town."

"I remember that place. It's still around?"

"And better than ever. Plus, they deliver."

"Perfect." He pulled out his phone and looked up the number. "What do you like?"

"I'm a meat pizza kind of girl, so sausage, pepperoni, ham, and whatever veggies you want to throw on top."

"Sounds good to me," he said, punching in the number to place the order. When that was done, he looked back at her. "I'm ready for the next letter."

"You want me to keep reading them aloud? You're not finding them too sweet and sappy?"

"Oh, they're definitely sappy, but I'm still interested in the content."

She picked up the next note. "I think they're in order, at least they have been so far, although there aren't any dates." She unfolded the paper and began to read aloud.

To My Love,

Last night was the most wonderful night of my life. You touched me with such tenderness. You kissed me with such passion and ferocity. I felt desired and loved. I never imagined it could be like this. And then you held me through the night. I told you I slept well, but I didn't sleep at all. I stayed awake, listening to the sound of your heartbeat, the swoosh of your breath. I didn't want to close my eyes. I didn't want to miss a second.

I wish you hadn't left so early. I felt like I needed more

*time with you. I have this fear that things are moving too fast
and yet not fast enough. I don't want to lose you. I'm sure you
would say that you're not going anywhere, but I can't seem to
believe that. I can't keep the worry out of my heart. If it were
just about us, then maybe I could be more confident...but it's
not just about us.*

*I just hope you know how much I love you. I should have
said the words last night. But sometimes the words don't
come when we're together. I'm afraid I'll say too much or not
enough. Maybe you feel the same.*

*Now the words are flowing, along with the questions and
the doubts. Am I foolish to believe that something so
wonderful could last forever? Because then I must be the
most foolish person on earth.*

"That's it," Juliette said, setting the note down. "Sounds
like they slept together."

He nodded. "And she's not sure of his feelings."

"I wonder what she meant when she said: *if it were just
about us, but it's not.*"

"Maybe one of them was married."

"I was thinking that, too. At first, it seemed like the
letters were written by a teenager, but maybe not, perhaps just
a very young woman."

"Did you ever write letters like this?"

"No," she said, with a shake of her head. "I had a diary
when I was very young. I used to write under my window
upstairs. I had the room with the sloping ceilings, and the sun
would come through the window and light up that corner. I
had big pillows to flop on, and I'd sit there and read or write
in my journal."

"About boys?" he asked with a teasing smile. "Your
future Romeo?"

"There were a few boys mentioned in my journal. I had a
big crush on Kyle Daniels. He was blond and blue-eyed and
oh, so cute. But he only had eyes for Tracy Stone. She was
also blonde and blue-eyed and oh, so cute." She paused. "I
wonder what happened to them. They were dating when I left

school."

"Did you keep in touch with anyone after you left?"

"My friend Cassie. She lives in Chicago now, but we've seen each other a few times over the years. Whenever she came to New York, we'd get together. I'm hoping she'll come to Fairhope sometime to visit her parents. She skipped Christmas here to go to her boyfriend's parents' house. But maybe Easter."

"So this is it for you? Fairhope is your permanent home?"

"I'd like it to be. I feel like it's the right fit for me."

He nodded, agreement in his eyes. "I do, too."

She looked around the kitchen. "It's kind of weird to be sitting here with you. Even stranger that I took this particular seat, because we had a table in exactly this location, and this was my seat."

"Old habits," he murmured with a shrug.

"I used to do my homework here while my mom cooked dinner." She thought for a moment. "So many of my memories involve food. I was either in here with my mom making dinner or in the bakery helping my dad. I guess it's not that unusual. Meal times are usually family times."

"They can be."

"I know your mother had issues, but did she cook for you?"

"Rarely. I usually cooked for her."

"What did you make?"

"I was really good at spaghetti and mac and cheese that came out of a box. Tuna was a popular favorite. Hot dogs occasionally."

"Anything from the fruit or vegetable section of the grocery store?" she asked with a smile.

"Not very often. Sometimes a neighbor would drop off apples or oranges."

"Did you live in a house or an apartment?"

"Lots of different apartments. Sometimes there were roommates."

"Male roommates?"

"Both male and female. Most of them were nice enough."

"You lived a very different life than I did," she murmured.

"I did. I don't want to paint it all black, Juliette. My mom was not a bad or evil person. She had problems, and she didn't handle them well, but she wasn't mean. She loved me in her own way, as best she could."

She had a feeling Roman had been defending his mother for a very long time, and she respected the fact that he didn't blame her for ruining his life or making it hard, because there was no doubt it had been difficult.

The doorbell rang.

"That was fast," Roman said. "I'll get our pizza. Don't read ahead. We're doing this together."

"I'll wait for you," she said, sipping her beer as he left the room.

While he was gone, she closed her eyes for just a moment and let herself remember the old days. She could almost picture her homework before her, her mom at the stove, the sound of the TV in the living room where her dad watched the news every night. But the images were blurry, the sounds not as sharp as she would have thought they'd be, sitting here in the room where it had all happened.

She opened her eyes, feeling a little disappointment that her memories weren't better, that the house hadn't made them brighter. Maybe she'd been a fool to think they would be any different here.

Roman came back into the room, and she put a smile on her face as he set down the pizza and then grabbed paper plates and napkins for them. She didn't want to think about the past anymore.

"So tell me about the Marines," she said as she grabbed her first piece. "About your friends—the guys in your unit."

"Well, Cole is probably my closest friend. He's from Texas, and he's got a big, loud personality. Jimmy is loud, too, but more of a flirt, more of a ladies' man. Henry is the quiet one. We sometimes forget he's in the room. But his instincts are razor-sharp. Then there's Walton; he comes from the Louisiana bayou, and he talks endlessly about fishing and crocodiles and all other kinds of swamp creatures. He's the most superstitious, too. He has all kinds of rituals to ward off evil. I found myself doing the craziest things just so I wouldn't break some superstitious rule. He took us to Mardi Gras one year, and I met his crazy relatives and finally understood where his beliefs came from."

She liked the softness in his voice when he talked about his friends. "You miss them, don't you?"

"I do. We've spent most of the past seven years together. We're brothers." He took a breath, then added, "I never had anyone in my life who watched my back until I joined the Marines."

"Not even your grandfather?"

"He did the one time—after the fire. I don't think I appreciated it at the time. But the guys I served with—they would die for me, and I would do the same for them. Knowing that there were men I could count on made me want to be the person they could count on."

"I'm sure you were that person."

"Until I got hurt."

"Probably protecting someone else," she guessed.

"You don't know that."

"Am I wrong?"

He shrugged. "There was a lot going on that day."

She knew he wasn't going to give her any more information than that. "Well, I don't know how any of you do what you do. It takes an incredible amount of bravery to face that kind of danger to keep our country safe."

"When I joined up, my interest didn't really come from a place of patriotism," he said candidly. "It was more about having no other real options that I could see. But once I got in it, traveled the world, saw what I was fighting for, I knew I'd made the right decision. I was proud. First time in my life."

She smiled. "So your friends...are they all in it for the long term? I don't know much about the Marine Corps. Do they kick you out after a certain age?"

"No, but you usually move on to less action-filled roles as you get older. Not everyone wants that. And even before that, sometimes you just get tired of the fighting, the deployments, being away from your family. It's a lot easier when you're single, when there's no one waiting at home for you."

"Are any of the guys you just mentioned married?"

"No, Jimmy just got engaged, but he gets engaged every other year and never seems to make it down the aisle. Henry will probably actually get married. He's been dating a woman he met in the first grade. I think things are getting serious."

"If he gets married, will you all be in the wedding?"

"Hard to say where anyone will be, but we'd certainly try to get there for him."

"What I do seems so trivial in comparison to your job. I make cake. The world really doesn't need more cake, but every day I make a couple more."

He laughed. "It's good cake. At least, that's what I hear."

"I should have brought you some cookies. Damn. I forgot. You caught me off guard with your call, and I just rushed right over here. One day you are going to taste one of them."

"Next time."

As he said the words so casually, she was reminded that just last night she'd told herself she should stop seeing Roman, but here she was again. And she wasn't in any hurry to leave.

It wasn't just because the letters had caught her interest; it was him. He was quite simply one of the most intriguing men she'd ever met.

He pushed the last piece of pizza in her direction. "That's yours."

She shook her head. "I'm stuffed. Save it for tomorrow. Pizza for breakfast is always a good choice."

"I would have to agree. So you want to keep reading?"

"Okay." She pushed her empty plate aside, and pulled out

the next note.

My Love,

I'm sorry about my father—what he said to you last night. It was wrong. You didn't mean to hurt me. And you didn't talk me into anything, either. I wish you had stayed around so I could have told you that.

I don't know where you are right now, but I hope you're safe, and I hope you come back, so I can tell you how much I love you. So we can figure out how to make this right.

You're the only man for me. It's you or no one. That might sound dramatic, but it's how I feel. Please come back to me. Please don't let last night really be our last night.

"Trouble in paradise," Roman said as she finished reading.

She frowned. "It sounds like her father doesn't like her lover."

"I got the feeling she might be pregnant."

"Maybe, but she doesn't mention a baby, and it seems like she would."

Eager to find out what happened, she grabbed the next note on the stack.

There was no salutation this time. The woman just dove right in.

I can't marry him. I won't marry him. I don't love him. Marriage can't be about money, about union of families, about business, about who's right on paper. It has to be about love.

I'm willing to fight for you, for us, but where are you? You have to fight with me. We can do this together. We can have what we want. I know we can.

She looked up. "The notes are getting shorter, more desperate. Even her handwriting looks scared." She turned the note toward Roman so he could see it. "Don't you think?"

"I don't know. It looks like words to me."

"The first few notes were much more descriptive." She looked into the box. "Two more to go."

"I'm on the edge of my seat."

Oh, my Love,

How I long for you. My heart aches. I didn't know that love could be so consuming. It's in the air I breathe. It inhabits my dreams. It makes me thirsty and ravenous, but nothing will fill the emptiness inside of me. I feel all is lost.

And then I see you again. You're across the street. You look so handsome. I can't quite believe how long it's been since I saw you.

You smile, that half-smile, the one that makes my nerves tingle, the one that makes me believe you love me, too, no matter what you say, what you do.

You tip your head. That small acknowledgment makes my heart pound against my chest.

And then you turn away.

I have seen your back so many times. I yearn to call your name. But I can't.

I'm such a coward. I wish I could be braver.

One day...

"One day what?" Roman asked impatiently.

"That's it. It just ends with three dots."

"Well, let's read the last one. I hope this story has an ending."

"I don't think she wrote these notes as if she were putting a book together," she said, but she kind of hoped there was a happy ending, too. "Last one, here goes."

My Dearest Love

I did it. I ran away from the marriage I didn't want and from the man I didn't love. But when I got to your house, I heard you had left town.

My heart broke in two. I had left it too late. I should have told you that I wouldn't go through with it, that I would find a way to say no, to be with you and not with him.

Now it's too late. You've chosen another life. I must let you go.

I want you to be happy. I want you to have children, to love and be loved. I want you to live the life you were meant to lead.

But in the dark of the night, I want you to remember me, the way we loved each other, the passion of a youth I'll never forget. I know it's my fault. I was too afraid to speak. I've never even been able to send you these letters. I want to. I can see the mailbox from my window.

Dare I go out there and at least let you know how I've always felt? Will that make you happy? Or will it make you sad and angry?

I wish I knew the answer.

Good-bye, my love.

"I'm going to cry," she said with a sniff. "This is not the happy ending I wanted."

"It's real life," Roman said, as she dabbed at her eyes with the napkin. "Not everyone gets what they want."

"I wonder what really happened. It sounds like she was being urged or forced to marry someone for money and at the last minute she bailed out, but it was too late. Her real love was gone."

"That's what I got from it, too."

"I wonder who she is." She sat back in her chair and folded her arms across her chest. "I want to find out."

He laughed and shook his head. "Of course you do, but how?"

"I don't know. She must have lived here. And there must be a record somewhere of everyone who lived here."

"Maybe in the county records, but you don't know that she lived here. Maybe he did. Maybe she sent the letters to him in the end, but he was married to someone else by then. He could have hidden them in the box under the floorboards so his wife would never see them."

"That's true. He would have a reason to hide them if he had married another woman. But she could have also hidden them away from her family—her father. I really want to know who she is—who he is. And what happened to both of them. Did he pine for her? Or did he find happiness with someone else? Did she fall in love again? Did she ever marry? Did they ever see each other?"

Roman smiled. "You are so caught up in this."

"I can't help it. Her love speaks to me. Her words are filled with so much emotion. I can feel her longing, her pain. I want to do something about it."

"This could have all happened a long time ago, Juliette."

"Or not that long ago," she countered. "Are you going to help me figure it out?"

"You mean, am I going to delve into someone else's life and maybe cause them more pain and turmoil? Sure. That sounds like a plan."

She made a face at him. "You always look at the glass half-full. We could be returning the letters to someone who really wants them. Or we could be telling someone about a love he never thought he really had."

"Which could break up a marriage or two, hurt someone's children…"

He did have a point. "It could turn out that way, but that's the pessimistic point of view," she said. "We could just take it far enough to see what we're dealing with, then make a decision."

"That's exactly what you said when you asked me to go with you to Cameron's house."

"Well, that didn't work out so bad. At least we know his father lives there, so it's not just his batty grandmother watching him. And I dropped it after that."

"His father who I never wanted to see again and who never wanted to see me," he reminded her.

"You both came through the encounter without any mortal wounds."

"You're going to do this whether I help you or not, aren't you?"

"I am," she agreed. "But I'd rather have your help. I know you're curious, despite your cynicism. You want to know what happened to them, too."

He stared back at her. "You're very persuasive."

She smiled. "Is that a yes?"

"I have to go down to the county offices tomorrow to

check on some permits. I could possibly go by the Hall of Records and see if I can get a list of the previous owners of this house."

"Would you? That would be perfect. I'd love to go with you, but I am swamped with baking this week, and I only have Susan's help for a few hours tomorrow. I might be able to do it later in the day, but I can't commit."

"Don't worry about it. I'll see what I can find out and let you know."

"You're being very nice, Roman."

He laughed. "Just saving myself time trying to argue you out of this idea."

"Smart man."

"Am I?" He gave her a bemused look. "When I left your apartment last night, I told myself I probably shouldn't see you for a while."

Her heart quickened. "Why would you tell yourself that?"

"You know why. There's something between us."

She licked her lips at his blunt response. "I'm not dating Doug, if that's a concern to you. I'm not interested in him."

Roman's gaze darkened. "I'm glad."

"Are you?"

"Yeah. But…"

She waited a moment, then said, "Are you going to finish that sentence?"

He let out a sigh. "Maybe when I come up with an ending. You know I'm leaving, Juliette. I don't know when, but it will probably be soon."

She swallowed hard at the reminder. "I know."

"So…I should walk you out."

She really didn't want to leave it like that, but Roman was already on his feet. She slowly stood up. "Do you mind if I hang on to the letters?"

"No, I think you should."

"Okay." She followed him out to the front door, not sure what to do next. *Should she kiss him? Should she say good-*

night and just leave?

While she was thinking about it, he grabbed her arms and hauled her up against his chest in a possessive manner that stole her breath away.

"Not so fast," he murmured. "I didn't get my kiss yet."

"I didn't think you wanted one."

"Oh, but I do."

His mouth touched hers with a heated warmth that melted her insides. She leaned into his kiss, inviting his tongue to tangle with hers, wrapping her arms around his neck as she pulled his head down.

It wasn't so much as a good-night kiss as a let's-keep-this-going kiss. But all too soon it ended.

Roman lifted his head, his gaze unreadable as he stared down at her. "That sweet mouth of yours packs a punch."

"Only with you," she murmured.

"I like that."

"I figured you would. And it's the truth."

"I'll see you tomorrow."

She nodded, then his lips touched hers again, one last teasing taste that she savored all the way home.

Ten

❯❯❰❰ ❮

"Juliette," Susan said. "We need more Wish cookies."

She stared at her assistant in confusion late Tuesday afternoon, realizing she'd been completely lost in thought. That had been happening a lot since she'd met Roman. She spent way too much time thinking about him. And last night's dreams had certainly been filled with his image.

"There's more in the back," she said. "I'll get them." She went into the kitchen and then brought out another tray of the popular cookies.

When she put them in the display case, an older woman with jet-black hair and bright-pink lipstick gave her a huge smile of relief.

"Thank goodness," the woman said. "I was afraid you were out of those cookies."

"How many do you want?"

"I'll take the whole tray."

"Really? All of them?" she asked in surprise. "There are thirty-six cookies here."

"And I have a lot of friends who want to make wishes. I'm Dolores Baker. I work at the Morning Glory Retirement Center. We're having a pre-Valentine's Day party tomorrow, and I can't tell you how many of the residents asked me if I was getting your Wish cookies."

"That's sweet," she said, grabbing a large box.

"My mother is one of those residents. She told me that fifteen years ago, as a widow, she bought a cookie from your father. She wished that she would find love again. It seemed impossible to her at the time; she was still grieving for my dad. But at the Valentine's Day Sweetheart's Dance, she met another widower, Malcolm Hodges. They started talking and they ended up married six months later. He made her happy for twelve years. Sadly, he passed away three years ago. I think these cookies are just what she needs to be hopeful again, even if it's just all fun."

She was touched by Dolores's story. "That's really sweet. I'm glad you shared that with me, and I hope these cookies bring a lot of happiness to all of your friends."

"I'm sure they will. And at the very least, they'll taste good."

She rang up the purchase, then said good-bye.

"I think that's it," Susan said, letting out a tired sigh as she finished with the last customer. "Busy day. And it looks like you're headed for an early morning with more baking. The orders continue to pour in. At some point, you may just have to say no. There's a limit to how much you can do."

"I can make it all work. I don't need much sleep."

Susan gave her a doubtful look. "I think you should reconsider the dessert order for the Wayfarer restaurant. It's just too big. They want six toasted almond cakes and six molten lava chocolate cakes, and they called it in twenty minutes ago for tomorrow's lunch. What were they thinking?"

"They said they were hoping for a miracle. I'm going to give them one."

"And kill yourself in the process."

"I'll be fine." She paused, looking at the clock. "You can go. I'll close down."

"Are you sure? I hate leaving you to handle all this baking on your own, but you know I'm no good in the kitchen."

She nodded. She had tried to use Susan a few times, and she just didn't have the enthusiasm or skill set for baking. "You've already worked hard enough today. Go and be with your husband."

"Okay, but you do need to start thinking about getting an assistant to help with the baking. I know you don't trust anyone, but you only have two hands."

"I am thinking about it. I just feel like I can't sell anything I haven't made myself."

"You have to get over that."

"I'm sure you're right."

Susan took off her apron. "I've been meaning to ask—what happened with Doug the other night? You never said how your dinner was."

"It was fine."

"That doesn't sound very exciting."

"It wasn't. We just didn't have any sparks."

Susan looked disappointed. "That's a shame. I was thinking you'd make a good mayor's wife."

She laughed at that. "I'd make a terrible politician's wife. I often speak before I think."

"That can be refreshing."

"Or career killing," she said, following Susan to the door. "See you tomorrow." After her assistant left, she locked the door and turned the sign to Closed, then started to unload the display cases, and put some of the items back into the refrigerator.

When that was done, she grabbed a quick bite upstairs, making some soup to go with a salad. Then she headed back downstairs around seven to start prep for the next day. She'd just re-entered the kitchen when she got a text from Roman.

Her heart zinged at just the sight of his name. She really needed to get a grip on her emotions. His text said he had some information for her.

She told him to come to the bakery. She was really curious to see if he'd discovered the identity of the letter writer.

He said he'd be there in about a half hour, so she decided to get some work done before then. Setting down the phone, she put on her apron and turned her attention to her prep work.

She was deep in flour, butter, and cream when her phone buzzed again with a text that Roman was out front. She quickly hurried out to the front door to let him in.

He looked better than dessert, she thought, his hair mussed from the windy evening, his cheeks glowing, his brown eyes sparkling.

"Cold out there, warm in here," he said with a grin, as he unzipped his jacket.

"I'm preheating the ovens. Come in the back."

He followed her into the kitchen, then pulled a big envelope out of his pocket before hanging his jacket on the hook by the door.

"So this is where the magic happens," he said.

"This is it." She waved her hand around the room. "But it doesn't look much like magic right now. I have a huge order due tomorrow by eleven, so it's going to be a long night."

"We don't have to do this now if you're busy."

"Of course we have to do this now. I'm busy but I'm also curious."

"Did anyone ever tell you curiosity killed the cat?"

"My dad used to say that to me a lot, but I'm not a cat, so I'm not worried."

She waved him toward a stool by the island counter. "Have a seat." He sat down and she took the stool next to him. "So what did you find out?"

"I went down to the county courthouse and was able to get the list of recorded deeds on your property."

"That's great."

"I have to warn you that this data doesn't reflect tenants. So if your letter writer was a renter and not an owner, she won't be in here."

"Got it. Let's start with the owners."

"Okay." He pulled a piece of paper from the envelope.

"It's not too long of a list. The house was built in 1917, and there have been seven owners in the last hundred years, four owners before your parents and two afterward, including my grandfather."

"Seven," she muttered. It wasn't a lot for a hundred years, but it reminded her again that her story was just one of the many stories the house would tell.

He arched an eyebrow, giving her a speculative look. "What did I say?"

"Nothing. Who are the owners?"

"Jeremy Bascom built the house and lived there for eighteen years. He moved out in 1933."

"That was during the depression. I wonder if he had to sell."

"Possibly. I was also talking to the woman in the recorder's office, and she told me that most deeds up until the 1950s were held in a man's name only, regardless of his marital status. So when I give you a man's name, it doesn't necessarily mean he was single."

"It's hard to believe that it wasn't that long ago that women couldn't own property in their own name. Who's next on the list?"

Roman consulted the sheet of paper in front of him. "Harry Sackmore. He owned the property from 1933 to 1958. Next was Max and Jane Grayson, from 1958 to 1972."

"Wait, are the Grayson sisters related to Max and Jane?"

"If those were their parents, I'd say so, but I don't know for sure."

"That's interesting. Who's next?"

"Connie Jacobson owned the house from 1972 to 1987, when your parents bought it. I don't know if she was a single woman or just held the deed in her name." He paused. "Do we need to go on with the owners after your parents?"

"There was just one, wasn't there?"

"Yes, Dee and Bill Hannington, from 2003 to 2016. Then my grandfather purchased the property. That brings us to now."

She thought about what she'd just learned. She had names, but she needed more.

"Let me ask you something," Roman said. "Was that bedroom and closet carpeted when you lived there?"

"I think so," she said slowly. "I feel like all of the bedrooms were carpeted."

"Do you remember your parents putting down new carpet?"

"No, not really. Why all the questions about carpeting?"

"Just trying to see if we can rule out anyone. If the carpet was placed over the boards where the box was hidden, then it probably happened before you moved in."

"That's true, but who knows how many times it was re-carpeted? I think we have to base our theory on the fact that the letters sound old-fashioned."

"I agree," he said with a nod. "Her language, and her concern about her father forcing her to marry, sound dated."

"So we need to research the four owners before my parents. That shouldn't be too difficult." She paused. "Maybe I should start with the Graysons."

He groaned. "If you want to start there, I'm out. You'll get further on your own."

She knew he was right, but she didn't want him to be out. She wanted him to be working with her. "Then let's start at the beginning. I wonder what we can find out on the Internet."

"Probably quite a bit. Do you want to start now?"

"I really do," she said, "but..."

"But you have cakes to bake. No problem. This can wait. Those letters have been hidden for years. There's no real urgency to figure out who owns them now."

"Except that I really want to, but it will have to wait until tomorrow night."

"I should let you get back to work."

"Or..." she said impulsively.

He gave her a wary look. "I don't think I like the sound of that."

"You could help me bake. I could use another set of hands." She couldn't quite believe she was asking Roman to help when she'd already turned away Susan's offer, but she just hated to see him leave again so soon.

"My hands?" he asked doubtfully. "I don't think I'll be much help."

"I'll tell you what to do."

"What are you making?"

"Toasted almond cakes with mascarpone cream and Amarena cherries, decorated with pink and red hearts."

"That sounds hard."

"They're not difficult, but they are time-consuming. And I need six of them. I also need six molten lava chocolate cakes. It's a special order for a private luncheon. That's why I could use the help."

"And you don't have anyone else to ask?"

"I really don't."

"You're going to regret this, Juliette."

She smiled. "I don't think so. You're a smart guy. And you said yourself you used to cook for you and your mom."

"I also said I made hot dogs and spaghetti."

"You can do it. I'm a great teacher."

"Well, you're filled with confidence tonight." He got to his feet and pushed up the sleeves of his sweater. "Fine. You're on. I am yours to command."

"Great." She stood up and moved over to the built-in set of drawers, pulling out an apron and a baker's hat. "First, you dress."

"You want me to wear an apron?" he asked doubtfully.

"And a hat. Health regulations."

"No one is here to see what I'm wearing."

"I'll see. And what happened to—*I am yours to command*?"

"Fine," he grumbled, putting the apron on and tying it behind his back.

She put the hat on his head. "You look sexy."

"I seriously doubt that," he said dryly. "Save your

buttering-up for the cake pans."

She laughed. "That's a good one. But you do look sexy, and if you do an amazing job tonight, I'll prove it to you." Her reckless dare brought a gleam to his eyes.

"Oh, yeah? What are you going to do?"

"You'll have to wait and see. First, you have to show me you can follow instructions and let me be the boss."

"I'm a good soldier," he said lightly. "What do you want me to do first?"

"Get the pans ready."

"Okay, that sounds easy."

"It is, but if you mess it up, the cakes won't come out of the pans, and we'll have to start over again."

"So a little pressure then. Way to build my confidence, boss."

"I just want you to know what's at stake," she said. "All kidding aside, Roman, these have to be perfect. This is my business, my brand, and it has to be amazing."

"I get it," he said, giving her a reassuring smile. "I'll do the best I can. But at any point you want to fire me, just say the word."

She probably shouldn't have hired him in the first place, but spending the night baking with Roman sounded a lot more fun than doing it by herself.

Juliette was tough, Roman thought two hours later, as he wiped the sweat off his forehead with a paper towel. She'd told him that she took her business seriously, and she hadn't been lying. Once they'd gotten into the baking, her instructions had been crisp, clear, purposeful, and her attitude had gone from sweet and easygoing to serious and perfection-driven.

He wished he could say he liked her less now, but it was just the opposite. He could see her passion, her drive, her determination to do well, to meet her own very high standards, and her willingness to do things over and over until they were done exactly the way she needed them to be done.

When she'd asked him to help, he'd sort of expected he'd be playing around in some flour, cracking some eggs, and watching her sweet, sexy body move around the kitchen, but instead he'd been taught how to make toasted almond cake, filling, icing, and pink and red hearts to add decoration to the top of the cakes. He'd felt a bit clumsy throughout most of the tasks, but he had to admit he'd enjoyed the work.

Glancing at the clock on the wall, he realized it was almost ten. The last almond cake was in the oven, but they had yet to start the chocolate cakes. Juliette still had a lot of work ahead of her. He had a feeling her enthusiasm for everything might be leading her into over-booking herself.

"One more to go," she said, giving him an absent-minded smile, as she checked the oven. "Then I'll let everything cool before I decorate. While that's happening, I can start on the chocolate cakes."

"You know it's nearly ten, right?"

"What?"

He pointed to the clock.

Dismay flashed across her face. "Oh, I didn't realize it was so late. I guess I'll do the cakes in the morning. That's probably a better plan anyway."

"What time do you get up?"

"Tomorrow—probably four."

"That's six hours from now."

"I'm used to going on little sleep."

"So am I, but at some point it catches up to you. You can't do your best work when you're exhausted," he said.

"I appreciate that, but I feel pretty good. I am sorry I kept you so long. I tend to lose track of time when I'm baking."

"I noticed that."

"Your help was invaluable, Roman. I feel better having gotten so much done tonight."

"I'm glad I was able to help a little. I like your drive," he said, stepping forward to wipe a smudge of flour off her cheek.

Her blue eyes sparked back at him, and suddenly he had a feeling that neither one of them was thinking about cake anymore.

"I like your willingness to learn," she said.

"What else do you like?" he asked softly.

She drew in an unsteady breath. "Your eyes, the intensity of your gaze. When you're looking at me, I don't feel like there's anyone else in the room."

"I know the feeling. What else?"

"Searching for compliments?" she teased.

"It's more that I want to know what you like."

"I like the way you kiss me, the way you hold me, pretty much everything about it."

"I like the way you kiss me back," he said softly. He slipped his arms around her waist and pulled her up against him. "I think I've earned my reward for being a sexy assistant in an apron and a hat."

She smiled at the reminder. "First, tell me what you like about me."

"Where do I start?"

"Anywhere you want."

"I like your hair, the way it curls up from the steamy ovens. I like the way your cheeks flush when you cook or when you talk or when you think I'm going to kiss you."

She put her hands on her cheeks. "Are they pink now?"

"A beautiful shade of rose—like your lips...your soft, sexy, tempting lips."

"Oh, my," she said, breathing in. "When I first met you, I thought you were a man of few words, but I'm liking the words you choose a lot better now."

"So, is it time for my reward?" he asked.

"Yes," she said, smiling back at him. "You've earned it in so many ways." Her hands slid around his neck as she pressed on tiptoe to kiss him.

The kiss started out soft, tender, but within seconds it became explosive and hot. He was fast becoming addicted to her taste, to the feel of her body in his arms, to the scents of sugar and cinnamon and vanilla that seemed to cling to her skin. She was sweet and sexy—a deadly combination. Not to mention smart and fun and eager to explore whatever she was curious about.

He tried to put a brake on his thoughts, but every kiss between them just made him like her more. He knew he should stop. She had to get up early. And this fire could so easily burn out of control. He didn't want to hurt her. He didn't want to leave her. But he was afraid both would happen—and probably too soon for either of them.

His body told his brain to shut up, enjoy the moment and not think about tomorrow.

It seemed like good advice, especially when her breasts pressed against his chest.

And then the oven timer went off.

The sound took a moment to register.

Juliette woke up first, pulling out of his embrace. "The cake," she muttered, her voice somewhat bemused. She ran into the corner of the counter as she hurried toward the oven, yelped with a hint of pain, then moved around the counter to open the oven.

She pulled out her cake and set it on the counter. Then she rubbed her hip bone.

"Are you all right?" he asked.

"Yes." She let out a breath. "It's fine."

"Good thing you set the timer. We might have forgotten about that cake."

"That's a good bet." She tucked her hair behind her ear with a somewhat self-conscious smile. "I tend to forget a lot when we start kissing."

He nodded in agreement, wishing she wasn't on the other side of the big island, but she seemed to like the distance between them now, and maybe it was a good thing. Otherwise, he would probably never leave.

"I did appreciate your help, Roman," she added. "It was nice of you to offer."

"I don't know if I exactly offered, but you're welcome. I should go. And you should, too."

She nodded. "I'll just clean up a few things and then head upstairs."

"Can I help?"

"No, you've done enough."

He frowned. "I don't like to leave you here alone."

"I'm here alone all the time. It's very safe."

"You have to go out to the street to go upstairs."

"Which is also very safe, and it's about a six-foot distance between doors. You don't need to worry about me."

"All right—if you're sure." He took off his apron and hat and set them on the counter.

"I do want to follow up on the information you got from the county on the previous homeowners. Hopefully, I can find some time to get online."

"I'll leave the paperwork with you. We can touch base tomorrow night."

"That would be good. It's going to be crazy until then. Should I come over to the house, and we can go on the Internet together? Wait, do you have Internet there?"

"I have a hot spot on my phone."

"That will work."

"But actually tomorrow night isn't good. How about Thursday?"

"Sure. What's going on tomorrow? Or would you rather not say?" She paused, frowning a little. "Do you have a date?"

"No, it's not a date."

"Then what are you doing?"

"I'm playing guitar at Mickelson's Bar. John Mickelson is a friend of my grandfather, and he persuaded me to sit in with one of the bands tomorrow night."

Surprise ran through her eyes. "Wait. What? You play the guitar well enough to play in a band?"

"We'll find that out tomorrow night," he said lightly. "I'm a little rusty."

"I have to admit, I'm surprised. You are a man of many layers."

He shrugged. "Not that many. Do you want to walk me out?"

She hesitated, then shook her head. "I'm going to stay right where I am, because I really do need to go to bed, and you really do need to leave, and if we end up at the door together, who knows what will happen?"

He smiled. "I'd like to find out."

"That's not going to happen tonight."

"Fair enough. Good luck with the baking tomorrow."

"Thanks. Good luck with the playing. Are you going to sing, too?"

"I don't think he'll be able to talk me into that."

"I bet you have a good voice."

"I don't know what you're basing that bet on."

"Gut instinct."

"You were shocked I played. Now your instinct tells you I'm a singer?"

She laughed. "Fine, I'll wait and see for myself."

His pulse sped up. "You're going to come?"

"Of course I'm going to come. You singing and playing the guitar—I wouldn't miss it for the world."

Eleven

—➤➤➤◄◄◄—

Wednesday morning passed in a blur as Juliette worked from four a.m. until eleven when she went to the Wayfarer restaurant to drop off her desserts, which were received with a great deal of awe and praise.

On her way back to the bakery, she stopped in at Donavan's for some much-needed coffee. She'd sent Susan to make the morning delivery to Donavan's, so she'd missed her early morning espresso.

Sara and Donavan were both working behind the counter, and she noticed that Roman's grandfather, Vincent, and his friend Max were chatting at their usual table with another gray-haired man.

She stepped up to the counter and gave Donavan a smile. "I am in desperate need of coffee."

"What can I get you?"

"I think I'll try the dark roast today. It smells so good."

"You've got it," Donavan said.

"You look tired," Sara commented, as she took her credit card and swiped it.

"I'm exhausted. I just finished up a huge order for a private lunch at the Wayfarer restaurant."

"That's a good place to show off your desserts."

"I hope so. The cakes turned out well, which is always a relief when I get a special order."

Donavan set down a mug of coffee in front of her instead of her usual to-go cup. "Why don't you sit down and read the newspaper or something? You've been going nonstop for days. The shadows under your eyes are getting bigger."

"I wish I could, but—"

"But nothing. Sit," Donavan ordered. "You have to pace yourself, Juliette. I recognize your need to make everything great immediately. But it's hard to build a steady business. You're going to need strength to keep all the balls in the air, so a few minutes here and there to breathe are absolutely required."

"I know you're right. It's just so hard to take those minutes when time is precious."

Donavan gave her an understanding smile. "From what I can see, you're doing really well."

"I actually do feel kind of proud of myself," she admitted. "I dreamed about owning a bakery for a long time, and I wasn't sure I could do it all by myself, but somehow I'm doing it."

"And you'll keep doing it, after you sit down and have some coffee."

"Thanks." She took her coffee over to a table and sat down. Someone had left a newspaper behind, so she browsed through the local news, thinking it had been a long time since she'd actually read a newspaper. Most information she got online. It did feel relaxing to actually be out somewhere and not have something pressing to do for a few minutes.

Sara brought over a sandwich on a plate and set it down in front of her.

"What's this?" she asked.

"I picked up sandwiches at Connor's Deli but then Eli called in sick, so I have an extra. It's turkey and jack cheese with tomatoes and sprouts. Will that work?"

"It's perfect."

Sara took the seat across from her. "So anything new

happening? Did you ever go out with Doug?"

"As a matter of fact, I did—last Sunday night. He took me to dinner at Gladstone's."

"Fancy," Sara said with a raise of her brow. "Doug does know how to charm the ladies. And then what did you do?"

She saw the expectant look in Sara's eyes and knew she was going to disappoint her. "He took me home and we said good-night."

"No kiss?"

"Just a peck."

"So will there be a second date?"

"No. Doug is great, and I think we could be friends, but that's it."

"Oh, too bad. Does he feel the same way?"

"I haven't heard from him since Sunday night, so I'm guessing yes. I don't have time to date right now anyway. What about you? How was your night with Tim after the movie festival?"

"It was really fun and there were definitely sparks when we kissed good-night. He had to go visit his sister in Kansas City, because she's having a baby, but he's texted me a few times since then."

"That's promising."

"We'll see." She pushed back her chair and stood up. "I better get back to work."

As Sara left, Travis came into the coffeehouse. His steps slowed when he saw her. He gave her a quick, curt nod and then headed to the counter. He didn't look much better today than he had over the weekend when they'd first met. His clothes were still wrinkled, his beard still scruffy, his skin pale and unhealthy looking. She really hoped Cameron was all right.

"Travis," Donavan said. "Your mother said you were back in town. It's so good to see you again."

"I heard you have a good business going here," Travis said, looking around. "It's nice."

"Thanks. What can I get you?"

"Actually, I didn't come here for the coffee; I'm looking for a job. I was wondering if you might need anyone."

"Oh, well, I'm sorry," Donavan said, giving him an apologetic smile. "We're not looking for any help right now."

"Okay," he said heavily. "If you hear of any openings anywhere, will you let me know? Can I leave you my number?"

"Sure," Donavan said, jotting down Travis's number. "Is there any kind of work you're particularly looking for?"

"Whatever will pay some bills. I've been selling cars the last few years, but there aren't any dealerships around here, and I need to stay close to home. I've got a kid now—a son."

"Cameron, right?" Donavan said. "He's come in with your mother a few times. He's cute."

"Yeah, I'm hoping this is a good move for him." He cleared his throat. "I'm good with construction, too. I can paint, whatever."

Juliette could hear the desperation in Travis's voice and judging by Donavan's sympathetic expression, she could, too.

"I will definitely keep my ears open," Donavan said. "You might talk to Mr. Prescott. He's right over there. He's doing a big remodel."

Travis cast a quick look at the men in the corner and shook his head. "Roman's grandfather? I don't think so. But anyone else—let me know."

"Sure," Donavan replied. "But maybe it's time to bury that old problem."

"Not my choice," Travis said shortly, then tipped his head and walked out of the coffee shop.

As Travis left, she couldn't help wondering what had happened to his wife, why his finances had gotten so dire. Her concerns about Cameron's well-being returned. Hopefully, Travis could find work somewhere in town. Roman probably could use his help on the remodel, but she knew that was a non-starter. Travis hadn't even wanted to talk to Vincent. Once again, the past was rearing its ugly head, and once again, she wondered who had actually started the fire. She wondered if anyone really knew.

But that was a worry for another day. She took her plate and mug to the counter, then headed back to work.

Her next break didn't come until after six, when she closed up the bakery and made her way upstairs. The short night of sleep was catching up to her, but she had to stay awake. There was no way she was going to miss Roman playing at Mickelson's Bar.

She took a shower to wake up, blew-dry her hair, applied some makeup, and then made some scrambled eggs for dinner. After that, she got on her computer with the list of names that Roman had gotten for her yesterday. She might as well do a little research before she left.

She started with the first owner, Jeremy Bascom. Twenty minutes later, all she'd found was an obituary notice that made no mention of a wife or children. She decided to move on to the next owner, which was Harry Sackmore, who'd owned the house from 1933 to 1958. She found out that Harry was a dentist and that he'd died in 1958. He'd been survived by his wife Leonora and his son Franklin. Franklin was a dentist like his father, and he'd died in 1986, survived by a wife, Carol.

Frowning, she jotted down notes, not really sure exactly what she was looking for, but her gut told her that the letter writer had been a single young woman—which took her to the Graysons. Max and Jane Grayson had bought the house in 1958 and lived there until 1972. They'd had two daughters, Martha and Cecelia. Max had worked at a law firm in town before his death in 1990. There was no information on Jane.

Martha and Cecelia had lived in Fairhope their entire lives. Martha had been on the staff of a different law firm than the one her father had worked at. She'd been a legal secretary until she'd retired in 2008. Cecelia ran the local nursery and volunteered for several charities.

She didn't need the Internet to learn more about them; she could just talk to them. They came into her bakery several times a week. But she wasn't quite sure how to broach the question of whether or not one of them had written letters to a lover and then buried them under some floorboards.

She couldn't imagine Martha loving anyone. Cecelia was definitely softer and nicer. Maybe it had been her. Or perhaps it hadn't been either one of them, but it was the best lead she had.

And it was interesting that there hadn't been any men in their lives, or at least no marriages. Was that because one of them still pined for the man she'd lost?

Perhaps that was why Martha was so bitter. Or maybe it was why Cecelia seemed so lonely.

Setting them aside, she looked for the last owner before her parents—Connie Jacobson. There were several Connie Jacobsons on social media, but no one listing their hometown as Fairhope. She tried for marriage and obituary listings and finally found a Connie Jacobson who had died of cancer in 1985, which was two years before the house had sold to Juliette's parents.

Connie had been survived by three sons: Nathan, Philip and Adrian. There was no mention of a husband. It looked like the sons had sold the house to her parents.

It was possible Connie had been the letter writer. Maybe her husband had left her or died.

She tapped a few more keys, looking for any other info she could find on the sons. Nathan Jacobson, which implied Jacobson was Connie's married name, was a realtor in town. Finally, another lead.

She closed the computer. She had three people to talk to now—the Grayson sisters and Nathan—but they would all have to wait until tomorrow. Checking her watch, she got up, grabbed a coat and headed out to Mickelson's Bar.

What the hell had he been thinking? He never should have agreed to play tonight, Roman thought, as he looked around the crowded bar. So far, he hadn't seen any familiar faces, but that didn't mean some people from his past wouldn't show up. And those who came could very well be people who didn't like him at all. He was not only putting his rusty guitar skills on display, he was also putting himself in a position for some nasty heckling.

He didn't really care what anyone said to him, but he did like John, the owner of the bar, and the last thing he wanted to do was create any problems for him.

He stood off to the side, adjusting the tension on his strings, while a guy set up the amps. He'd met Bobby, the drummer, and David, the bass guitarist, and they both seemed like good guys. Hopefully, he could keep up with them.

As the door to the bar opened, he found himself looking for a certain pretty brunette with dazzling blue eyes, but Juliette had not shown up yet. He told himself she might not come. She had to be exhausted from all the work, but somehow he thought she would be there, and he was both excited and a little wary about her presence. He found himself wanting to impress her, and it had been a long time since he'd felt the need to do that for anyone.

But it wasn't Juliette who walked in; it was Donavan and her younger sister Becky. While Becky went to the bar, Donavan came over to him.

"Are you playing?" she asked, surprise in her eyes.

"The guitar gave it away, huh?"

"Yes. I can't quite believe it."

"Me, either. John Mickelson caught me in a weak moment."

"I remember when you used to sit on the pier and strum your guitar. I can't tell you how many girls showed up there accidentally on purpose to hear you play."

"I don't remember that," he said.

"You were in your own world when you had that guitar in your hands. Actually, I think you were in your own world a lot of the time. It's what made you so interesting. You were elusive."

"Elusive? I wasn't trying to be, but okay."

"Roman Prescott?"

He turned his head to see a woman with bright copper-colored hair walking toward him.

"Is that you?" she asked. "I'm Vanessa Henderson. Remember me?"

He didn't really, but she looked vaguely familiar. "Vanessa, sure. How are you?"

"In disbelief that you're actually here. I heard you were in town, but you haven't shown up anywhere before now."

"I've been working for my grandfather. How are you?"

"I'm single again," she said.

"Again?"

"I was married for a couple of years—silly mistake. But you know me, I can be impulsive. Remember that time we made out at the movies?" she asked with a mischievous smile. "We should do that again sometime."

He cleared his throat. If he'd made out with her, he had absolutely no recollection of it. "I need to get ready for my set."

"Maybe we'll talk...later."

"Maybe," he said, knowing he would do everything to avoid that.

Donavan was all smiles when Vanessa walked away, and he looked in her direction.

"See," she said. "Not everyone in town has bad memories of you." She lowered her voice. "But Vanessa? Really? I always thought she made that up about the movies and your make-out session."

"I don't remember it, but let's keep that between us."

"You've got it. And now I'm pretty sure she did make it up. Good luck tonight."

"Thanks."

As Donavan left, Bobby came over with a young woman in her early twenties. She had long, black hair and dark eyes, a bohemian look to her flowy clothes.

"This is Fiona," Bobby said. "Our singer."

"Good to meet you," he said, shaking her hand.

"Likewise. I haven't seen you around here before."

"Just got back into town."

"You ready to rock?" she asked.

"Definitely."

They went over the first few songs they would be playing. Fortunately, he knew the first one really well and the second two he could keep up with. After that, who knew...

He took a deep breath as he got onto the stage. He couldn't remember the last time he'd played for anyone but himself. Hopefully, he wouldn't embarrass the band.

Fiona stepped up to the mic, and with a *one-two-three*, they were off.

He felt ridiculously rusty at first, even though he'd practiced a few hours earlier in the day. It was very different playing on a stage in front of people than in an empty house. But once the music and beat started flowing through him, he began to relax.

Fiona's voice had a raspy, almost magical quality, that instantly quieted the crowd, and all attention turned to the band.

By the end of the first song, he was feeling it. And halfway through the second song, he thought he might get through the night without any problems.

Then Juliette walked through the door, and he lost his focus for a second, hitting the wrong chord.

He quickly corrected and hoped no one would notice. He watched her make her way to the back of the room. Damn, she was pretty. Even in the dim light, she seemed to sparkle.

He forced himself to look away from her and focus on the music. He wanted to get it right, not just for the band or the crowd, but for her.

They played three more songs before ending their set to a round of applause. As he got off the stage, he saw Doug standing with Juliette. That stopped him in his tracks.

He headed to the bar and got a beer from the bartender, feeling instantly deflated by the sight of Juliette and Doug together. She'd said she wasn't interested in him, but he'd seen

Doug change a girl's mind many a time.

John Mickelson came over and gave him a slap on the back. "I knew you were still good, Roman."

He looked into the silver-blue eyes of his grandfather's friend. "Thanks. It was fun."

"You can come back any time."

"I might take you up on that."

"How are things going for you around here?"

"They're all right," he said, taking a swig of his beer.

"Your grandfather is happy you're back."

"It's not for too long."

"That's what he said. Can I offer a suggestion, even though it's none of my business?"

He gave a nod. "Sure."

"Your grandfather would love nothing more than to give you his business, but he doesn't want you to feel obligated to take it, if your heart is somewhere else."

He stared at John in surprise. "He's never told me that."

"Well, Vince isn't one to say much about what matters to him. But you're his family—his blood. He's proud of you."

"From what I can see, except for this latest remodel, his business is pretty much done."

"Not if you turn the house on Primrose Lane into a winner. Your grandfather has a great eye, and he knows how to make the most out of a house. He's a good manager, but he needs someone to build the business up to what it used to be."

"I'm a Marine, not a contractor."

"I know you're a soldier. And from what I hear, you've been a damn good one. But if there comes a time when you decide to make a change, you might want to give construction and Fairhope a chance. I know one man you'll make very happy with that decision."

He wondered about that. He'd never really thought much about his relationship with his grandfather. They didn't speak about emotions or feelings or anything personal. They were blood, but they were strangers in a lot of ways.

"You know, he wanted your dad to take over his

business," John added. "But Brett couldn't hammer a board without hitting his thumb. If there was a paint can to trip over, he'd somehow end up on his back with paint all over him."

He was shocked to realize it was the first time anyone, outside of his grandfather or mother, had ever mentioned his father to him. Even when he'd lived in Fairhope before, the subject had never come up. Although, that might have been because he had rarely spoken to adults during those few rebellious teenage years.

"Your grandfather was disappointed that Brett wouldn't carry on his business, but the man just didn't have the talent for it. He was a good musician, though. You must have gotten those genes from him. He played guitar, too."

"I had no idea."

"Seriously? Your grandfather never told you?"

"We don't talk about my father."

"Well, your dad was very talented. He had a band in high school."

He was more than a little surprised at that. "A band, huh?"

"Yeah. I don't think your grandfather liked it much, but Brett did what he wanted. That seems to be the Prescott way."

"I don't know anything about my father. He wasn't with my mother longer than a few months after I was born, and then he died when I was three. I didn't meet Vincent until I was fifteen. By then, my dad had been gone a long time, and my grandfather didn't like to talk about him, so we didn't."

John nodded with understanding. "Well, they butted heads a lot. Brett had his head in the clouds, and Vincent is a practical sort. He didn't like that Brett wouldn't ever take his advice."

"Do you know what drove them apart? Was there a specific incident?"

"There was. Brett dropped out of college without telling your grandfather. He sold everything Vincent had given him and took the cash and went to California. Vincent didn't find him for almost a year. Brett said he just didn't have the nerve to tell him he hated school. They had some big confrontation. Vincent came back and said they were done. That's all I know. You should ask your grandfather, if you want to know more."

"I doubt he'd tell me more," he murmured. "I can't believe my father didn't tell my grandfather he was leaving school."

"Like I said, he was headstrong and stubborn."

As John stepped behind the bar to answer something for the bartender, Roman thought about what he'd just learned. He'd given up on asking his mother for information about his father, because it always made her cry, and when he'd broached the subject with his grandfather, the reaction had been anger. So he'd let it be, figuring he didn't really need to know about a man who'd given him nothing more than a last name.

But knowing that his father liked music…somehow that changed things a little, fleshed out the ghostly figure in his head.

"Roman, you were amazing."

He turned his head to see Juliette's bright smile and dazzling blue eyes. "Thanks. You're being generous as usual."

"I'm really not. I was actually quite impressed. Everyone was. I've been to bars where people just keep talking when the band plays, but you had everyone's attention."

"I think that was Fiona."

"She was good, too."

"Can I buy you a drink or are you still working on that one?" He tipped his head to the quarter-full glass of wine in her hand.

"I'm just going to finish this. I'm afraid if I drink anymore, I'll fall asleep with my head on the bar."

"I'm surprised you're awake at all after your marathon night and morning."

"I wanted to hear you play."

A wave of emotion ran through him at her simple words. He didn't quite know how to handle it. He cleared his throat.

"I saw you talking to Doug." He was sorry the instant he brought up the other man's name, but it was too late.

"I figured that's why you didn't come over to say hello." She paused. "You're not going to like this—"

"Then maybe don't say it," he suggested.

"But I think you should consider the fact that maybe you, Doug, and Travis need to hash out the past so you can all move on."

He sighed. "It's over. Forget about it."

"Look, I wasn't going to bring it up again with Doug, but he did it himself."

He drank the rest of his beer in one long swallow. "I don't care what he thinks, Juliette."

"He cares what you think."

"No, he doesn't."

"Yes, he does. He said you think he turned on you, but he didn't."

"He just wants to win an election, Juliette. He'll say whatever he thinks will make him appear like a good guy."

"I'll admit that he's self-serving. He doesn't really pretend not to be. I told him that he's probably the only of you who can actually find out what truly happened, what everyone said, and that if he wants to get to the truth, he might try looking for it. His father was the chief of police. He can speak to him, or he can ask to see the case file. Maybe there are transcripts of the interviews each of you had. There's a truth that I don't think any of you know. And if Doug wants to prove that his father didn't protect him by going after you, then he's going to need ammunition."

"He doesn't want to prove that. Whatever he said to you was just to make points, get you on his side."

"I told him I was on the side of the truth."

He would have preferred if she'd said she was on his side.

"Oh, and I saw Travis at Donavan's today," she continued. "He looked as bad as he did on Saturday, and he was asking Donavan for a job. He said he was desperate to find work. I think Cameron's well-being is still up in the air."

He didn't really know how to feel about Travis. Because Doug's dad had been the one to press him about confessing his guilt, he'd always blamed Doug more than Travis, but the two of them had always been better friends with each other than with him. He had no doubt that they'd made sure their stories matched up, or their fathers had made sure of it.

But Juliette was right about one thing—Travis's unemployment situation didn't bode well for Cameron. "I'm sure he'll find work. His father was well-liked in the town. Maybe Doug will give him a job. Did you tell him he was looking?"

"He said he hadn't talked to Travis in years. He seems to blame Travis for some sort of betrayal, along with you. I think the three of you should talk."

"And I think you need to back out of this and worry about your own life," he said sharply.

She flinched at his harsh statement, but her eyes were still defiant. "I will back off, but I have one more thing to say. Travis said he's good at construction. That's it, I'm done."

"No way. I am not going to hire him, and my grandfather wouldn't consider it, either."

"It's been a long time, Roman. People grow up; they change. It sounds like you changed. Can't you let Doug and Travis change, too?"

She had a point, even though he didn't want to hear it. But had they changed? Doug seemed pretty much the same. Travis—who knew? He seemed to have a lot of other problems that had nothing to do with their shared past.

"So, are you going to play again?" she asked, changing the subject.

"No, there's a new band coming up next."

"I think I'll go home then."

"I'll walk out with you."

She set her glass on the bar. He grabbed his guitar, and then they left the bar.

"Where did you park?" he asked.

"I didn't; I walked."

"Seriously? I thought you didn't like walking or running unless there's a ball involved," he teased.

"I felt like I needed the exercise and the fresh air to wake up. It's only about a mile. And I figured it would be early enough to walk back on my own."

"I've got my truck; I'll give you a ride."

"It's really not that far," she said, somewhat halfheartedly.

"And I am really not going to let you walk home."

"Okay, you can give me a ride."

"That was fast," he said with a laugh.

They walked down the street to his truck. He opened her door and put his guitar behind the seat, then waved her inside. He slid behind the wheel a moment later and started the engine. As he pulled away from the club, he said, "This part of town is a lot nicer than it used to be. That yoga studio over there used to be a strip club."

"The Kitty Kat Klub," she said. "I remember the three K's lined up on the neon sign."

"And I remember when I snuck in there with Doug and Travis."

"Wait, you three did something besides smoke in the park?"

He gave her a dry smile. "We did a lot of things. One of the girls that Doug was dating had a cousin who worked there. She let us in through the back door. We lasted about three minutes on the main floor before the bouncers kicked us out."

"See anything you liked?"

"Definitely," he said. "We were actually a little stunned, I think. Not that we acted anything but cool."

"Of course not. Who was that older man you were talking to at the bar? Your conversation seemed intense. I waited to talk to you, because I didn't want to interrupt."

"That was John Mickelson, the owner. He's been friends with my grandfather for forty plus years. He started telling me stuff about my father. It was strange. He was talking about someone I don't remember at all."

"What was he saying?" she asked curiously.

"He said my father apparently couldn't hammer a nail and that my grandfather had wanted him to go into business with him, but it wasn't in the cards. He also told me my dad dropped out of college without telling my grandfather. He sold his belongings and ran off to LA to find his true passion—whatever that was. Oh, and I guess he used to play the guitar."

"So you have something in common with him. How does that make you feel?"

"I honestly don't know."

"Does it make you want to know more about him?"

"Maybe."

"Hasn't your grandfather told you about him?"

"No. Maybe if I'd asked, he'd have answered, but I never did. My dad wasn't part of my life. I had other problems to worry about."

"That makes sense." She paused. "You know what I liked most about your music tonight?"

"What's that?"

"I could feel emotion coming from your strings. You don't like to show how you feel. You've got the tough guy mask on almost all the time. But tonight was different. You were part of a group. You were engaged with the music. It was like it released something in you, opened a gate or a lock."

"I don't know exactly where you're going with this, but I will admit that music was always an escape for me."

"When did you start playing?"

"I was about eight or nine. One of my mom's boyfriends was a guitar player. He taught me how to play, and he left me a guitar when he took off. I kept playing it." He thought about all the dark nights when music had blocked out reality. But realizing how much he was giving away, he cleared his throat and said, "Baking must be like that for you."

"It wasn't in the beginning. I told you, right after my parents died, I couldn't go near the kitchen, but then it became a safe place for me again."

"And Fairhope is an even safer place."

"Yes. But I don't feel like I ran away from New York. Fairhope is a nice place to live, and it suits me more than the big city. I think you like it, too, even though you probably wouldn't admit it."

"It's not all bad."

"High praise," she said dryly.

"Speaking of praise, how did our cakes go over today?"

"They're *our* cakes now?" she teased.

"I feel I have somewhat of a claim on the toasted almond cakes."

"They were amazing. The restaurant loved them on sight, and they called me later to tell me that everyone at the party raved about them."

"Congratulations."

"Thanks. Hopefully, I'll get more business out of it."

"I think you're going to have more business than you can manage. You might have to consider hiring someone and letting go of some of your control in the kitchen, not that that would be easy for you. You are as tough as any drill sergeant I've ever had."

She looked surprised at that. "I'm not tough. I'm sweet—everyone says so."

"Not in the kitchen, babe."

"What do you mean?"

"You're cutthroat. I was afraid for my life when I dusted the pans wrong."

"You were not," she said with a frown. "And I just wanted to get everything right."

"Which you did. Just saying you might come across to some people like a creampuff, but you've got a lot of steel in your backbone."

"I'm trying to find a way to take that as a compliment."

"It *is* a compliment. You run a tight ship in the kitchen,

and you should. You have high standards, and I respect that."
He pulled up in front of her bakery and shut off the engine.
"Like you, I don't believe in doing anything halfway."

"That's true. If you're going to go for something, you
have to go all in. That's what my dad always said."

"Smart man." As he looked at her, he knew he wanted to
go all in—with her. But how could he? His future was
uncertain. And he'd just said he didn't believe in doing
anything halfway. Starting something with her that he might
not be able to finish...it seemed risky and potentially
painful—for both of them.

"You're staring, Roman," she said softly.

"I don't know what to do about you."

"Do you have to *do* something?"

"I don't want to give you the wrong idea, Juliette."

"Which would be what? That you like me a little?"

"I like you a lot, but you know I'm probably going to
leave. If I pass my physical to get reinstated, I could be gone
quickly."

"I know you have decisions to make and a career you
love. Everything you said is true. I'm staying and you're
probably leaving. I'm building a business that takes a lot of
energy and the last thing I need is a complicated social life.
But...I really want to kiss you right now and worry about
tomorrow—tomorrow."

Her soft confession stole the breath from his chest. "Then
kiss me."

She leaned forward and he met her halfway, their lips
touching off an immediate wave of heat. He couldn't
remember the last time he'd made out in the cab of a truck—
probably when he was a teenager, and he felt a little like a
teenager now, driven by desire for a beautiful girl, who could
easily upset all of his plans. But it was impossible to think
with Juliette's sweet mouth under his.

They were good together. The chemistry was
unmistakable, and he wanted to get her into bed. He wanted
to take his time with her. No more hurried, rushed, good-

night kisses. Just him and her, a soft mattress, a long night...

But there was always a morning. The last thing he wanted to do was hurt Juliette.

And the last thing he wanted Juliette to do was to hurt him. They were treading into dangerous territory.

So he had to retreat.

He'd done it before in battle. If there was no immediate way to win, back up, fight again another day. That's what he'd do—in a minute...or two.

And then someone banged on the window.

They jolted apart.

He stared in disbelief at the woman knocking on Juliette's window. "You've got to be kidding me."

"It's Martha Grayson," Juliette muttered, as she opened the door. "Miss Grayson. Is something wrong?"

"I was just going to ask you that. He's not attacking you, is he?" Martha gave Roman a glaring look. "Are you all right?" she continued. "Should I call the police?"

"No, he's not attacking me. Everything is fine," Juliette said. "I don't know why you'd think it wasn't."

"It looked like you were struggling."

"I wasn't struggling," Juliette said. "I was kissing him."

"Well, that was a stupid idea. Are you getting out now? I just want to make sure you get safely inside."

Juliette flung him a questioning look. He shrugged. It was just as well they said good-night, and he doubted Martha was going to leave them alone together anyway. "I'll talk to you tomorrow. Thanks for coming tonight."

"You're welcome. I had fun."

"So did I," he said, as they exchanged an intimate look.

Juliette got out of the truck and closed the door. He started the engine and drove down the street, thinking that Juliette wasn't going to get away from Martha as fast as he was.

Twelve

—➤➤◄◄◄—

"You really should stay away from Roman Prescott," Martha told Juliette. "I know a young woman like yourself can get caught up in a man as handsome as that, but he's no good."

"Roman is a good person," Juliette defended. "You should get to know him. You should judge him by who he is today and not who he was as a teenager."

Martha looked taken aback by her remarks. "You weren't here when he was terrorizing the town and a leopard doesn't change his spots."

"But a man can grow up," she pointed out. "And if Roman had been guilty of anything, then it seems like he would have ended up in jail, which didn't happen."

"Just because he got away with something doesn't mean he's innocent. You know, his father was nothing like him. He was always at the top of his class. I don't know how he sired such a wild one."

"Roman's father was an A student?" That didn't sound like the guy who'd sold his belongings and dropped out of college.

"Oh, yes. Brett was smart and funny, too. Everyone liked him. He used to bag groceries at the market. He always helped me out to my car. I heard he left school and ran off to California. I guess once he got there, he forgot all about his good upbringing. It's a shame. I'm sure Vincent was disappointed. He always wanted a son to follow in his footsteps."

"Maybe Roman will do that," she suggested, knowing that was just wishful thinking on her part. Roman's heart was in the military. He wanted to go back, and she needed to remember that, not fantasize about him staying in Fairhope to build houses and be her boyfriend.

"I don't see that happening," Martha said. "Anyway, I should go home."

As Martha mentioned the word *home*, Juliette was reminded of her earlier research and her connection to the Graysons. "One second, I wanted to ask you something," she said. "I understand that you once lived in my old childhood home on Primrose Lane."

Martha's eyebrows arched in surprise. Then she slowly nodded. "That's right. I forgot you lived there as a child."

"Why did your family move out of the house?"

"My parents wanted to get a smaller place after Cecelia and I had left home, so they sold the house and moved into a condo. We did love growing up there, though."

"When you lived in the house, do you remember a secret hiding place under the floorboards in the downstairs bedroom closet?"

Martha's eyes widened. "What?"

"Roman found the secret hiding place during his demo work on the house and thought it was a little odd." She didn't want to mention the letters until she got a feel for what Martha knew.

"I never knew about any hiding place like that. My father used the room as a study, so I was rarely in there. Was there something hidden inside?"

"Roman said it was a box of letters," she said.

"Letters?" she said faintly. "From who?"

"There weren't any names mentioned."

"Oh, well, then it will be impossible to find the owner."

She was actually starting to think it might be very possible, and that she might be talking to the owner right now. Martha definitely knew more than she was saying.

"It would be a shame to just throw them away," she said.

"What else can you do?" Martha asked. "If the person who wrote the letters wanted to keep them, they wouldn't have left them behind."

"I suppose that's true."

"I have to go," Martha said abruptly.

"Of course. Good night."

As she watched Martha hurry down the street, she wondered about her odd response. Her attitude toward the letters had been off. Why? Were they hers?

Martha would be the last person she could imagine writing such beautiful, romantic love notes.

On the other hand, the woman had never married...

She pondered that thought as she unlocked her door and walked up the stairs to her apartment.

If Martha were the owner of the letters, she'd made it clear that she didn't want them.

But if she wasn't the owner...

She sat down on the edge of her bed and kicked off her shoes. There was another woman to consider in this scenario—Martha's sister, Cecelia, who definitely seemed more the type to write a love letter. Maybe she needed to talk to her. But she had a feeling it would be better to do that without Martha around.

She flopped back on her bed, suddenly exhausted, but as she stifled a yawn, her fingers touched her still tingling lips, and her thoughts fled back to Roman.

Things were getting hotter each time they were together.

But like Roman, she didn't know what to do about it. She just didn't want it to end...and she knew it had to.

She couldn't think about that now. But someday she was going to have to face reality, and she had a feeling it was going to hurt.

As Roman signed off on a delivery of sheetrock and wood Thursday afternoon, he felt a little overwhelmed by the enormous amount of work in front of him. Demo was one thing. Building was going to take more time, more skill, and more help.

His grandfather had come by earlier and told him he was looking into subcontractors for sheetrock, electrical, and plumbing and was just waiting for some people to get back to him. In the meantime, Roman should just keep doing what he was doing.

He was happy to keep working, but his physical was in three days. What if he was cleared to go back to duty? How was he going to let his grandfather handle all this on his own?

Even if Vincent could hire subs, they would bill at a higher rate than laborers, and the budget would go through the roof.

He was surprised that his grandfather didn't seem to understand that. He'd always been excellent at estimating time and materials, but everything about this project seemed different than the ones his grandfather used to run. Had he lost some of his mental sharpness? Or was he letting some sentiment about the house drive his decisions?

With a frown, he realized he was just wasting time wondering when he could give his grandfather practical help by just getting back to work.

He was about to do that when the doorbell rang. He strode down the hall and opened it, thinking—hoping—it might be Juliette.

It wasn't. It was Travis.

He wore jeans, a long-sleeved T-shirt, and a baseball cap on his head. His beard was as ragged as it had been a few days ago, and there were dark shadows under his eyes. Juliette was right; Travis still looked like hell.

"What are you doing here?" he asked shortly, not in the mood to deal with Travis.

"I was just down at the lumber yard. They said your grandfather is looking for laborers."

"Seriously, Travis?"

"I need the work," Travis said, a bitter edge to his voice.

"And you think you and I are going to work together?" He was stunned that Travis would show up and ask for a job after everything that had gone down between them.

"Look, we have a past, but that doesn't matter. I'm worried about the present. I lost my job. My mother is having health issues. My wife took off and has no interest in raising our kid. I have been all over this town looking for work. If you have work, I can do it. We don't have to talk. We don't have to be friends."

"Just like that, I'm supposed to forget you tried to send me to jail? You think my grandfather has forgotten that?"

"You did the same to me."

"No, I didn't."

"That's what Chief Winters said."

"I didn't talk to the police at all. I sat there in silence for hours. And then the chief came in and told me you and Doug gave me up."

"He said the opposite to me."

Travis's story matched the one Doug had told him. *Had Chief Winters turned them against each other?* He was still thinking about that when he saw a car pull up in front of the house and Doug Winters got out.

"What is going on?" he muttered.

Doug paused when he saw Travis on the porch, but then he squared his shoulders and came forward.

"Did I miss the reunion notice?" Doug asked.

"What are you doing here?" he asked.

"We need to talk about the fire." Doug shot Travis a look. "It's good you're here, too. Saved me a trip to try to find you."

"I don't want to talk about the fire. I'm looking for a job," Travis said. "I'm a grown man with a kid to feed. That old story isn't of interest to me."

"Well, it is to me," Doug said. "Let's go inside."

Without waiting for an invitation, Doug pushed past him and then Travis followed.

The three of them stood awkwardly in the empty living room.

"You got chairs anywhere?" Doug asked.

"I don't think you'll be staying long enough to sit," he said, folding his arms across his chest.

"I might be. I was talking to Juliette last night and she said if I really wanted to know the truth, I should look for it." Doug let out a breath. "So I went down to the police station today and I asked them for the case file regarding the fire. I read through each of our statements and the other interviews that were conducted. It seems that none of us actually accused the others of setting the fire."

"What?" Travis asked in surprise. "That can't be true."

"It is true. My father played us off against each other."

"Even you—the golden boy?" Roman asked.

"Even me," Doug replied, looking him straight in the eye. "I think he wanted to make sure I never talked to either one of you again. It worked."

He thought about that. It made sense. "All right," he said slowly. "So we weren't rats, but no one stepped up and confessed. Unless none of us were guilty. I know I didn't set the fire."

"Neither did I," Doug said.

"Or me," Travis put in. "I was the last one in the park, but I stopped smoking when you guys left. Kathy Marson snuck out to meet me. We made out for a while, and then she went home and so did I. Everything was fine."

"You never said you were with Kathy," Doug said with a frown. "I didn't see that in the file."

"I didn't tell anyone. I didn't want to get her in trouble for sneaking out after curfew. And her house had just burned down. She was devastated. But she knew I didn't have anything to do with it."

Doug nodded. "I believe you, Travis, and I believe you,

Roman, because it turned out there were two other suspicious house fires in the county that year. They weren't in Fairhope, but they weren't that far away. One of those houses was located next to a park as well. The other was near a school playground. No suspects were ever arrested."

He was surprised at that new piece of information. "I don't remember hearing about that."

"I don't, either," Travis said.

"It wasn't in the newspapers," Doug admitted. "The police report said the fire investigators couldn't find a definitive link. But I believe the real reason there was so little follow-up on this fire was because my father was protecting me. He probably wasn't a hundred percent sure I was innocent. I'd been disappointing him all year. And he hated you, Roman. He thought you led me down the wrong road."

"Only you were right there next to me, not behind me," he reminded Doug.

"I know." He handed Roman the file folder. "You can read through it. You'll see that I'm telling you the truth."

"So what do you want from me now?" he asked.

"I don't know. We were friends once. Maybe at the very least we could stop being enemies. This is a small town. If we're all here, we're going to run into each other."

"I'm not staying that long," he said. "And let's be honest—your real reason for trying to clean this up is so your run for mayor won't be tainted."

"That was a big part of my motivation," Doug admitted. "But it was also about finding out what my father did back then. I have big plans for my future, and I don't want any surprises."

He actually appreciated Doug's honesty about his ambition.

"What do you think, Travis?" Doug asked.

"I'm hoping that this new information means Roman might hire me." Travis's gaze swung to him. "Does what Doug found out change anything?"

He pondered that question. Was he really going to hang

on to an old grudge that had obviously been based on misinformation? And wasn't he just as guilty for believing in their betrayal as they'd been for believing in his?

"Yes," he said, giving Travis a nod. "I'll hire you by the hour for the next three days. My grandfather will have to sign off on anything beyond that, but if you are an asset, I'll recommend that he do that. There's a lot of work, so if you're good, you'll probably stay busy."

"All I need is a chance," Travis said, relief in his eyes.

"You've got it." He looked at Doug. "I will not impede your efforts to be mayor."

"Thank you. In return, I'll make sure that Martha Grayson and some of the other town criers have the correct information regarding the fire," Doug said dryly.

"How do you think your father will respond to that?" he asked.

"He won't love it, but I'm happy that he didn't do anything illegal during his investigation. He just didn't work that hard to get to the real culprit. But even if he had, it's doubtful he would have found the arsonist. Neither of the other two fires has ever been solved." He paused. "If you want to stay here, Roman, you can start over with a clean slate."

"I'm not sure it will be that clean even if we wipe the fire offense away. I wasn't exactly a choir boy."

Doug smiled. "True. We did have some fun back then."

"Yeah, we did," he muttered.

"The best was putting that bulldog in the lake," Travis added, his expression much lighter now.

"I really thought he'd just jump off and swim back," he said. "I didn't think the entire fire department would come out to rescue him."

"I thought the best time was when you put crime scene tape around the principal's car, and spread ketchup on the ground," Doug said. "He had a day off but everyone thought he was dead for a while."

He groaned. "I don't think we need to rehash the old

days."

"Well, if we do, we should do it over a beer," Travis said. "Do you have any, Roman?"

"I have some in the fridge," he admitted.

"Along with some chairs?" Doug asked. "Looks like we're going to stay long enough to sit."

"Looks that way," he agreed, leading them into the kitchen.

Juliette left the bakery in Susan's capable hands around four o'clock on Thursday afternoon. She'd been thinking about her conversation with Martha all day, and she really wanted to talk to Cecelia Grayson while she was at work and not with her sister.

Cecelia managed the Bella Terra nursery down by the bay. The nursery consisted of a red brick building, a greenhouse, and two acres of plants.

She made her way into the main showroom and asked a saleswoman if Cecelia was there. She was directed to the outdoor patio, where she found Cecelia with her hands in a big pot of soil.

"Hello, Juliette," Cecelia said with a welcoming smile. "I can't believe you're away from your bakery. There's always a line in there now when I pass by."

"It has been busy with Valentine's Day around the corner. You must be selling a lot of flowers as well."

"Oh, absolutely, but we're really more about long-term plants here. Can I help you? Are you looking for something in particular?"

"Actually, I wanted to talk to you, if you have a moment."

"Of course." She wiped off her hands on a nearby towel. "What is it?"

"I don't know if you're aware of this, but I grew up in a house on Primrose Lane—the same one you grew up in."

Surprise passed through her expression. "I didn't know that. What a coincidence. I loved that house."

"So did I. I had to move because my parents died unexpectedly."

"Yes, I remember that horrible accident," Cecelia said with sympathy in her eyes. "It was so tragic; you were so young. I didn't know your parents well, but I'd visited your father's bakery, and your mother used to come here and buy plants for her yard."

"She loved to garden," Juliette said. "Unfortunately, I didn't inherit her green thumb."

"Well, you have other talents."

"Anyway, I've had thoughts of buying the house back, but right now it's being remodeled, so I'll have to wait and see what Mr. Prescott wants to sell it for when he puts it on the market. In the meantime, I've been spending a little time there. My friend, Roman, is handling the construction."

"Yes, I heard that." Cecelia didn't look too happy at the mention of Roman's name. "I'm sure the old house needs a makeover."

"That seems to be the consensus. The other day Roman was pulling up some carpeting in the downstairs bedroom, and he found a box filled with love letters. We're wondering if you might know anything about them."

Cecelia's face paled, and there was not a doubt in Juliette's mind that Cecelia knew about the letters, no matter what she said next.

"Letters?" Cecelia echoed, her voice shaky.

"Love letters to a man. There aren't any names, but the letters are beautifully written. Roman and I didn't want to just throw them away, so we thought we'd try to find the owner."

"You read the letters?" Cecelia asked tightly.

"We did," she admitted. "We were hoping to find a clue to the writer's identity, but what we found was a rather haunting love story. It starts out filled with hope and giddy desire and ends with heartbreak. I have to admit we're kind of curious about what happened."

Before Cecelia could speak, Martha came through the door, giving them both a surprised look.

"Juliette, what are you doing here?" Martha asked.

"I wanted to ask Cecelia about the letters I found," she said, deciding not to beat around the bush. "The ones I told you about last night."

"She told you last night?" Cecelia muttered to Martha.

"And I told her that I didn't know anything about any letters," Martha said, sending Cecelia a pointed look.

"It seems like you both know something," Juliette cut in, drawing their gazes back to her.

"It's none of your business," Martha said sharply.

"Stop," Cecelia said. "It's fine."

"Cici," Martha said warningly.

"It's all right, Martha," Cecelia said. "I don't mind telling her. I wrote the letters."

It was exactly what she'd thought. "But you never sent them, did you? I wasn't sure, because in the last letter you were looking at the mailbox and thinking about mailing them."

"I never sent them. I couldn't. He was married by then. I couldn't break up a home. It was too late." Cecelia's eyes had a faraway look in them, as if she was being swept back in time. "I wrote those letters fifty years ago. I can't believe you found them now."

"Why didn't you take them with you when you moved?" she asked. "Why leave them hidden under the floorboards?"

"I meant to take them with me, but I was away when my parents decided to get the house ready to sell. When I came back, they'd laid down new carpet in that closet. I couldn't rip it up because of some old letters. And I certainly couldn't tell my parents about the letters. They would not have been happy with my behavior, my father, especially. That's why I hid them in a box under the floorboard in the first place."

It all made sense now. "Can I ask who the man was?"

"That's none of your business," Martha interrupted. "It was a long time ago, and Cecelia has let all that go. I can't believe you're bringing it up again. You have no idea how much pain you're causing her."

"I'm sorry; that's not my intent."

"It's all right," Cecelia said, giving her a troubled look. "I admit I'm a little shocked, but I'll be all right."

"Would you like the letters back?" She felt a little guilty for having asked about Cecelia's old lover. Martha was right; it was none of her business. The letters were Cecelia's real life; they weren't for someone else's entertainment.

"Say no," Martha told her sister.

Cecelia hesitated. "I think I would like them back."

Martha let out a long, annoyed sigh. "That's the wrong decision. Let me take them and destroy them. You do not want to read them again. I remember how sad you were for days and months on end. I don't want to see you go down that road. There's no point. Life has moved on."

While Martha was being her usual bossy self, Juliette was touched by the clear love Martha had for her sister. It gave her a dimension that Juliette hadn't seen before.

"It was all a very long time ago," Cecelia said. "I would like to see the letters again. Did you bring them with you?"

"No. I wasn't sure you were the owner. I was just guessing."

"You guessed correctly," Cecelia said with a sad smile.

"I can bring them to you tomorrow, or you can come by the bakery if you'd like."

"I'll do that," Cecelia said with a nod. "I'll get them from you. I don't want to put you to any trouble."

"This is a bad idea," Martha said. "I don't like it at all."

"Well, they're not your letters," Cecelia said, standing up to her sister.

"Just don't come crying to me about your heart breaking again," Martha said harshly, then turned on her heel and left the patio.

"Don't mind her. She does have good intentions," Cecelia said. "And thank you for taking the time to track me down. Most people wouldn't have tried that hard to find the owner of a bunch of old letters."

She looked into the older woman's eyes. "Your words were beautiful. You evoked so many emotions in me when I read them. I have to admit; I was completely caught up in your story. I was hoping it had a happier ending than what I read."

"I've had a happy life," Cecelia said. "And the man I was writing about was also happy in his choice. We just weren't happy together. Sometimes, that's the way it is. You have to accept what you can't change."

"I have a hard time doing that," she confessed. "Even when people tell me no a hundred times, I still think there's a way to get a yes."

Cecelia smiled. "That's a good trait. You're a strong, modern woman. You have confidence and determination. I was not like that, especially not when I was your age."

"It was a different time."

"That's true. We weren't brought up to speak our minds. I think that's partly why no one can shut my sister up anymore. Once she found her voice, she couldn't stop talking."

She smiled at the quiet humor in Cecelia's eyes. "I guess I understand but Martha is a bit terrifying."

"I know she takes things too far. She judges too quickly and she has trouble with forgiveness, but she's been a loyal sister, and there are things she's gone through in her life that have made her bitter. It's not an excuse, but maybe it's an explanation that will help you understand a little better." Cecelia paused. "She was rude to Roman the other day. I told her to give that boy a chance, but once she makes up her mind about someone, it's hard to change it."

"Roman is a good man. I'm sure he made mistakes when he was younger, but he's a soldier. He fights for our country. He was injured in the line of duty. Martha needs to back off."

"I will tell her that, and so should you, if you feel inclined."

"I did tell her that last night, but she didn't want to hear me."

"She heard you; we'll just have to see if she decides to listen."

She nodded. "I should get back to the bakery."

"I'll come by tomorrow and pick up the letters. I have to admit I need a little time to get ready to read them again."

"I'll see you then." As she walked out of the nursery, she was happy to have solved half of the mystery, but she was still curious about Cecelia's old lover. Was he someone in town? It seemed likely since Cecelia had lived in Fairhope most of her life. Although, it was certainly possible the man in question had moved away years ago.

She probably wasn't going to find out the answer, unless Cecelia had a change of heart about sharing between now and tomorrow. But why would she? It was her personal business and it had obviously been a painful breakup.

As she got into her car, she impulsively pulled out her phone and called Roman. She knew he would be interested to hear what she had found out. Plus, she just really wanted to talk to him.

He answered after a couple of rings, and she was a little surprised to hear male conversation in the background. "Hi, it's me," she said. "Are you out somewhere?"

"No, I'm in the house. Hang on a second." He paused for a moment. "Okay, I moved. It's quieter here."

"Who is at the house with you? It sounds like you're having a party."

"Not a party, but we have had a few beers."

"You and who else?"

"You're not going to believe me."

"Doug," she guessed.

"And Travis."

"How on earth did that happen? Last I heard, you were mortal enemies."

"Things have changed remarkably fast," he agreed. "Travis came by looking for work. I was about to turn him away when Doug showed up with the old police files on the fire. Apparently, he decided to get more information, as you obviously encouraged him to do."

"I'm glad he did, especially since it sounds like whatever he found out has brought the three of you together again."

"We're talking. I wouldn't say we're best friends, but it's clear that there were a lot of misunderstandings surrounding our police interviews. And it turns out there might have been an actual arsonist involved. Doug discovered there were similar fires started elsewhere that were never solved."

"So none of you were responsible?"

"Nope. I believe what the other guys have told me, and they seem to believe me."

"I'm so glad," she said, genuinely happy he'd been able to get rid of that dark, hanging cloud.

"I didn't think I cared that much, but now that we've cleared the air, it does feel good. Of course, Doug admitted that he went to the lengths that he did to protect his run for mayor and future political ambitions, but I appreciated the fact that he owned up to it."

"This is great. I'm really happy for you. And I think I have to remind you that some of this might have happened because I stuck my nose into it."

His laugh warmed her heart. "No doubt, Juliette, no doubt. What have you been up to today? Baking like a madwoman?"

"Definitely, but I do have some other news."

"I can't wait to hear it."

She settled into her seat, thinking how nice it felt to have Roman to talk to. "I figured out the identity of the letter writer."

"No kidding? Who?"

"It's someone we both know—"

"If you tell me it's Martha, I don't know what I'll say," he said dryly.

"It's not Martha; it's her sister, Cecelia."

"How did you figure that out?"

"I got an inkling when Martha was lecturing me about being with you last night."

"Wait, she was lecturing you? I'm sorry. I should have stuck around until you got into the house."

"It was fine. I didn't care what she had to say, but to get her off the subject of me and you, I told her we'd found letters in her old house. She got the strangest look on her face even though she said she had no idea what I was talking about. So I went to see Cecelia today, thinking she'd give me a better answer, and she confessed that she was in love with a man who married someone else. Apparently, she was out of town when her parents had the room and closet carpeted, and she just figured the letters were lost forever. I told her she could come by tomorrow and I'd give them to her."

"That's amazing, Juliette. There is nothing you can't figure out, is there?"

"I'm having a pretty good week," she admitted.

"I suspect you have a lot of good weeks. You tend to accomplish everything you set your mind to." He paused. "So who was Cecelia's lover?"

"She wouldn't tell me. And Martha scolded me for asking."

"Wait—Martha was there, too?"

"She came in during our conversation. She tried to shut it down, but Cecelia wouldn't let her. It was interesting to see their loyalty and love for each other. Martha can be a mean-spirited person, but she adores her sister. Cecelia alluded to something in the past that had made Martha bitter and unforgiving. I wonder what that was."

Roman groaned. "Not another mystery to solve, Juliette—you just figured this one out. Can't you at least take a breath in between?"

She laughed. "Yes, I can take a breath, and I'm not planning to add that to my list, just commenting."

"Well, I'm glad you can give Cecelia back her letters. It's better than throwing them out."

"It is." She paused. "I'll let you get back to the guys. Are you rehashing old times?"

"More than I'd like, but that's what a few beers will do."

"What about Travis? Do you feel like hiring him now?"

"I told him I'd hire him for three days. My grandfather will have to sign off on anything longer than that. If Travis does a good job, then I see no reason why he can't continue."

"That will be good for Cameron and probably Donna, too." She was proud of Roman for being able to put the past aside to help out Travis.

"I hope so." He let out a breath. "I missed you today."

The husky, sensual note in his voice made her heart skip a beat as his words felt far more intimate than the conversation they'd been having.

"I know," she admitted. "It seems like forever since I saw you, and it was just last night."

"I was going to see if you wanted to get dinner, but I think I've had a few too many beers for that, and I'm not sure I'll get either of these guys out of the house any time soon."

"You should hang out with them. I have tons of baking to do. I'm going to get a quick bite and get down to it."

"Don't work too hard."

"I will work as hard as I need to." She wasn't quite ready to say good-bye, and she didn't want to hang up the phone without making a plan to see him. "So tomorrow they're having the love boat parade."

"What on earth is that?"

"It's a parade of brightly lit boats just after sunset. They also have live bands and other entertainment on the pier while it's happening. Do you want to come and check it out with me?"

"Don't tell me you're providing desserts for that, too?"

"No. I gave the parade a pass, so I could be free to wander around."

"I'll meet you down there. I have some subcontractors coming late in the afternoon to give me some bids. But once they're done, I'll head to the pier."

"Great. I'll see you there."

She found herself smiling as she drove back to the bakery. It had been a long time since just hearing a man's voice on the phone had made her so happy. She just wished this particular man didn't have one foot out the door.

But it didn't matter how often she told herself to hold back, to guard her heart, to try to stay away from him; she just couldn't do it. She liked him too much. For better or worse, she was in this til the end.

Thirteen

———⟫⟫⟪⟪———

"That call must have been from a woman," Doug told Roman as he returned to the kitchen.

"Why would you say that?"

"Because you have that look on your face that you used to have when Amy Downing called you."

"Amy Downing," he echoed with a laugh. "That is a name out of the past. Do you know what happened to her?"

"I do," Travis put in. "She married a lawyer who became a state senator in Illinois last year. They have three kids and apparently quite a bit of money. Oh, and I saw a picture of Amy recently, and she's still hot, my friend."

Roman laughed. "How do you know all that?"

"My mother is friends with her mother."

"I told you that you should have called her after graduation," Doug reminded him. "You blew it."

He shook his head. "I didn't call her, because it was over. I told her I was going to enlist, and she said have fun, but don't think I'll be waiting around for you to come home."

"Ouch," Travis said. "You never told us that."

"It wasn't exactly news I wanted to spread around."

"So who put that grin on your face today?" Doug asked. "Or do I have to ask? It's Juliette, isn't it? You've got a thing for her."

He couldn't deny it, but he also didn't want to talk about it. Because Juliette was far more important to him than he wanted to tell these guys, so he just shrugged.

"I knew she was into you when she brought you up on our date," Doug said.

"Wait, you dated Juliette?" Travis asked. "Are we going to have another problem on our hands? Because I don't want to be in the middle of some love triangle."

"There's no triangle," Doug said. "Juliette is into him, and he's into her."

"Thanks for the recap," he said dryly. He reached into the fridge and pulled out another beer.

"You should be careful," Doug said, a more serious note in his voice now. "She's going to be hard to leave. And you are leaving, aren't you?"

"That is the plan," he admitted. "Juliette knows that." He took a long draught of beer, not wanting to think about the moment when he might have to say good-bye to her. He sat back down at the table. "So, who's going to the love boat parade tomorrow?"

"I'll be on the water," Doug said. "I'd invite you on the boat, but we're full."

"That's fine." He turned to Travis. "What about you?"

"I thought I'd take Cameron over there. He likes boats."

"What happened to your wife?" Doug asked Travis. "If you don't mind me asking."

"Since you already asked," Travis said, his lips drawing into a tight line, "she left us about six months ago. She said she was bored with being a wife and a mother, and she read some book about traveling and hiking and finding herself, and the next thing I knew she was gone. Oh, and she took most of our savings for her trip."

"Sorry," Doug said. "That's rough."

"Yeah," Travis said. "I understand why she left me, but not why she left Cameron. She hasn't called. I can't reach her. He can't talk to her. It's like she died, only she didn't. But I'm going to try to make things right for Cameron and for my mother, who has her own issues." Travis looked at Roman. "She said you and Juliette were checking up on her."

"Only because Cameron looked a little lost before you came back."

"I had no idea she was as scattered as she is. I won't be asking her to babysit again." He paused. "I do appreciate your looking out for my kid."

"When Juliette sees someone in trouble, she doesn't look away."

"You don't, either," Travis said quietly.

He felt a little guilty that he'd tried to look away when Travis first arrived at the house. "You give me more credit than I deserve."

"I think we should get some food," Doug interrupted. "How about I order in?"

"Since none of us are up for driving, I'd say that's a good idea."

Doug nodded. "By the way, your guitar skills have certainly improved." He turned to Travis. "Roman played at Mickelson's Bar last night."

"So you kept up with that. Good for you."

"Thanks. Someone call for some Chinese food or something. I'm starving."

"I'm on it," Doug said, pulling out his phone.

"I need to call my mom," Travis said. "I just want to make sure Cameron is good for another hour."

"Call your mom," Roman echoed with a laugh. "Now, it really does feel like old times."

⌖

Juliette was lucky enough to find a spot near the pier. The great thing about driving a small car was that it fit in anywhere.

As she walked through the parking lot, a dozen or so people stopped her to say hello and offer a compliment about her bakery or one of her desserts, and each comment broadened her smile and deepened her sense of belonging.

Fairhope was becoming her town again. She felt connected to the community. She might not have made a lot of close, personal friends yet—mostly because she hadn't had the time—but she was definitely starting to feel like she fit in. It was what she'd wanted, what she'd come back for, and it felt good.

"Juliette, wait up."

She paused as Sara hurried to catch up with her. "Hi, Sara."

"I'm glad you came; I wasn't sure you'd be able to tear yourself away from the bakery."

"I probably shouldn't have torn myself away, but I didn't want to miss the parade. And, frankly, I could use some fresh air. I was beginning to feel like a big bag of sugar."

"Sometimes I feel like a big bag of coffee beans," Sara said with a laugh. "The scent sticks to my skin."

"Maybe we better not get too close to anyone," she joked. "We'll make them hungry for dessert and in the mood for coffee."

"Which would be great if we were working tonight, but Donavan and I agreed that we will do the Sweetheart's Dance on Saturday, and that is it—at least until Easter."

"My thoughts, exactly. So where is your handsome Rhett Butler tonight?"

"You know his name is Tim, right?"

She laughed. "Okay, Tim."

"He should be here soon. What about you? Where's your Romeo?" she asked with a teasing smile.

"Roman also said he'd meet me here."

"You two are destined to be together."

She knew Sara was joking, but there was a part of her that wanted to believe that, too. She was just afraid destiny was going to throw her a curve ball.

"What did I say?" Sara asked, giving her a concerned look. "Your smile just went dark."

"Nothing."

"Are things not going as well with Roman as you hoped?"

"They're going better than I hoped. That's the problem. I don't know what I'm going to do when it ends."

"Maybe it won't end."

She wanted to be the optimist who could believe that, but she was having trouble getting there. Fortunately, Sara's attention was drawn to Tim, a tall, skinny man who greeted her with a hug.

"Do you remember Juliette from the movie festival?" Sara asked.

Tim nodded. "Nice to see you again."

"You, too. You look a lot different tonight."

"I was happy to leave Rhett Butler behind."

"Looks like the boats are getting ready to start," Sara interrupted. "Let's get a good spot on the pier."

"You two go ahead," she said. "I'm going to keep an eye out for Roman."

"See you later," Sara said, as Tim put his arm around her waist, and they walked off together.

There were certainly a lot of couples out tonight, she thought, as she wandered through the crowd, feeling a little too single. She shouldn't be surprised. Love was in the air. And she was doing her best to contribute to that love with her Wish cookies. She'd already had a couple of people stop by the bakery to tell her that they'd gotten a date for Valentine's Day after making their wish on her cookies.

She liked that her father's tradition was continuing, and she enjoyed being part of other people's happiness. But she was starting to wonder if she should have wished for something for herself while baking some of those cookies.

As she wandered down the path, she saw Roman coming in her direction, and just like that, her pensive mood brightened up.

He smiled when he saw her, and she couldn't help thinking that he smiled a lot more these days. He talked more, too. Maybe he was starting to feel like he fit in as well.

Any thought of not kissing him *hello* vanished, as he grabbed her hands and pulled her in for a warm, lingering kiss that told her he was as happy to see her as she was to see him.

"I'm so glad you came," she said, a little breathless from his kiss.

"I'm so glad you're here."

"I guess we're both pretty happy right now."

He grinned. "I guess we are." He tipped his head down the path. "I saw an empty bench back that way. Want to check it out? Get away from the crowds?"

"Sure." She followed him over to the wooden bench that was farther away from the start of the parade but had a perfect view of the water. "This is great."

He put his arm around her shoulders, and she couldn't help but snuggle up next to him.

"How did today's baking bonanza go?" he asked.

"Very well. I'm keeping up—barely. But the next three days will be crazy. I just got an order today for a Valentine's Day wedding cake."

"What? Valentine's Day is Tuesday. It's Friday. Who decides to order a wedding cake four days out? I hope you said no."

"I never say no," she confessed with a sigh. "It's so romantic. The couple was going to get married in the spring, but her father is ill, and she doesn't want to wait that long. So they decided to do it on Valentine's Day in her parents' backyard."

"How big is this cake supposed to be?"

"Big enough to feed about forty people. So probably three good-sized layers. I can do it," she said, trying to infuse some confidence into her voice. "I have to do it."

He moved a little away from her, dislodging her head from his shoulder.

"Hey, I was just getting comfortable," she protested.

"What are you trying to prove, Juliette?"

"What do you mean?" she asked warily.

"You're not superhuman. You can't bake everything everyone wants you to make."

"I'm building a business, Roman. I have to put myself out there. I have to push right now."

"Is it really just about building the bakery up?"

She didn't like the challenge in his voice or the way he was looking at her, as if he knew something about her she didn't know—or didn't want to know. "What does that mean?"

"Forget it."

She sat up straighter. "No, I'm not going to forget it. You want to say something, say it."

"Fine. I think your reasons for taking on so much work, not to mention solving other people's problems, are more about keeping yourself too busy to think. You're running away from yourself."

"That's ridiculous."

"No, it's not. You came back here to recapture your childhood, but I'm guessing that the memories aren't as sharp as you thought they would be, that you don't feel your parents' presence, you don't hear their laughter, you can't remember what their favorite foods were or what flowers your mom planted in the spring every year. As long as you're fixing other people's lives and working at a breakneck pace, you don't have to acknowledge that."

She stared back at him. She'd once thought he was a man of few words, but he certainly seemed to have plenty to say now.

"I'm not trying to hurt you," Roman added, regret in his eyes. "But you have to slow your pace down, or you'll burn out or drop from exhaustion. I don't want to see that happen. And I have seen it happen."

"Are you talking about yourself now?"

"Yes. I was guilty of a similar obsession when I first got into the Corps. I had to be the best at everything. I had to prove I was not the irresponsible kid everyone thought I was. I was relentless in my ambition to be better than I used to be."

"There's nothing wrong with ambition, with wanting to

be the best."

"As long as you're honest about it. I thought if I could be someone else, someone better, that would change everything. I could say I'm a soldier and nothing else would matter. I would suddenly be transformed. But that's not the way it worked. I was a good soldier, but I was also a kid who grew up with an addict for a mother. I had to learn how to trust in the people next to me, not just myself."

It was the most revealing thing he'd ever said about himself, and she was touched that he trusted her enough to share his story. "How did you learn how to stop running away from yourself, how to trust?" she asked.

"My staff sergeant locked me up for twenty-four hours one day. He told me when I was done fighting myself, then I could fight for others. Only then could I be the soldier he needed me to be. I was nineteen at the time and mad as hell about it, but all those hours with nothing else to do did finally make me stop and think about everything. He was right. I was a better soldier after that." He paused. "And you'd be a better baker if you didn't take on such a ridiculous amount of work, if you acknowledged that you can be happy even if you don't remember or relive every moment of the past."

"You're not exactly...wrong," she said slowly. "I did think that coming home would feel more like home than it has. Don't get me wrong; I love Fairhope. But it's not the same. And I don't see my parents around every corner the way I thought I would." She paused. "I feel better when I bake. I can control my kitchen. Everything turns out beautiful. Outside, it's not always that way."

"No, it's not."

"But I mostly take on too much work, because I hate disappointing people. I don't like to say no. I don't want to be seen as weak or unable to manage my business. It's my dream job, and I have to be successful. There's nothing else I want to do. This is it."

He nodded. "I get it. But you can say no and still be successful."

"I'm going to have to work on that."

"I'm sorry if I came on too strong," he said.

"I guess I should be grateful you didn't try to lock me up somewhere for twenty-four hours," she said dryly. "Did that really happen, or were you embellishing?"

"It really happened," he said with a smile. "I was a hardhead. He wanted to knock some sense into me. It worked."

"Do you..." She hesitated over her next question, then decided since they were being so honest, she would ask it. "Do you forgive your mother for the way she treated you?"

He thought about her question. "Yes," he said finally. "It's taken a long time, and sometimes I still feel some anger, but I know that her addictions were always about her, not about me. She loved me, but she wasn't meant to be a mother."

"That seems like a very healthy perspective."

"I've had a long time to make my peace. Being angry with her didn't accomplish anything."

"I was really angry when my parents died," she confessed. "I was mad that they took that trip without me, which is crazy, because I would have died with them, so I should be grateful I wasn't invited."

"But you felt left out."

"Before and after," she admitted. "I've never said that to anyone. It sounds absurd. They're dead, and I'm angry with them for dying without me."

"They just got on a boat, Juliette. That's all they did."

"I know. I just wish they hadn't."

He nodded and then put his arms around her. "I wish that, too."

He held her for a few minutes, then said, "Hey, you're missing the parade."

She turned around and they settled back against the bench as the brightly lit boats made their way across the water in front of them. "They're so pretty," she murmured.

"Not as pretty as you, but not bad."

"Now you're going to sweet-talk me?"

He laughed. "I hope you know that I just want you to be happy."

"I want you to be happy, too." She turned to look at him. "So, your physical is Monday?"

"Yes."

"Are you nervous?"

"Not about doing it, but the results could determine the rest of my life, so that's unsettling."

"You're in good shape; it seems likely you'll pass—don't you think?"

"I still get some ringing in my ears. It's better but I don't know if it's good enough."

"Won't they just extend your disability then?"

"I don't know what's going to happen," he said, tightening his arm around her. "I'm sure there are jobs I'll be offered if I can't go back to my unit."

"Would you take a different job?"

"I should. It's all about service. It's never been about what I want to do but what the Marines need me to do. The Corps has been my life, my family, my job for thirteen years. I can't imagine leaving, but I also can't imagine not being able to do the work I was trained to do."

A wave of sadness ran through her at his words. He was being honest, but that honesty was breaking her heart. How could she even want him to leave *everything* for her?

Maybe going back to his job wouldn't mean the end of their relationship. Soldiers fell in love, got married, and still served. But her life would have to come second to his. She'd have to follow him. How could she do that? How could she give up this life she was building?

She knew she was getting way ahead of herself, but time was moving fast. Next week Roman could be gone. She didn't know whether she should make the most of whatever time they had left or start pushing him away now so it wouldn't hurt so much.

However, the idea of pushing him away when he felt so

good right next to her seemed impossible to fathom. So, she wasn't going to do it. Decision time would come soon enough.

They watched the boats for the next half hour, comfortable with silence now.

"That must be Doug's boat," Roman said, breaking into their quiet to point out a large yacht with a flag for the University of Alabama's Crimson Tide football program.

"Speaking of Doug. What happened last night?"

"We talked everything out—me, Doug, and Travis."

"So you're all buddies again?"

"Looks that way."

She turned to face him. "You're starting to fit into this town, Roman. Both of us are. I left when I was a kid; you left when you were a teenager. We came back as adults, and I think we've both been trying to figure out our places."

"You definitely fit, Juliette. You're like Donavan. You give and give to this town, and you are part of the heartbeat, just like she is."

"I would like that. And that has nothing to do with recapturing the past."

"Got it."

"I hope now that you and Doug and Travis are on the same page, the news can get out to the rest of the town. I would love to shut Martha up."

"I suspect you'll get another chance, hopefully, before she tries to get me arrested for kissing you."

She laughed at the reminder. "For a minute, I thought that knock on the window of your truck was a cop."

"She was worse than a cop."

"She gave me quite the talking-to. But now that I know there's something in her past making her act the way she does, I'm going to see if I can find out what it is."

"Of course you are," he said with a wry smile.

"And I still want to find out who Cecelia wrote those letters to. I can't help being curious, Roman. I spend a lot of time alone with butter and flour and sugar—my brain tends to wander off into whatever puzzle I'm trying to solve. By the way, Cecelia never came by to get her letters. I wonder if she's having second thoughts about taking them back."

"That's possible. Some people like to leave the past alone."

"I think my parents would have liked you," she said.

He raised a doubtful eyebrow. "Really? I've never been very popular with parents."

"That was when you were a teenager, I'm guessing. What about now? I'm sure there have been women in your life."

"I never met any of their parents."

"So no one serious?"

He shook his head. "Nope. What about you? Did you break any hearts when you left New York?"

"Not a one. I dated, of course, but never that seriously." She paused, realizing the parade was coming to an end. "Let's walk back to the pier. I think the band is going to start soon."

"Sounds good."

When they got back to the center of the action, she saw Cecelia and Martha waiting in line at a booth run by a local wine bar. Not far away was Roman's grandfather. There was something about his stance, the fierceness of his gaze aimed at the Grayson sisters that gave her a jolt, that told her she might just have stumbled on the answer to one of her questions.

She stopped abruptly and put her hand on Roman's arm. "Look at your grandfather."

"Where is he?"

"Over there." She tipped her head in Vincent's direction.

"He's just standing there," Roman said in bewilderment. "What's the big deal?"

"He's not just standing there. He's watching Cecelia."

Roman's brows furrowed. "I guess—maybe."

"No maybe about it. His gaze is on her."

"I know where you're going with this, but you're taking a big leap. My grandfather was happily married for a long time."

"So was Cecelia's lover," she reminded him. "They're about the same age."

"Yes, and they have both lived in this town for most of their lives. My grandmother has been dead for twenty plus years. If they were carrying a torch for each other, wouldn't one of them have done something about it by now?"

"It depends on how much their breakup hurt, how betrayed they felt, how scared they would be to take another chance and risk all that pain again. You heard the sorrow in Cecelia's voice when we read the letters."

"I suppose it's possible, but there's nothing for you or us to do about it. You told Cecelia about the letters. You have to let her make her own decision."

"But your grandfather might not know about them. Maybe they need a gentle push in the right direction. They've both been eating my Wish cookies all week. Sounds like they have something to wish for."

"My grandfather may like shortbread cookies, but I can tell you for certain that he doesn't think they're magic."

"We should try to get them in the same room or in the same place," she continued on, dismissing his opinion. "I wonder if they're going to the dance tomorrow night. That would be a good place for them to meet up."

"I doubt my grandfather is going to the Sweetheart's Dance."

"You should get him to go. And I'll encourage Cecelia. If she doesn't come by the bakery tomorrow, I can take her the letters and talk to her about the dance."

"Juliette, didn't you just say you had nonstop work to do?"

"There's always time for love," she said.

"Well, you're on your own with this one. I can't mess around with my grandfather's love life."

"But we're so good when we work together. And don't you want to see your grandfather happy?"

"I think he's happy enough."

"Oh, come on. Anyone is happier with love in their life.

All you have to do is ask him about Cecelia."

"That's all, huh? My grandfather and I talk about nails and plumbing and electrical; we don't talk about women. He doesn't ask me questions, and I don't ask him. That's the way it's always been."

"You could change that. I have an idea."

"Wait, hold on," he said, as she started down the path. "What are you going to do?"

"Tell your grandfather about the letters. If he's not the person they're about, then he won't care."

Roman grabbed her by the arm. "Cecelia didn't tell you who she was writing about. You should respect that."

She wavered slightly. "I'm not going to say the letters are about him. I just think we should tell him about the letters. He is the owner of the house, after all." She pulled away from Roman and walked quickly down the path. "Mr. Prescott," she said, drawing Vincent's attention to her. "Hello."

He gave her a nod. "Miss Adams, Roman. What's this I hear about you hiring Travis Hastings?"

"I was going to talk to you about that. He needs a job, and you need help."

"I thought of the two of you didn't speak," Vincent said, a puzzled expression on his face.

"We did a lot of speaking yesterday. I'll fill you in later. It's a long story."

"All right, but if he doesn't do a good job, he's out."

"I told him that," Roman said.

"There's something I wanted to tell you, Mr. Prescott," she interrupted. "Roman found a metal box filled with love letters hidden under the floorboards in the downstairs bedroom."

"What?" he asked, his face tightening. "Love letters from who?"

"There aren't any names mentioned," she said. "But we figured out that the letters were from Cecelia Grayson to someone she once loved."

Looking at him in the shadowy light, she couldn't quite

tell if he paled or if she just wanted to believe that.

"I don't know anything about any letters," he said gruffly. "Why do you think they belong to her?"

"Roman looked up who owned the house before my parents, and—"

"You looked it up?" Vincent interrupted, giving his grandson a hard look. "Why did you do that?"

"Originally, I thought the letters might belong to Juliette's parents, but when it was clear they didn't, we thought we'd see who else owned the house," Roman explained.

"Where are the letters now?"

"I have them," she answered. "I told Cecelia I'd give them back to her."

"She knows you found them?"

Juliette nodded. "Yes, she said she wrote them, but she never said who they were about."

Vincent's gaze drifted back to Cecelia and Martha. "Well, that's her business. I'm glad you found them and that she'll get them back. Excuse me, I have to speak to someone."

As Vincent left, she turned to Roman, excitement running through her body. "It's him. He's her lover; I know it."

Roman slowly nodded, his gaze reflective. "I think you're right. And those letters might explain something about why he bought the house."

"Maybe because he was in love with her when she lived there."

"It's possible."

As she looked at Roman, she suddenly realized that in her enthusiasm to match up Vincent and Cecelia, she was overlooking Roman's personal history. "I hope you know I'm not trying to say that your grandfather didn't love your grandmother or your father or his life."

"I didn't think you were saying that."

"Okay, good. So, what do you think we should do now?"

"Nothing."

"Roman," she protested, disappointed in his answer.

"I don't know what you want me to say. You've told them both about the letters. Whatever happens next is up to them."

He was right. It was their move. "I will give Cecelia back the letters." She smiled at his sigh of resignation. "Then I will be out of it."

"I'll believe that when I see it."

As he finished speaking, she saw Travis come down the path, with Cameron riding high on his father's shoulders, a big grin on his face. "Look, Roman. Look how happy Cameron is."

"As happy as I've seen him," Roman admitted. "Travis, too."

Travis saw them and came over to say hello. When he reached them, he set Cameron down on his feet.

"Hi, Juliette," Cameron said. "Did you see the boats?"

"I did. They were really pretty."

"I was just going to get Cameron some hot apple cider. Anyone want one?" Travis asked.

"That does sound good," she said.

"I'll go with you," Roman told Travis, leaving Cameron with Juliette.

Cameron slipped his hand into Juliette's and gave her a shy smile. "I got my wish," he said. "The one I made on the cookies."

"You did? That's wonderful." She saw his gaze drift to his father. Travis and Roman were laughing about something as they stood at the back of the line for refreshments. "Was it for your father to come home? Wait, you don't have to tell me. It's your wish."

"It wasn't just for him to come home. It was for his face to look like that," he said, pointing to his father.

"You wanted him to be happy again," she murmured, thinking how sweet a wish that was.

"He used to look like that all the time, until my mom left. Then he was always sad. But now he's back."

"I'm so glad."

"I'm sorry I took your cookies without paying," Cameron added, giving her another guilty look. "I can pay you back from my allowance. Daddy says I can start making five dollars a week if I help Grandma more."

"You keep your money, Cameron. Save it for something really special."

"I want to buy my dad a new fishing rod when I have enough. My mom broke his when she left."

She frowned at that piece of information, not feeling too much regard for Travis's missing mother. But she certainly wasn't going to say anything to Cameron about it.

"Hot apple cider," Roman told her, as he came back with a steaming paper cup.

"Hmm, smells delicious," she said, inhaling the scent as she blew on the hot liquid.

"We need to let it cool down, buddy," Travis told his son. "I'll hang on to it until then. You'll burn your mouth."

"There's Sam," Cameron said, letting go of Juliette to point to a friend of his. "Can we go over there? Sam is my best friend."

"Sure," Travis said. "I'd like to meet your best friend." He gave Roman and Juliette a nod as they walked away.

"Travis looks a million times better," she said, as she carefully sipped her cider. "This is good. You didn't get any for yourself?"

"Not really a cider fan. I guess having a job has eased some of Travis's worries," Roman said.

"Cameron told me that he wished on the cookies for his dad to be happy again. Looks like his wish came true."

"It's another Valentine's Day miracle due to your special cookies," he teased.

She laughed. "It is. Speaking of cookies..." She ended that thought with a sigh. "I don't want to leave, but I have to go back to the bakery. There's just too much to do. I can't wait until morning."

"I know. I'll walk you to your car," he said, putting his arm around her shoulders as the band started to play.

"You should stay and have fun," she said, sipping her cider as they slowly made their way to the parking lot.

"I might go back for a while."

"Good, because you've been working hard, too. And as much as you don't want to talk about it or admit it, I'm pretty sure that you're worrying just a bit about your physical on Monday."

"I'm trying not to."

"How is that working out?"

"Not that well. There's nothing I can do about it. I've done my part on the rehab. I just have to see what happens."

Roman definitely had a fatalistic attitude about some things. She couldn't blame him. Not wanting things too much was a protective instinct he'd learned as a child.

"Well, I'm keeping good thoughts," she said. Although, secretly she had to admit she had mixed feelings about his upcoming physical. She wanted him to be completely well, but being back at one hundred percent would take him away from her. Still, it was what he wanted, what he deserved, and she couldn't go against that.

As they reached her car, instead of opening her door for her, Roman pressed her back against it and took his time exploring her mouth with his tongue.

She felt enveloped by his body, by his warmth, feeling both safe and protected and wildly reckless all at the same time. It was the kind of feeling he always drummed up inside of her—like she could take the biggest risk because he'd be there to catch her if she fell.

Unfortunately, he couldn't protect her from falling for him. Somehow, she was going to have to find a way to save herself.

He stepped back and opened her door for her. "Try to sleep at least a few hours tonight."

"I will. Tomorrow will be crazy. I don't know when I'll come up for air, probably not until the dance. I hope I see you there—maybe you and your grandfather."

He shook his head. "You never quit. Even if I get him

there, you don't have time to wrangle Cecelia into going."

"I'll just talk to her when she stops by; that won't take much time."

"No promises, Juliette, but I'll do what I can."

"You'll make it happen; I have confidence in you." She gave him a quick kiss. "I'll see you later."

—➤➤◄◄◄—

Roman got to work early on Saturday. Travis arrived by nine, and they quickly fell into a natural groove. He realized as he worked alongside Travis that they were both quiet by nature. Doug's big personality had always been the center of their trio.

They talked a bit here and there, but mostly it was about the work. Seeing how good Travis was at following directions and working independently gave him hope that he'd finally found another person his grandfather could count on.

With his physical and career decisions looming, he wanted to get some help lined up. He'd interviewed several subs the day before and had some good leads to present to his grandfather. Hopefully, he'd take them.

As he heard his grandfather's big, booming voice, he left Travis in the back bedroom while he went out to greet Vincent. "I'm glad you're here," he said. "I already got one bid on framing out the back end of the house this morning."

"From the guy you talked to yesterday?" Vince asked in surprise.

"Yes, one of his jobs fell through, so he can start next week if you like the price. It seemed good to me." He moved over to the stack of wood where he'd left the estimate. "Here you go."

"I'll take a look. How is Travis working out?"

"Good. He's a hard worker. He's very motivated because he needs to take care of his son and his mother. I think he's just what you need to handle a lot of the easier but more tedious labor."

"I can't believe you boys just kissed and made up," Vince said gruffly.

"We didn't go that far," he said dryly. "But it turns out Chief Winters made a point of turning us against each other to try to get someone to confess to the fire—someone other than his son."

"Well, I knew that. I just didn't know which one of those two did it. I had my money on Doug. He was entitled."

"None of us did it. It was probably the work of an arsonist who started two other fires in the county that year, but I doubt we'll ever know for sure."

"An arsonist, huh? You're confident you can believe Doug and Travis?"

"I am," he said with a firm nod. "Doug went down to the police department and came back with the actual file. I read the interviews and the investigative notes. It's all there."

"Why did Doug do that?"

"I think he was trying to get in front of any problems before his run for mayor."

"Makes sense."

"I did want to say something I should have said a long time ago—thanks for bailing me out back then, standing by me, even though you didn't know if I was innocent or guilty. I always wondered why you didn't ask."

"I knew you were innocent; I didn't have to ask. You were a troublemaker, yes, and you had your problems, but you cared about people. Not many people saw that, but I did. You gave your jacket to a homeless man and told me you lost it. I saw that guy wearing it outside the drugstore, and he said you gave it to him."

He shrugged, feeling awkward about that old incident. "I probably didn't like the jacket."

"And you saved that skinny kid with the glasses from a fight. I was coming back from work and saw a bunch of kids behind the convenience store. And there you were, pulling that kid away from some bullies. I would have stopped, but you had it under control." Vincent paused. "You were always better than anyone thought—better than *you* thought. When you first joined the Marines, I didn't like it, but it made sense. You felt good when you could help someone else. Your father was a little like that—in a different way."

"What do you mean?" he asked, surprised that Vincent had actually brought up his father.

"Brett liked to encourage people to follow their dreams, too. They were usually musicians, artists, or poets. I wanted him to have a practical job, a solid income, a normal life. But he wanted to travel and work when he wanted. It was all about freedom for him. Of course, he used my money to get himself that freedom. He never recognized that."

"That's why you didn't talk to each other? Because he sold the stuff you gave him?"

"It wasn't the money; it was the betrayal. And then it was too late. Words were said that couldn't be unspoken. I've regretted the choices I made back then, but there's nothing I can do about them now." He exhaled. "I also regret that I didn't keep in touch with your mother after Brett's funeral. She disappeared, but I could have tried harder to find her and you. I should have been there for you."

"I used to think that, too," he admitted. "But in the end, you were there when it counted. You probably saved my life when you picked me up and brought me here."

"I just wish I'd done it sooner. Have you spoken to her—your mother?"

"She's sent me a few emails. She's sober—three years running."

"You going to see her?"

"Not any time soon. I think we're better off apart for now."

"I agree."

He took a breath, not sure he should risk ruining what was the most personal conversation he'd ever had with his grandfather, but he had promised Juliette he would try to speak to him about Cecelia. The timing seemed right with Vincent in a reflective mood. "Speaking of regrets and not having the chance to make things right…maybe you should talk to Cecelia Grayson about the letters she wrote."

His grandfather's eyes darkened. "Why would I do that?"

"Because I'm fairly certain they're about you. I saw the way you looked at her last night. It was you, wasn't it? That's why you wanted to buy this house. It had something to do with her having been one of the residents."

His grandfather didn't answer right away, and there was both pain and anger in his eyes now.

"Look," Roman continued. "You don't have to talk to me about it, but as you just said, you don't always get a second chance in life. If you do, you should take it."

Vincent stared back at him. "It was a lifetime ago," he muttered.

So his grandfather was admitting it. He was somewhat stunned. "What happened?"

"Timing. Her father." Vincent shook his head. "A lack of courage."

"But you did love her."

"It wasn't enough."

"Could you try again?" Juliette had really rubbed off on him. He didn't usually get involved in other people's love lives.

"We're old now. There's no time left."

"You're not dead yet," he said bluntly, because that's the kind of plain talk his grandfather understood. "If there was ever a time to take a chance, it's now."

"I can't imagine her reaction if I even said hello to her after all these years."

"You don't say hello?"

"Sometimes our eyes meet, but then one of us looks away."

"So next time, don't look away."

"Next time?" Vincent asked warily.

"We should go to the Sweetheart's Dance tonight. Everyone will be there—probably Cecelia. And it's for a good cause. The ticket sales are going to support the homeless shelters in town."

"I know that, but if I'm going to a dance, I'm not going with my grandson," he said roughly.

He grinned. "I admit you're not my choice of a date, either. We can meet there. Maybe we won't end up alone at the end of the night."

"You've got your eyes on Juliette," Vincent said with a gleam in his eyes.

"Hard not to," he admitted.

"She's a beauty," his grandfather agreed. "And spunky, too. Reminds me of your grandmother." He took a breath. "I don't want you to think I didn't love your grandmother, because I did. We had a good life together. If she was alive, I'd be with her, and I'd be happy."

"I understand."

"Cici and I had a different story."

"It looks like your story might have another chapter."

"We'll see. I definitely have some things to think about."

He hoped his grandfather didn't think too long, didn't waste this moment in time, but it was up to him now. He'd done his part.

Fourteen

"**Y**our apartment is cozy and cute," Cecelia told Juliette as she wandered around the studio Saturday afternoon. "It reminds me of my first place. I felt so independent, so modern, to be on my own." Her smile was a bit sad. "That was a long time ago."

"Please, sit down." She waved Cecelia toward one of the two chairs at her small kitchen table. While she'd been swamped in the bakery downstairs, when Cecelia had shown up, she couldn't resist taking a break and inviting her upstairs so she could talk to her before she handed over the letters.

"I don't want to take up too much of your time," Cecelia said.

"Don't worry about it. I could use a few minutes off. My day started around four, so I've already put in twelve hours."

"That's so early. I don't know how you do it."

"It's a busy time of the year for me, but I love it."

"That's the way it should be." Cecelia's gaze strayed to the metal box between them. "I still can't quite believe you found that."

"Roman was the one who discovered it under the floorboard. He thought the letters might belong to my parents; that's why he called me about it. But we soon realized that they'd most likely been written years before. Can I say again how beautiful your writing is? I felt like I was experiencing the same emotions you were. I was completely caught up in your story."

"That's sweet of you to say. I've always felt more comfortable writing than speaking. Words come easier when I don't have to say them out loud." She drew in a breath. "You want to know the whole story, don't you?"

"If you have any interest in sharing—yes. I think I know the man you were writing about."

"I had a feeling you might figure that out." She paused, gathering her thoughts. "I met Vincent when I was nineteen years old. He was twenty-three and so handsome, so worldly. I had seen him around, but the first time I spoke to him was in the drugstore. He had a cold, and he asked me if I knew what medicine he should take." She smiled to herself. "It shouldn't have been romantic at all, but when he smiled at me, I felt a fluttering in my heart that I'd never felt before."

"That's sweet," she whispered, once again caught up in Cecelia's story.

"It seemed like fate had thrown us together. We probably wouldn't have met otherwise. My parents were very protective of me, and Vincent was a diamond in the rough, you know? He was a construction worker, and my father had bigger plans for my future. But I didn't care about those plans. Vincent and I saw each other whenever I could sneak out to meet him. Being with him was...exhilarating."

Juliette smiled at the love in Cecelia's eyes. The years were fading away as she told the story, as she remembered the girl she'd once been.

"I fell madly in love with him," Cecelia continued. "I couldn't eat, couldn't sleep, couldn't wait until I could see him again. He was my world. It was all him—every breath that I took." The gleam in her eyes dimmed. "Until my father found out about us. I know it will seem silly to a woman of your generation, but fifty years ago, my father ruled our house. What he wanted for his children was all that mattered, and he wanted me to marry the son of the senior partner at his law firm. He said it would make his career, that he would be named a partner, that he would never have to worry about being fired, and that we needed the security. My mother had a lot of health problems, and her care was expensive."

"It sounds so mercenary," she muttered.

Cecelia nodded. "It was all about the money. The man in question—he wasn't bad. He was even somewhat attractive. I just didn't love him. And I couldn't talk to him the way I talked to Vincent. He and I could discuss anything. We could share our dreams and not feel foolish. That wasn't the case with the other man. I didn't know what to do, Juliette. I didn't know how to say no to my father. And it wasn't just about him; it was about my mother, too. She was ill, and I did want the best care for her."

"It sounds like a complicated situation. But you had a sister. Why couldn't Martha marry him and save the family?"

"Martha was already engaged. Her fiancé was in medical school. He was someone my father approved of, because he was going to be a doctor. He thought his girls would have dream lives as the wife of a doctor and the wife of a lawyer."

"So you broke things off with Vincent and agreed to marry the other man?" she asked, eager to hear the rest of the story.

"Yes. It was the most difficult thing I ever had to do. Vincent was angry and hurt. The pain in his eyes almost killed me. He thought I was weak and a coward, and he wasn't wrong. He said horrible things, and I felt like I deserved them." Cecelia's chest heaved as she tried to breathe through the painful memories. "Vincent left town shortly after our breakup. He said he couldn't stay and watch me marry someone else. For the next year, I planned my wedding and tried to pretend my life wasn't ending. But as the date neared, I got cold feet. I knew I couldn't go through with it. I couldn't marry this man when I loved someone else. It wasn't fair to him or to me. I finally got up the courage to call it off."

"That must have been incredibly difficult."

"It was awful," she said with a shudder. "I hurt him terribly. I felt so bad about that."

"Did you go to Vincent then?"

"Yes. I found out where he was living, and I went to find him. I wanted to tell him I was sorry, that I loved him and only him, but when I got there, I saw him in a pub with another woman. They had their friends with them, and they were toasting to Vincent's engagement. I watched him kiss her, and then I left without saying a word. They got married a few months after that, and six or seven years later, they came back to Fairhope with a son."

"I'm so sorry," she said. "I really wish your story would have ended differently."

Cecelia gave her a watery smile. "It was my own fault. I didn't have the courage to pick the man I really wanted, to go against my father, to stand up for Vincent. I know Vincent was disheartened by my lack of strength. He didn't believe I loved him enough."

"I'm sure he understood that your father was too powerful for you to fight."

"At some level, perhaps, but every man wants a woman who will fight for him. At any rate, I tried to be happy that Vincent had found happiness with someone else. He deserved that. His wife was a good woman. I got to know her a bit over the years."

"Really?"

"It's a small town. Our circles sometimes intersected. I don't think she knew anything about the romance I had with Vincent. I never told her, and I don't think he did, either."

"Did you ever come close to marrying anyone else?"

Cecelia shook her head. "No. I never met a man who touched my heart in that way. There were some men I cared for. One I lived with for a while, but he eventually left when he realized my heart was not there for him. I wasn't really lonely; I had Martha."

"Wait! What happened to Martha's fiancé?"

"He finished medical school and decided he didn't want

to marry her after she'd waited all those years. So he broke it off."

"And she never found anyone else, either?"

"Actually, she did. She was engaged again in her thirties, but that man died in a freak skiing accident. After that, she gave up on love. She said we were destined to be spinster sisters. She was right. She's been there for me, and I've been there for her."

She thought about Cecelia's words as another thought occurred to her. "Is Martha why you never talked to Vincent after his wife died? Did you feel like you couldn't break the sister spinster bond? Because surely you must have thought about it."

"I might have had a passing thought, but it was too late. Thirty years had passed before his wife died. He had a son, a grandson. Our time was over."

"It's never too late," she said, daring to push a little, because it was clear that whatever Cecelia had felt for Vincent, it was still there.

"You say that because you are young, because you still see forever. I see my time left in years."

"Then you should make the most of those years."

"Martha and I are a pair. We're the Grayson sisters."

"You'd still be sisters. If she loves you, she'd want you to be happy, just as you'd want her to be happy if the situation were reversed."

"I don't know about that," Cecelia said. "Martha can be very controlling. She's a lot like my father. Even if I wanted to try...I'm sure Vincent still hates me. He can't even say hello to me when our paths cross. He always looks away."

"Maybe he needs a reason to keep looking—a smile, a welcome. One of you has to make the first move. And it has to be you, because you're the one who broke things off. You have to be the one to take the risk now."

"I don't know if I could."

"You should go to the dance tonight. Vincent will be there. What better time to reconnect than at the Sweetheart's

Dance?"

"I'm sure Vincent won't go to that. He's not a dancer."

"He might go. Roman is trying to talk him into it."

Cecelia smiled. "So you and Roman have a plan, do you?"

"It's mostly my plan," she admitted. "It only extends to getting you both in the same place. The rest is up to you. I will say one thing, though. When I told Vincent that Roman found love letters hidden away in the house, he was shaken. I think he bought the house because you once lived there."

"I wondered about that when I heard that he had purchased it. I loved that house, and I especially loved the backyard. We had a hammock between the trees back then. I used to sit there in the summer and dream about my life, my love, my future. But Vincent didn't share my love for the house. He said those walls kept me away from him. In that house, my father was king. I couldn't go against him. And Vincent and I could never meet there." She paused. "I didn't understand why he would buy my old home."

And now she understood exactly why Vincent wanted to change it. "I have this crazy idea that he wants to rip down the walls that kept you apart. It won't be your father's house anymore; it will be his...maybe yours."

"That would be insane. It's been so many years, and so many people lived there after me. You lived there."

"I loved that house, too," she said, wondering why it felt suddenly more like Cecelia's home than hers. "I was devastated when I had to leave. When I came back here, I told myself one day I would buy it. But then I saw that the Prescotts were changing it completely, and at first, it really threw me. I felt like they were tearing up my past."

"I understand, dear."

"But now I'm starting to realize that the house has seen more stories than mine. It was foolish to think it was waiting for me to come back." She paused. "Will you come to the dance tonight? If not for Vincent, just come and have fun. I'll be there. I'm bringing desserts."

"I'll think about it," Cecelia said, as she got to her feet.

"Don't forget this." She stood up and handed Cecelia the metal box.

"Thank you for these, Juliette. I doubt I would have gone as far as you did to find the owner."

"Roman says I always go too far," she said, as she walked Cecelia out of her apartment and down the stairs.

"Sometimes that's what it takes to be special."

She laughed, thinking special was a nice way of saying pushy, but she'd take it.

As she watched Cecelia walk down the street, she really hoped she'd come to the dance.

What a miracle it would be if Cecelia and Vincent could find their way back to each other. Cecelia was interested. Hopefully, Vincent was, too.

⟶⟫⟪⟵

The Sweetheart's Dance was held in the recreation center, but the usually plain auditorium had been turned into a romantic haven for the evening with pink streamers, bouquets of flowers on high-standing cocktail tables, black-and-white photographs of famous romantic couples through the years adorning the walls, and romantic music coming from a band on the stage. *When the people of Fairhope went all in on a holiday, they went all in,* Roman thought, as he perused the room.

He didn't care that much about the decorations; he was far more interested in finding one beautiful brunette.

When he saw Juliette, his heart jumped a beat, and he felt a tightness in his chest.

She was standing in the back corner of the room with a dessert buffet bar set up in front of her. Next to her table was coffee from Donavan's, manned by Sara and Donavan. All three women wore cocktail dresses, but he only had eyes for Juliette.

He loved that she'd left her hair down and loved even

more the short, dark-red, spaghetti-strapped dress that hugged every beautiful curve. He couldn't wait to get his hands on those curves. It was the main reason he'd come to the dance. He knew he'd have an opportunity to do just that. He wasn't a big fan of dancing, but if it meant he could hold on to Juliette for a while, he was on board.

He made his way to her table, happy to see her gaze light up when she saw him. He waited for her to hand the couple in front of him two chocolate-covered roses and then he stepped up. "How's it going?"

"Wonderful. I'm so glad you came, Roman."

"I can't believe you're here and looking more relaxed than you should be with your workload."

"I'm not thinking about any of that right now. It feels good to be away from the ovens."

Donavan moved over to say hello. "Nice to see you, Roman. You clean up well."

"Thank you. You ladies look beautiful tonight."

"Would you like some coffee?" Donavan asked.

"No, thanks. I'm good for now on coffee and dessert."

"Well, have fun," Donavan said as she went to help a middle-aged couple who had questions about whether the coffee was actually decaf.

"You do look handsome in that suit," Juliette said. "I'm a little surprised you own one."

"Don't get too excited. This is the only one. I usually don't wear it for happy occasions." Her face fell a little, and he mentally kicked himself for bringing down the mood. "But tonight is different."

"It is a happy occasion," she agreed. "It will be even better if your grandfather and Cecelia show up."

"I made my pitch yesterday."

"So did I. Cecelia is still in love with your grandfather. She thinks it's too late, but I say it's never too late."

Juliette certainly didn't have the word *quit* in her vocabulary. "What else did she tell you?"

"The whole story. Her father wanted her to marry

someone in his law firm that would ensure the future of his job, and she didn't say no. Eventually, she called it off, but by then your grandfather was engaged to your grandmother. Oh, and she did tell me that Martha was dumped after waiting years for her fiancé to finish medical school and then the next time she took a chance on love, her fiancé died."

"That's rough. I almost feel sorry for her."

"I think it explains why Martha is such an unhappy person."

"I guess everyone has a story, don't they?"

"They do. What did your grandfather say?"

"That he hasn't spoken to Cecelia in years."

"She said the same thing; that even when they cross paths, they just look at each other and then someone looks away."

"Word for word, he told me the exact same thing."

"So they're both super aware of each other. We have to get them together."

"We put out the invitation. They have to do the rest." He could see the impatience in her eyes. "I know you want the best for them, but love happens between two people—not four."

She smiled at that. "I know that, but we can give them a little push."

"We've already done that."

"Hang on one second," she said, moving to the table to hand out some more desserts.

As she did so, his gaze moved toward the door, and he saw his grandfather walk into the room, along with his friend Max, who wheeled in next to him.

As Max fell into conversation with a woman, Vincent moved a few feet away, his gaze sweeping the room. He saw Roman and gave him a short nod, then continued looking around the hall.

"Your grandfather is here," Juliette said with excitement, moving next to him. "One down, one to go." She grabbed his hand. "Wait, there's Cecelia. She just came in with Martha.

Our plan is working."

He smiled. "Calm down. Nothing has happened yet. They just walked in."

"The hardest part was getting them both here."

"I'm not sure that was the most difficult part."

"You're right. How do we get them to talk to each other? Maybe you could go over and get your grandfather and walk him over to Cecelia."

"Yeah, that's not going to happen," he said dryly. "Just give it a few minutes."

She waited for about thirty seconds, then said, "I can't just do nothing. Watch my table and hand out desserts to whoever wants them. There's no money involved. It's all free. You can do it."

He knew he could do it; he just didn't want to. But Juliette was already walking away. He moved behind her table and almost immediately was deluged with people wanting desserts. Sara gave him a hand when he had to go looking through plastic bins for more cookies, but otherwise he was on his own.

At one point, he saw Juliette talking to Cecelia, then he lost track of her.

"What's this?" Doug asked, approaching the table with an attractive redhead. "You're working desserts now, Roman?"

"Just holding down the fort for Juliette."

"So things must be going well there," Doug said, a knowing gleam in his eyes.

"Who's your friend?" he asked, ignoring Doug's comment.

"This is Valerie Marks—Roman Prescott."

"Nice to meet you," she said, extending her hand.

"You, too," he replied.

"Valerie is in public relations," Doug added. "She's going to help me with my campaign."

"I am not just going to help you; I'm going to get you elected," Valerie said confidently.

"Sounds like you're set," Roman said, thinking that Doug

and Valerie made a good match. Not that he expected Doug to get serious about a woman right now. He had one goal on his mind and that was being mayor. "What can I get you?"

"We want some of the Wish cookies," Valerie said, slipping her arm through Doug's. She gave him a sideways glance. "I already know what my wish is. What about you?"

"Same as yours," Doug said with a laugh. "Two Wish cookies, Roman."

He handed them each a cookie on a napkin. "Here you go. Enjoy."

As Doug and Valerie moved away, he saw Juliette and Cecelia in conversation. He also saw that his grandfather had seen Cecelia as well. He knew what he needed to do and that was not to get his grandfather to move; it was to get Juliette out of the picture.

"Sara, would you mind keeping an eye on the table?" he asked her.

"Sure, no problem."

He moved across the room as the band began to play. "I think this is my dance," he told Juliette.

"Oh, but—"

He cut her off. "You promised."

"You go and have fun with this handsome young man," Cecelia said.

"All right. We'll talk later."

"I'm sure of it," Cecelia said.

As he pulled Juliette onto the dance floor, she said, "I was just about to take her over to your grandfather, Roman. He kept getting into conversation with other people, but he was finally free."

"I know, but I told you that the next move had to be theirs. Look." He swung her around so she could see his grandfather approaching Cecelia. "I knew he wasn't going over there while you were with her."

"So you didn't want to dance with me; you wanted to get me out of the way."

He laughed. "I did want to dance with you, and I also

wanted to get you out of the way. You can say thank you."

"Thank you," she said with a grin.

They fell silent as they watched Vincent say something to Cecelia. She murmured something back. And then they stopped talking, but their eyes never left each other.

"I'm so nervous," Juliette whispered to him.

"Me, too," he admitted as they just swayed to the music, their attention on the older couple.

"Oh, my God, they're going to dance," Juliette said, her arm tightening around him.

To his amazement, Vincent took Cecelia's hand and led her to the dance floor.

"It's working," Juliette added, excitement in her voice.

"I think it is," he agreed.

Vincent and Cecelia weren't dancing particularly close, and there was tension in both of their bodies, but it was the kind of tension that spoke of a lingering attraction. Was it possible that these two could find their way back to each other? He hadn't actually believed that until now.

His grandfather caught him looking and gave him a rare smile, then he pulled Cecelia a little closer.

"Did you see that?" Juliette asked.

"I did. But I think they're just going to dance; I doubt they'll announce an engagement when the band stops playing."

She made a face at him. "I know I'm way too involved in this, but it just makes me so happy to see them taking the risk. Thanks for helping to get him here."

"As if I could resist you. You're a force of nature, Juliette Adams."

"I just want people to be happy."

"I want you to be happy."

"I am, but…"

"No," he groaned. "No *buts*…"

"I should probably get back to my table."

"Or you can let everyone get their own desserts." He pulled her up against his chest, wrapping his arms around her.

"How does that sound?"

"Like a really good idea," she said with a soft sigh.

"Then let's dance."

She wrapped her arms around his neck as their bodies swayed in perfect rhythm.

They danced through the next three songs without a thought to breaking apart. But when the band went for a faster song, Juliette suggested they take a break. It was fine with him. He didn't want to dance as much as he wanted to hold her.

They walked back to the dessert table, hand-in-hand.

"Everything is pretty much gone," she said. "Just two Wish cookies left."

"Looks like you might have two takers," he said as his grandfather and Cecelia approached the table.

"Hello, Roman," Cecelia said in her sweet voice.

"Nice to see you," he said.

"We wanted to thank you," Cecelia added, her gaze encompassing Juliette. "Both of you. You encouraged us to come here, and, well, it's been very nice." She looked at Vincent with her heart in her eyes. "I can't believe we haven't spoken all these years."

"I didn't know you wanted to," he said gruffly.

"And I didn't know you wanted to. What a pair of old fools are we."

Vincent took her hand. "We're going to keep talking."

"We will," she promised. "Anyway, we wanted to say good night," she added, turning back to them.

"Good night," Roman said.

"We're really happy for you," Juliette put in. "I have two of my Wish cookies left. Would you like them?"

Cecelia shook her head. "I already got my wish."

Vincent smiled at Cecelia. "So did I."

And with that, the two of them walked away.

"That was the most romantic thing I've ever heard," Juliette said, dabbing at her eyes.

"It wasn't bad," he said, not willing to admit his chest had tightened at the look of love in his grandfather's eyes.

"It was better than *not bad*. You have quite the gift for understatement, Roman."

"True. So are you happy now that you got them together?"

"I am. But—"

"Another but?"

"I could be happier if you danced with me again."

"You've got it."

—➤➤◄◄—

"I don't want this night to end," Juliette said as she walked out to her car with Roman. Most people had left the dance already. It was almost midnight, but she'd been reluctant to call it a night until the band had packed up their instruments and they'd been forced out of the hall.

Roman smiled at her. "Does it have to end? Just because the dance is over doesn't mean we have to go home." His finger ran down the side of her face. "We could take a walk, get coffee somewhere, go back to one of our places…"

She was tempted to say yes to any and all suggestions, but there was a logical part of her brain that was screaming caution. "It's too cold to walk, no place still open to get coffee, and I have to go to work in like four hours."

"Timing is everything," he drawled. "I'll say good night then."

She put her arms around his neck and pulled his head down for a kiss. His lips were hot in the cold night air, and her head spun from the rush of desire she felt for him. Kissing Roman was like quicksand. Every touch of his mouth took her deeper. She was never going to get out, but then again, she didn't really want to, not as long as he stayed with her.

But he wouldn't be with her…not forever.

The thought gave her strength to push him away.

He stared down at her with a serious gleam in his glittering eyes. "Juliette, we have a few hours until morning."

Her nerves tingled at the promise in his eyes. "I—I can't," she said. "It's not that I don't want to, Roman. But my work is so busy and your life is up in the air."

"I know," he said, a husky note in his voice. "I should get to bed, too. I want to get a good workout in tomorrow before my fitness tests on Monday."

"Fitness tests? I thought it was a physical."

"It's both. I'm flying to South Carolina, to the base at Parris Island, tomorrow night. The tests will start around ten in the morning on Monday. I'll be done by three and be back here around ten o'clock Monday night."

"I didn't realize you had to go somewhere else for the tests. What do they make you do?"

"Everything from running to pull-ups, agility and dexterity tests, rifle skills. The list goes on."

"Do you feel ready?"

"For everything but the results," he said soberly.

"I'm sure you'll do great. Will you let me know how it goes?"

"Yes, but I won't know anything official Monday. It will probably take a few days."

"Maybe you'll have a better idea, though."

"Maybe."

The mood had definitely changed with the turn in their conversation.

She took her keys out of her bag. "If I don't talk to you before Monday, good luck. I really do mean that." Her voice caught a little as a wave of emotions ran through her. "I want you to have everything you want."

"I know," he said, meeting her gaze. "I want the same for you."

She wished what they both wanted was the same thing, but it didn't appear that it was. She gave him a watery smile. "I'll talk to you later."

"Don't work too hard." He shut the door behind her and then stood there with his hands in his pockets as she drove away.

She didn't take her eyes off the rearview mirror until she had to turn the corner.

She had to fight the urge to turn around and go back to him—take whatever time they had left and enjoy every second. But she was afraid to make herself even more vulnerable to the heartbreak she saw coming.

She didn't want him to go back to the Marines. She didn't want him to leave Fairhope, but it wasn't her call. It was up to him to go or to stay.

She hated feeling powerless. It reminded her of when her parents died, when her aunt had taken her to New York, when nothing in her life had been under her control.

Was she really going to give all the power to Roman?

She was still thinking about that when she entered her apartment.

Fifteen

➤➤◄◄◄

The last time Roman had made the trip from Fairhope to the Marine base at Parris Island, South Carolina, he'd been eighteen years old and a new recruit, not at all ready for the world that awaited him.

Back then, he'd arrived late at night, and had been immediately thrust into a whirlwind of events. He'd gone through processing, gotten a haircut, received his uniform and gear, and undergone a medical evaluation and a strength test. Then it was on to meeting his drill instructors and learning about the Marine Corps, before moving on to a grueling camp that tested him physically, mentally, and emotionally.

As he walked under the sign that said *We Make Marines*, he felt like he'd come full circle.

Watching the new recruits run by, he was stunned by how young they looked. He was only thirty-one, but he felt like an old man in comparison. These boys would become men very quickly, though. He knew what was waiting for them. He also knew not all of them would be able to handle the pressure. They thought they could now, because they knew nothing of what they would see when they were deployed to fight, to be the first boots on the ground, to face fears others could only imagine. But they would find out. And they would be well-trained.

It really did seem like a long time ago that he had been that young. But today wasn't about his past but rather his future. When the group of runners passed, he continued on to the fitness center, where he'd begin his day of testing.

It felt strange to see uniforms again, to salute, to be back in the Corps. This had been his world for thirteen years, and he'd loved being part of it. He'd never thought he would leave, but having been forced to be out of it the past few months, he had to admit that his perspective had started to change. He'd seen another world, one he might like just as much, and that life included a woman he didn't want to lose.

But he also didn't want to lose his career. Would he have to choose?

That question had been worrying him almost as much as whether or not he would be fit enough to have a choice.

Only one way to find out.

He jogged up the steps, then paused as the door to the center opened, and a man in uniform came out. The square-faced, hard-jawed, bald man was very familiar. Sergeant Jerry Woods, his first drill instructor, had been both his hero and his tormentor. He couldn't believe he was still here, still training recruits.

As he saluted, he realized the sergeant was now a major.

Major Woods stopped and gave him a hard look. "Roman Prescott?"

"Good memory. Congratulations on the promotion, sir. It's good to see you again."

"Thank you. What are you doing here?"

"I'm trying to get my job back. I've been on medical leave for a few months. I'm here for an evaluation."

"Right," he said with a nod. "I heard what happened to your unit. I was proud to hear how you handled yourself, how you protected your fellow soldiers. I wasn't surprised, though. I can pick winners from the first day of boot camp."

He'd never guessed that his drill instructor had thought he was a winner, especially not during those first weeks. "I appreciate you saying that now. I didn't think that was your opinion back then."

The major cracked a smile. "I like to give my recruits something to strive for."

"You always did that."

"Good luck today. Remember what I always told you—"

"You can do more than you ever thought you could," he finished.

"Don't forget it."

"I won't." As the major left, he moved into the fitness center and signed in for his scheduled tests.

He felt charged up after seeing Major Woods. The man had always inspired him to do better. Hopefully, that would be the case today.

For the next several hours, he was put through a series of grueling tests and then a thorough medical evaluation. When he was done, he had just enough time to grab his bag from the motel where he'd spent the night and head to the airport. While he was waiting to board his plane, he called Juliette, eager to hear her voice. Unfortunately, his call went to voicemail.

He felt incredibly disappointed. It felt like forever since he'd last spoken to her, but she was probably up to her elbows in flour and sugar.

He left a brief message. "It's Roman. I'm getting on a plane in a few minutes. Call me back if you have time. Everything went well," he said, then hung up, feeling frustrated that they hadn't connected.

She'd been on his mind all day, through the three-mile run, the stomach crunches, the push-ups and pull-ups, through the hearing and vision tests, even at the rifle range, which was not a good place to have a woman in your head.

He put his phone back in his pocket and stretched out his legs, feeling a weary ache in his muscles. He'd pushed himself to the limit today. He'd done everything he could. Now it was up to the medical evaluation board, and he had no idea what would happen.

He knew most of his results were good, but the hearing was still an issue. He didn't know how bad it was, because the lab tech running the test had been non-committal. There had also been some limit to the range of motion in his shoulder. Were the problems enough to kick him out of the Corps or at the very least get him reassigned?

He really wished he knew. He was tired of waiting, tired of wondering.

On the other hand, he wasn't quite ready to hear the final decision. Because then he'd have to deal with reality, a reality that might take him away from a woman who'd become very important to him, a woman who wanted nothing more than to put down the deepest roots possible in the town she'd been born in. She wasn't going to want to follow a man around the world. She needed the roots, the community, to be happy. She'd left New York to get them, and she was well on her way to her goals. He couldn't ask her to change those goals for him.

Could he?

—◆▶◀◆—

Damn. She'd missed Roman's call. Checking the clock, Juliette saw it had come in fifteen minutes earlier. Maybe he was still waiting to board his plane. She wiped her hands and called him back.

"Hello?" he said.

"It's me. I wasn't sure if you'd gotten on the plane yet."

"I've got about five minutes."

That was nowhere near long enough for everything she wanted to say to him, but she'd take it. "How did it go?"

"It went well. I passed all the combat-ready tests. It's down to the physical limitations. There was some improvement since my last medical evaluation. Will it be enough? I have no idea."

He sounded a bit down, even though he'd just said everything had gone great. "Well, you did everything you could do. When will you find out?"

"Soon. I talked to the commander of my unit, and he said there's something coming up they'd like to use me for, if I get cleared. He was going to see what he could find out."

The idea of him leaving soon made her feel weak, and she pulled over a stool and sat down. "Where would you go?"

"I honestly don't know anything more than that."

"Do you feel ready to return?"

He didn't answer her question right away, then said, "I would be ready if I needed to be." He paused. "How are things going with you? Are you baking right now?"

"I am. I just finished the wedding cake. It looks amazing. They're picking it up in the morning, so I'm relieved to have that done. But I still have a dozen more orders to fill before tomorrow afternoon."

"You're not going to sleep, are you?"

"Does putting my head down on the table count?"

"No. You should take a little break, just so you don't accidentally pour rum into a carrot cake."

"Hmm, that's not a bad idea for a combination."

He laughed. "I wasn't trying to give you ideas."

"I know, and I am making sure to be careful, because I do realize that I'm working on a lot of caffeine and not much else. But Valentine's Day is tomorrow. I want it to be perfect for everyone. Oh, hey, did you talk to your grandfather?"

"No, why?" he asked warily.

"He and Cecelia are having dinner together tomorrow night at his house, and he asked me to make them a cake. Isn't that amazing?"

"I can't believe you took another order for a cake."

"Didn't you hear me? It's not about the cake; it's about your grandfather and Cecelia."

"I heard you. I'm glad they're still talking."

"He sounded happy when he spoke to me, like *really* happy. Wouldn't it be incredible if they got together after all this time?"

"It looks like they're heading in that direction. I hope

Martha doesn't get in the way."

"So do I. She could ruin things. On the other hand, I don't think Cecelia will let anyone stop her if she decides to go for it this time."

"What time is the dinner?"

"They said they're meeting about seven thirty, so I told him I'd bring the cake by at eight-thirty. He'll be my last delivery."

"You really need to get some help."

"After tomorrow is over, I am going to look into that." Silence fell between them. There were so many things she wanted to say but in light of all the uncertainty, she didn't know if she should say them. Unfortunately, she seemed to have little restraint when it came to Roman. "I missed you today."

"Right back at you," he said, a tender note in his voice. "I guess I'll see you tomorrow after all the crazy baking is done."

"I can't wait," she murmured. "Have a safe flight."

"Don't fall asleep in the cake batter."

"I'll try not to." As she ended the call, she found herself smiling and feeling a lot less weary than she had a few minutes earlier. She could do this. She could get through the night and the day and then she'd see Roman again. She didn't want to think past that moment. For now, it was enough.

Juliette was standing in the kitchen of Roman's grandfather's house, pulling his cake out of its box on Tuesday night, when Roman entered through the back door.

Her heart jumped with the sight of his handsome face and she almost dropped the cake. That would have been a disaster. She carefully put it on the counter, then turned to look at him.

He was closer than she'd thought, slipping his arms around her waist, lowering his head to kiss her hello. It was a long, tender kiss, filled with promise—at least she hoped that was promise and not just wishful thinking.

"You're still alive," he teased, as he lifted his head to give her a smile.

"I am. I made it through the day. Who knew Valentine's Day would be so harrowing? This is my last delivery."

"How's it going with my grandfather?"

"Let's take a peek," she said, leading the way into the hall. They crept quietly toward the dining room, then paused so they wouldn't be seen.

Vincent and Cecelia sat close together at one end of the table, which was lit with candles and decorated with flowers.

"Wow, did he do all that?" Roman muttered.

"It's beautiful. I wonder if he cooked. There aren't any dishes in the sink."

"He probably ordered out." He paused. "He looks like a teenager in love."

"Cecelia looks young, too. They found their way back to each other. I still can't quite believe it."

"You're the one who made it happen," he reminded her as they made their way quietly back to the kitchen.

"And you," she said. "I'm just glad our meddling had a good result."

"Me, too. We make good partners in crime."

"I don't know if we'll rob any banks together, but I get your point."

He smiled. "I have a feeling you could talk me into anything."

And she had a feeling that the one thing she couldn't talk him into was what she wanted most. That thought was depressing, and she was suddenly overcome with exhaustion. She'd been running on adrenaline for too many days, and she didn't think she could handle an emotional conversation right now.

"I should go," she said abruptly. "You can serve them the cake in a few minutes."

"Don't you want to do that?" he asked in surprise. "It's

your dessert."

"It's theirs now. I'll leave it to you."

He followed her out of the house. "Juliette, wait. Why are you rushing away?"

"Because," she said with a helpless shrug. "I can't talk to you right now."

"Why not?"

"I don't want you to tell me that you're leaving. And I know you will. Maybe not tonight, or tomorrow, but soon. When I'm not so tired, I'll be able to handle it better. I'll wish you well and offer to throw you a good-bye party and pretend everything is great." Her voice caught, and she had to blink back a sudden welling of tears behind her eyes.

"Hey," he said softly, taking her hand. "Nothing is decided."

"Isn't it, Roman? You're in good shape. You'll go back to the Marines. Maybe it won't be your exact job, but it will be something. I want that for you, because you want it. You're a soldier. That's your life. I just need a little time to…I don't know…sleep." She pulled her hand away from his. "Happy Valentine's Day. I'll see you around."

She walked quickly to her car, hoping he wouldn't follow. She didn't want to cry in front of him.

<hr />

As Juliette pulled out of the driveway, he felt torn between going after her and letting her have the space she'd asked for.

He'd seen the emotion in her eyes and knew she was barely holding it together, and he'd hated to see her so vulnerable. He'd wanted to reassure her that whatever was between them wasn't ending, but he didn't want to lie to her.

He didn't know what was going to happen with his job, where he'd be a week from now or a month or a year. The uncertainty had always been okay with him before. He'd never had anyone to worry about except himself.

Still pondering the best move, he went back into the house. He'd just entered the kitchen when his grandfather and Cecelia walked in.

"Roman," his grandfather said with surprise. "I heard someone in here; I thought it was Juliette."

"She just left. I was supposed to bring you the dessert, but you beat me to it."

"Oh, the cake looks lovely," Cecelia said, eying Juliette's latest masterpiece of chocolate and strawberries. "She is so talented. And chocolate and strawberries are my favorite combination." Cecelia turned to Vincent. "You remembered that?"

"We dipped strawberries in chocolate on our second date," he said. "I've never forgotten the look of joy on your face."

"I can't believe you remember that," Cecelia said in wonder.

"I remember a lot of other times, too," he told her.

"So do I," she replied.

As his grandfather and his love exchanged a poignant look, Roman felt very much like a third wheel. He cleared his throat. "I'm going to get out of your way and let you enjoy your night."

"You can stay and have cake with us," Cecelia suggested.

"No, he can't," Vincent said, shaking his head.

Roman laughed. "I really can't." The last thing he wanted to do was cramp his grandfather's style.

"You don't have a date tonight with Juliette?" Cecelia asked, giving him a speculative look.

"She's about to collapse from all the baking."

"Oh, I'm sure that's true. But I bet she'd still like to spend some time with you."

"She actually told me she wanted to go home and sleep," he said. "Anyway, you two have fun."

"Tell Juliette thank you," Cecelia said. "Not just for the cake, but for everything. When you see her," she added with a mischievous smile.

"I will do that. When I see her," he echoed.

"Make that soon," Vincent told him. "Don't let pride or fear or doubts keep you apart. You don't want to wait too long to be with the one you love. Sometimes you don't get a second chance."

"I think that's what I said to you."

"Oh, there's one more thing." Vincent walked across the room and picked up an envelope from the counter. "I left this for Juliette, but I guess she didn't see it. Can you give it to her?"

"What is it?"

"You'll find out when she opens it," his grandfather said with a smile.

"All right." He figured the envelope gave him another reason to go to her now.

She'd told him she didn't want to talk to him tonight, but he couldn't wait until tomorrow. Maybe he couldn't promise the future, but he could at least tell her how he felt.

⟶⟫⟪⟵

The kitchen of her bakery looked like a disaster zone. The pots and pans were piled high in the sinks. On every available surface she saw remnants of her mad baking marathon of the past twenty-four hours with flour, sugar, cinnamon, excess dough, miscellaneous fruits, chocolates, and jams all waiting to be cleaned up.

Juliette sighed as she looked at the mess. She really wanted to turn off the lights and go upstairs, but she was too conscientious for that.

Even though Valentine's Day was over, the bakery would be open tomorrow, and while they'd be putting out desserts that were already baked, she would still need to throw a few bread loaves from the refrigerator into the ovens in the morning and make some batches of chocolate chip and oatmeal raisin cookies, which would be back in popularity now that the Wish cookies were done.

Those cookies had done the trick for at least a few people, she thought with a smile, as she started to wipe down the counter. Several people had told her yesterday that they were sure their Valentine's Day plans were the result of the cookies. She was happy to be a part of the tradition her father had started. But she was also eager to put it behind her until next year.

She was a little overwhelmed by her own turbulent emotions about Roman and all the couples falling in love around her. Seeing Vincent and Cecelia together had made her heart ache with happiness for them, but she also couldn't help thinking about all the years they'd lost.

She'd always thought love was easy, that when it was right, everything worked out. That's the way her parents' relationship had looked to her. Of course, she had no real idea what they'd gone through. She'd been a child, watching the two people she adored. Had they fought? Had their courtship been more complicated than she'd heard? Had they ever wondered if they could go the distance? Would they have made it forty, fifty, sixty years together if they'd lived?

She'd never know, but they'd be happy forever in her mind, and maybe that was all that mattered.

The bakery bell pealed, and she jumped.

It was probably Roman.

A part of her wanted to stay in the back and hope he just went away, but as the bell rang again, she didn't think he was going to leave.

She walked out to the front and opened the door. "Roman, it's late, and I told you I didn't want to talk."

"But I do." He pushed past her and walked through the store and into the kitchen. When he saw the state of the room, he had one word. "Wow."

"I usually clean as I go, but not today," she said defensively, pushing a strand of hair off her face. "Now do you see why it's not a good time to have a conversation? The flip side of a romantic Valentine's Day is a mess like this."

He gave her a smile that warmed her up despite her best

effort to keep him at arm's distance. "I'll help you clean up." He took off his jacket and hung it on a hook.

"You don't need to do that."

"But I'm going to." He rolled up his sleeves and went over to the sinks.

"You didn't come over here to wash dishes."

"No, I came over to see you. I have a few things to say, but they can wait."

"Maybe you should just say them and go."

He turned on the water. "Or you can go upstairs and lie down while I take care of this."

She couldn't believe he was offering to clean up the kitchen. "I can't let you do that."

"You're not letting me," he told her, giving her a purposeful look. "I'm doing it. So stand and watch or go upstairs and relax—your choice."

"I have another choice," she said. "I'll help you. It will go faster."

While he washed the bigger pans and loaded the smaller items into the dishwasher, she put ingredients away, wiped down the counters and took out the trash.

When she came in from the back alley, she found herself smiling at the sight of Roman in soapy dishwater up to his elbows. If the truth were told, he'd never looked sexier than he did right now.

"What?" he asked, giving her a speculative look.

"Just thinking how hot you look right now."

"Yeah, sure," he said with a laugh.

"It's true. You continue to surprise me. I've never had anyone offer to clean up my kitchen before."

"Then you've been hanging out with the wrong people."

He set the last dish in the drying rack and wiped his hands on a towel. "If you hadn't been working tonight, I would have liked to take you out for Valentine's Day."

"What would we have done? What's your idea of a romantic evening?"

"Well, for you I would have skipped the desserts,

because nothing compares to what you make, and I wouldn't have wanted you to do any work for our date."

"So, then what..."

He tilted his head. "I would have taken you down to the water, rented a boat—maybe Doug's big yacht, if he wasn't using it—and we could have sailed across the bay." He paused. "Do you like boats?"

"I love them. That would have been fun, Roman." She felt a little sad that she'd missed out on that.

"It wouldn't have mattered what we did, as long as we were together," he said quietly.

"You're right." A knot grew in her throat. "I like everything we do together, including this."

A smile curved his lips. "Who knew all I had to do were a few dishes to warm your heart?"

"You warmed my heart from the beginning—well, maybe not the very beginning," she amended.

"You did not like me tearing down your house," he said. "But we seem to have gotten past that."

"Well, it wasn't your idea; you were just helping your grandfather. How could I blame you for that?"

He stepped forward, taking her hands in his. "I told you I came over here to talk to you."

"And I still think we should save any more conversation for tomorrow or the next day or maybe a long time from now."

"I don't want to end this, Juliette."

"Really?" Hope sparked within her.

"Really. Look, I don't know what's going to happen, but I think we should work it out together."

"Together?" she echoed. "How can we? It's your choice what you do with your career, not mine. I won't ask you to give up the Marines for me. I won't ask you to stay in Fairhope. It wouldn't be fair. You are who you are, and you have to do what makes you happy."

"Are you done?"

"For the moment."

He squeezed her fingers. "Yesterday when I was taking all those tests, you were right there with me. You were running, doing push-ups, pull-ups—everything."

"Wow, I'm very active in your thoughts," she said lightly.

He grinned. "Yes, you are. But my point is that I couldn't stop thinking about you. At first, when I walked onto the base, I thought this is where I belong. This is where I feel comfortable, where I know who I am, but at the end of the day, all I wanted to do was see you again. When I called you on the phone from the airport, and you didn't answer, I couldn't believe how disappointed I was. I had never felt like that before."

"I did call you back."

"And made me very happy."

"So what do we do? Wait and see what happens? As you know, I'm not very patient with inaction."

"My gut tells me that I'm not going to be cleared to go back to my old job. They need me operating at one hundred percent, and I still have limitations. That means a reassignment, or I might be able to terminate my contract early."

She drew in a breath at his words, not wanting to let herself believe he might actually stay. "You might still get to a hundred percent, Roman."

"Or I might find that being a contractor in a small coastal town is where I belong now."

"Do you think you'd like that?"

"Fairhope has grown on me. My grandfather is here. But the real lure is you. This is where you want to be—where you've found happiness. And I'm not talking about the past anymore. You're building a life for yourself."

"It has room for you in it."

"Good, because I'm falling in love with you. Since I met you, you have changed my life. You have pushed me to get involved, to care about strangers, to make up with my friends, to do better. And you've brought the light back. My only concern is that I'll bring you down."

"You won't do that. You push me, too, Roman. You make me think about things longer, and you call me out when I'm lying to myself."

"I'm glad you think that's a good thing."

"I've never felt like my real self with a man before. You see me—the real me—and that feels good."

"It goes both ways." He paused. "Before I start kissing you—which, by the way, is going to happen really soon—my grandfather asked me to give you something."

He walked over to his jacket, pulled out an envelope and brought it back to her.

"What's this?" she asked.

"He said I'd find out when you did."

She opened the envelope and pulled out two pieces of paper and stared at them in shock. "Oh, my goodness. It's a deed, Roman. It's a deed to my old house."

"Seriously?"

"And a note from your grandfather."

"What does he say?"

She read the note aloud: *Juliette, I bought the house to feel connected to the woman I once loved, but you gave her back to me. And now I'm giving you back the house you love so much. I will transfer this deed into your name. I'll sell the house to you for what I bought it for. If you need a loan, I'll finance one for you. I'll finish the remodel, but you'll have full say over what you want done from here on out. Thank you again for bringing Cecelia back to me.*

"I cannot believe he's going to give you the house and include the remodel in the same price he paid for it," Roman said.

"It's too generous."

"Well, it's what he wants to do. You're not going to try to give it back to him, I hope. Because he's a stubborn man."

"And I'm a stubborn woman."

"Don't I know it, but my grandfather will still be a tough fight."

She set the papers down on the counter. "The truth is,

Roman, I don't want the house anymore."

He raised an eyebrow. "I can't believe that."

"It's true. It's not the house that will make me happy. I know that now. It's you, and my business, and this town that bring me joy. When I'm ready to move somewhere, I want to start fresh in a place that's all mine, that's going to tell the next part of my story...and maybe yours." She took a breath. "And even though I would love to stay here, if the Marines take you away, you might find me stowing away in your backpack."

"I would like that."

"And I like that you want to include me in the decisions, so I want to do the same. I want to give us a chance to find out where this love takes us."

"Me, too."

She let out a breath. "This is all moving so fast. A few minutes ago, I thought you were leaving, and I didn't know how I was going to say good-bye. Now you might stay, and I'm hoping I'm not deliriously tired and this is all a dream."

"It's not a dream. It's very, very real."

She laughed. "I can't believe it. I finally found my Romeo."

"And if you call me that, I'll have to…"

"Have to what?" she teased.

"Kiss you senseless."

"In that case, Romeo, Romeo, Rom—"

He cut off her words as he made good on his threat, kissing her long and hard, with passion and tenderness and love. He lifted his head and smiled at her. "You know what's funny?"

"What?"

"I never ate one of your Wish cookies, but I got my wish anyway."

"Well, it's too late now. They're all gone. The magic is over until next year."

"The magic was never in the cookies, Juliette; it was in you. You've changed people's lives in this town: Cameron,

Donna, Travis, Cecelia, my grandfather, Doug, me—probably even Martha."

"I'm not so sure about that, but there's still time."

"For everything we want," he agreed.

"Everything is really just you," she confessed.

"And you," he whispered. "Let's go upstairs and get you to bed…"

THE END

Author's Note: I hope you had fun with Juliette and Roman in SWEET SOMETHINGS and that you enjoyed your time in Fairhope. This book was actually part of a collaborative project. I was approached by the creators of a movie called COFFEE SHOP to write a book in their world. I thought how fun it would be to have characters cross over between a movie and a book. The book and movie are completely separate and independent stories, but some familiar characters do appear in both. In the movie COFFEE SHOP, you'll get to see Donavan's story. To find out where you can buy the movie, go to www.barbarafreethy.com/sweet-somethings.

About The Author

—➤➤◄◄◄—

Barbara Freethy is a #1 New York Times Bestselling Author of 52 novels ranging from contemporary romance to romantic suspense and women's fiction. Traditionally published for many years, Barbara opened her own publishing company in 2011 and has since sold over 7 million books! Twenty of her titles have appeared on the New York Times and USA Today Bestseller Lists.

Known for her emotional and compelling stories of love, family, mystery and romance, Barbara enjoys writing about ordinary people caught up in extraordinary adventures. Barbara's books have won numerous awards. She is a six-time finalist for the RITA for best contemporary romance from Romance Writers of America and a two-time winner for DANIEL'S GIFT and THE WAY BACK HOME.

Barbara has lived all over the state of California and currently resides in Northern California where she draws much of her inspiration from the beautiful bay area.

For a complete listing of books, as well as excerpts and contests, and to connect with Barbara:

Visit Barbara's Website:
www.barbarafreethy.com

Join Barbara on Facebook:
www.facebook.com/barbarafreethybooks

Follow Barbara on Twitter:
www.twitter.com/barbarafreethy

Made in the USA
Lexington, KY
24 January 2017